Shadow Men

'In *Shadow Men*, Jonathon King captures the intrigue, lyrical beauty, and darkness of the Florida Everglades better than any other writer I know of. His account of corporate greed in the midst of an Edenic paradise is a warning for our times'   James Lee Burke

'Cleverly plotted, with a diverse set of entirely believable characters – most importantly the mass of contradictions that is Freeman – this is an edgy thriller made all the more enjoyable by its quirky setting'   *Good Book Guide*

'Jonathon King gets better with each book . . . another absorbing mystery from a writer who deserves to be better known'   *Sunday Telegraph*

A Visible Darkness

'This is the second Max Freeman mystery and his creator Jonathon King has hit the ground running with another atmospheric thriller that exposes the dark, violent and poverty-stricken underbelly of Florida's glittering façade'
Irish Independent

'Top class . . . The Miami background is just fine, and this is an author with a big future'   *Independent on Sunday*

The Blue Edge of Midnight

'With his first novel, King jumps into James W. Hall territory and lands firmly on his feet . . . King uses descriptions of places and environment to reveal character and attitude, much as Hall, James Lee Burke, and Robert B. Parker do . . . skillful writing, original characters and evocative settings initiate a welcome new series'

Publishers Weekly

'A remarkable debut . . . King's writing is gritty, vivid, and suspenseful. Jonathon King is a natural storyteller'

Harlan Coben

'*The Blue Edge of Midnight* is a terrific book that begins the run of a great new talent in Jonathon King. From start to finish it is full of true character and jagged surprises. King adds new dimensions of depth and substance to the modern crime novel'

Michael Connelly

Jonathon King is the author of *A Visible Darkness* and *The Blue Edge of Midnight*, a *Los Angeles Times* bestseller and winner of the Edgar Award. A journalist for over twenty years, he has covered crime and criminal courts and is now a national award-winning news feature writer for the South Florida *Sun-Sentinel*. Visit his website at www.jonathonking.com.

SHADOW MEN

Jonathon King

ORION

An Orion paperback

First published in Great Britain in 2004
by Orion
This paperback edition published in 2005
by Orion Books Ltd,
Orion House, 5 Upper St Martin's Lane,
London WC2H 9EA

1 3 5 7 9 10 8 6 4 2

A CIP catalogue record for this book is available
from the British Library.

ISBN 0 75286 571 4

Printed and bound in Great Britain by
Clays Ltd, St Ives plc

www.orionbooks.co.uk

This is for my mother, Arlene Hall,
in honor of her fortitude.

And in Memory of Cindy Cusano,
a beautiful woman, and more than just a victim.

They picked a moonlit night to make their escape because it was the only way. And now it was killing them. The first shot sizzled through the humid air as if it were underwater, and he heard it a millisecond before it found the muscled flesh of his son's shoulder blade and made the ugly sound of a wet, dull punch.

The boy gasped and stumbled, and his father caught him under the arm before he went down.

"Papa?" his other son said from a few steps ahead, the fear in his young voice like an uncharacteristic cry. The father could see the pale glow of the younger boy's face in the moonlight and the outline of his body against the sky above the horizon, and he realized he had made targets of his sons.

"Down, Steven!" he called out. "Down in the ditch!"

All three scrambled off the piled hump of Everglades muck and limestone marl and slid down the embankment to the edge of the water below. Two of them were breathing hard; the third was bubbling wet air and blood through the new hole in his lung. They did not need to speak. They had known instantly from the sound of the report who was hunting them, and they knew the odds of surviving.

"Robert?" the father whispered, holding his seventeen-year-old son to him, now pressing his hand over the exit wound in the boy's chest to stop the ragged sound of death coming through his sweat-soaked shirt. "Oh, God, Robert, forgive me for what I have brought you to."

The other boy moved across the dirt to them, his face so close he could feel his father's breath on his cheek.

"Papa? Is Robert OK, Papa?" he said, and the father could feel the tears in his son's voice but could not answer. He had never lied to his children, and he did not want to break that vow this close to the end.

The father looked up to the high edge of the earthen berm they had all helped build, the foundation of the road they had all worked to create. Beyond it was a canvas of stars that had stunned them their first few nights out here in the wild Glades and then comforted them for weeks with a seeming physical closeness to God himself. But the clear crescent moon had betrayed them. The elevated roadbed was the only way back through the swamp to civilization. On a cloud-locked night it would have melded into the darkness and been impossible to follow to freedom. So they picked this night, planning to use the glint of moonlight on the canal water to guide them and the ribbon of black dirt to walk upon.

"We need to move, now, Steven," the father said. "Across the water. You are the strongest swimmer. Take your brother's good arm and I will get his belt and we will sidestroke together. If we can get to the mangroves on the other side, God will give us cover."

He could feel his son's head nod. He was the determined one, the one who thought all things possible, the one with the optimism and strength of youth. He would believe. The father took his shirt off, knotted it in the middle and put the lump of fabric over his son's exit wound, then tied the ends over the entrance hole on the boy's back. His own tears were running now.

"Get ready, Steven, we have to move quietly," the father said, and then hesitated once more, feeling in his pocket for the gold watch of his own father and then slipping the thick disk deep down into his leather boot, hoping it might be protected there from the water.

They slipped into the warm water and pushed slowly out. The satchels they carried floated at first. Their underwater strokes were both smooth and strong despite the load of the older boy's weight. They caught a rhythm and began to make progress.

The second shot was from closer range and it tore through the father's satchel, causing the bundle to bob in the water. The marksman had mistaken it. They were more than halfway across, and as the other boy stroked harder, the father kicked stronger. In seconds their boots touched mud. The father's next stroke touched the slick root of a mangrove. The boy let go with a soft exultation, "We made it, Papa!" and the third shot entered the back of his neck and opened a gaping wet hole in his throat that yawned like the ragged mouth of the devil himself.

The father looked back once and saw the outline of the rifleman and the tilt of his hat against the stars. He was standing in the bow of the shallow Glades skiff he'd always used for hunting. He had tracked them by water, letting his low angle paint their moving bodies against the sky, just as his was now. When he heard the familiar clack of the big Winchester's lever action, the father wrapped his arms around his boys in a final act of protection, whispering a prayer in their ears and refusing to believe he had seen the eyes of his killer glow red under the brim of his hat.

CHAPTER 1

I was sitting in a chaise longue on the patio of Billy Manchester's penthouse apartment. The multihued blue of the Atlantic lay out before me. Close to shore its color today was a green-tinted turquoise, then the darker blues at the reef lines and then an almost steel blue out to the horizon. From this height the layers were sharply bordered, and the smell of the salt still carried up on the southeastern breeze.

"This is really eighty years old?"

I should have known better. Never question Billy after he has presented you with something as fact, unless you crave silence from the man.

"I mean, it's interesting stuff, but isn't it kind of incredible that no one's seen it since, what, 1923?" I said, trying to redeem myself.

"Mayes said no one had ever opened his great-grandmother's hope chest. He said he wasn't even sure anyone in the family even knew it existed," Billy answered from inside the apartment, on the other side of the threshold to his sliding glass doors.

In my hand was a computer printout of what Billy called the last letter. Mark Mayes, a college student in Atlanta, had sent it to Billy with an inquiry asking him for representation in a legal action based on a handful of originals. Mayes had found them, yellowed and nearly dried to crumbling in his great-grandmother's attic in the family home. With great care he had unfolded each letter and read it. When he was done he had a new and profound respect for his long-dead great-grandfather and the two uncles he had rarely heard mentioned. He was also convinced that they had perished in the Everglades in the summer of 1923 while working for a private company trying to build the first highway across the great swamp. It wasn't a lark. The kid had offered up a small family inheritance to pay Billy's retainer.

This had all been explained to me during my first two beers from Billy's refrigerator. I suspected my friend and attorney was loosening me up.

"Another R-Rolling R-Rock?" Billy said, stepping out onto the patio with a sweating green bottle in hand.

"So you went and took a look at the originals," I started, but caught myself, "and they're convincing. I mean, there's no way to fake something like this?" I reached out and accepted the beer, smiling. Billy only raised his eyebrows.

"I stopped at M-Mr. Mayes's family home while v-visiting an acquaintance in Atlanta," Billy said. "He's a difficult young m-man to d-disbelieve, Max. And although I'm n-no expert, if these are f-fakes, he went to a lot of t-trouble preparing them."

Billy's stutter flowed through my ears now with only the most subtle recognition. It was something I'd gotten used to. Billy is a stress stutterer. His speech is flawless when he talks to you over the phone or even from the other side of a wall. But face-to-face, even among friends, his words jam up behind his teeth, always left behind and trying to keep up with his brilliant mind.

"The original sc-script is very faded. But the d-dates are compatible. The building of the Tamiami Trail had b-been off and on b-but wasn't completed until 1926."

Billy sat down in the chaise next to mine. He was wear-

6

ing a pair of shorts and a silk shirt of some expensive designer brand. He stretched out his trim legs and crossed his ankles. His chocolate-colored skin was smooth and tight, and his profile was equal to any *GQ* model or film actor as he looked out onto the horizon.

"Now, whether his c-conjecture about the f-fate of his relatives is correct, will t-take us time to investigate," he said.

I stopped tipping my bottle just at that point where the first swallow is down your throat and you are breaking the bubble for the next.

"Us?" I said, separating the bottle from my lips by only inches.

The twitch of a grin started at one corner of his mouth, but Billy's eyes did not leave the sea.

I was driving into the sun, leaving the coast behind, all the noise and heat, traffic and clutter, convenience and luxury that it inevitably drew. After a relatively short commute on the seventy-mile-an-hour bumper-car ride called I-95, I headed west on a two-lane asphalt road and then turned into the entrance to the state park. I pulled my pickup truck into a designated visitor's spot and clipped my officially purchased parking pass on the rearview mirror. It took me three trips to carry my supplies across the crushed-shell parking lot to my canoe, which was flipped under a group of sand pines near the boat ramp to the river.

On each trip across the lot I cut my eyes to the front door of the park ranger's station. I could detect no movement behind the windows, although the ranger's Boston Whaler was tied up at the dock and I knew he was still on duty.

More than three years ago I had walked away from a ten-year career as a cop on the streets of Philadelphia. In a shootout during a cheap Center City stickup, I had killed a child. The fact that I had taken a round in the neck and that the kid had been a tagalong with the stickup man made the shooting team rule the death as "justified." But I could never find a place for that term in my own head. I took a disability payout and moved here, to a place completely different from the city where I'd been born and raised. It did not take me long to realize that sometimes it's more what you bring with you than what you leave behind. I also found out that what I had brought was not welcome.

I locked the truck, and with my supplies of canned food, some extra water and Billy's new reading material secured in the bow, I pushed my boat off onto the dark water of the river. Without looking back I took three strong strokes to gain momentum and began gliding farther west. In minutes I was into a rhythm, reaching out with the paddle, digging into a purchase of water and pulling long strokes, then following through with a subtle feathering of the blade that sent a small funnel trailing behind.

The river is wide here, bordered by rimrock forests of slash pine. Farther west the water narrows and the land flattens into a low collection of mangroves spiked with an occasional bald cypress. The late afternoon sun had already begun to spin the clouds with pale streaks of pink and orange, and the air was losing its scent of salt as the mix of ocean water was overwhelmed by fresh spilloff from the Everglades. Two miles in, the banks narrowed again and I slowed my pace and eased into the tunneled canopy of the upper river. I stopped stroking and let the canoe drift into the shadowed silence. Here the deep green of oak, red maple and pond apple trees dominated, and when the water is high the place seems more like a flooded forest than like a river. A traveler learns to read the currents and flow in order to follow the natural trench, but I have paddled the river's length in both moonlight and spackled daylight so many times, I know every turn by rote.

In the deep shade the temperature dropped several degrees and I stripped off my sweat-soaked T-shirt and pulled a long-sleeved version from my bag. With my arms up and elbows wrapped in the material I stopped at the sight of a great blue heron standing on a moss bank only twenty feet away. The bird was nearly four feet tall, with a third of its length in the S-curve of its neck. He stared at me with one angry yellow eye, and I stared back. The instant I pulled the shirt down over my face the animal squawked once, and by the time my head popped through the collar he had already taken flight, his long, crooked wings flapping elegantly through the tunnel of foliage and out toward open sunlight.

I was now working south against a light current, and about a mile in, I came to the two tall, gnarled oaks that marked the entrance to my shack. The shallow water trail behind them was obscured by an overgrowth of filigreed maidenhair ferns. Thirty yards back from the river I stroked up to my small dock, looped a line over a four-by-four piling and climbed out. I bent and checked the first three steps leading up the staircase to the stilted cabin. Out here there was always a film of moisture on any flat surface. Had anyone used the stairway, they would have left a print. I don't get many visitors, and those I do get, I don't like unannounced. The steps were untouched, and I shouldered the first load of supplies and went up to the single room I called home.

The shack dated back to the 1930s, when a rich northerner built it as a hunting lodge. It was later abandoned for several years and then reopened as a research station for biologists studying the water flow and animal life on the edge of the Glades. Billy had somehow picked up the lease from one of his innumerable contacts and offered it to me when I first came to South Florida.

Most of the place was constructed of Dade County pine, possibly the densest, toughest wood in nature. Legend has it that frontiersmen in Miami had to cut and nail the wood while it was still green because it was impenetrable after it dried. A row of cabinets hanging on one wall may have dated back to the original owner. Windows are centered in all four walls, and the high ceiling is shaped like a pyramid with a cupola at the apex, which lets the warm air rise and escape while drawing cool air up from the shade below.

I started a pot of coffee on the shack's single-burner propane stove. There was also an ancient potbellied stove in one corner, but stoking it took time and I do not do well waiting on coffee. While it was brewing I put away supplies, then put my clean clothes in the old oak armoires that lined one wall, and added two new books to the stacks on the top mattress of the bunk bed. It was an odd collection that included new and old Florida history, travel books that I'd read and reread while waiting out the rain as a bored cop on night patrol, and some Southern literature, including a masterpiece by an old *Philadelphia Daily News* columnist that I always carried with me. The only other pieces of furniture were the two straight-backed wooden chairs and an enormous slab of butcher-blocked mahogany that served as a table.

By the time the coffee was ready only a weak light was leaking through the western window. I poured a cup, lit the clear glass oil lamp and set both on the table. I picked up the sheaf of transcribed letters that Billy had given me, and in the silence of my own corner of the Glades began to reread the sketchy account of Cyrus Mayes, an out-of-work schoolteacher whose eighty-year-old story had set a rough stone of unknown truth rolling in my head. My familiar but often unhealthy grinding had begun.

My Darling Eleanor,

Forgive me for my past letters if they have caused you distress or undue worry for us. This time I send you good news.

After our long and fitful train journey we arrived at the port of Tampa. It was my hope that here the boys and I would find work, at least on the docks as we are strong and physically able and eager. Alas, we find that here too is a crush of laborers in our same predicament. By gathering with a common group of men at daybreak, Steven and Robert or I have been picked for a single day's work, but it is not enough to sustain us or gain on our economic station. We were on our final dollars of savings when God's face shone on us this day.

At the gathering, a foreman who seemed to be careful in his selections singled all three of us out to join another twenty men. We were loaded into trucks and our future labors explained. The foremen offered us all two months of steady work for the Noren company on a road building project to the South. We will be given room and board and $75 a week each. The project is some distance away, but we are promised to return in eight weeks or to

11

sign on for additional time if we wish.

We shall be leaving at dawn tomorrow my darling, and in my heart I believe this is our chance to gain the capital we need to start a new life for us all.

I have used some precious few cents to secure stationery and postage, but I do not know when I might have the chance to write again.

Steven and Robert send their love and know that we think of you and young Peter always. Join us in prayer that this new opportunity will bring us our dreams.

Your loving husband, Cyrus

I got up and refilled my cup. Billy, in his role as my personal Florida historian, had told me of the back-busting efforts of men and machines to build a road across the southern Everglades. In the first two decades of the 1900s, Miami had become a thriving frontier city. Real estate, tourism, trade with Havana and the constant import of money from the Northeast on the new rail lines to New York had given the miracle city a growing reputation. Entrepreneurs on the west coast of Florida were jealous. They wanted a piece of the action, and a few were convinced that a road connecting Tampa and Miami would be the golden pipeline.

Mayes's following letters were only a glimpse of how the plans of businessmen had underestimated the Everglades. In long dispatches written at night by candle or lamplight, Mayes described how he and his teenage sons had been taken by boat to Everglades City, a fishing village that had become the supply depot for the road project. From there the men were taken several miles out into the swamp along a crude earthen berm to the worksite. At the end of the line was the monstrous Moneghan dredge, manned and serviced by the laborers. The dredge was an ever-moving, forty-thousand-pound beast sent to dig into the muck and water and tangle of wild jungle that was the Glades. The men cleared the way and the dredge scooped up a deep canal of earth and crushed limestone and piled it onto the ever-lengthening berm that would become the future roadbed.

"It is a horrific and awesome machine," Mayes wrote. "As it digs, its power rattles the very ground for fifty yards in all directions, shaking the world like a mass of jelly."

The workers lived at the work site, sleeping in wooden barracks, and Mayes's first letter from the camp listed the new and exotic dangers.

"At night when the dredge goes silent, the snakes come out from their hiding. Just last night Robert pounded some unknown species to death with his boot heel after finding it in his bedding."

A man called Jefferson was mentioned as the designated sharpshooter, assigned to kill any of "the numerous alligators that creep in while we are in the water trying to move and secure the machinery." In their first two weeks Mayes reported witnessing the death of two workers. One fell from the high dredge rigging and into "a mass of watery muck which quickly sucked him into the earth before any of us could reach him. No attempt was made by the foremen to recover his body and we do not know if the incident was even recorded." The second death was the result of a dynamite explosion, "of which there are several each day to crumble the limestone bed below us for dredging."

"We learned early to constantly be attuned to the call of 'fire in the hole.' Yet, some oblivious crewman was at work too near when the blast ripped his arm away from his body. Despite our efforts to retrieve him and the crew doctor's attempts, the blood ran from the poor man until he expired."

Mayes wrote that the man's wrapped corpse was loaded onto the cart that delivered the very dynamite that killed him and sent on the trip back to Everglades City. It was by this same means that Mayes had been able to surreptitiously send out his letters. Early on he "befriended the elderly Negro who regularly delivered the tons of explosives to the camp. I ascertained immediately his admiration for my father's pocket watch and though it was a heavy price to pay, my darling, he has promised that in exchange he will deliver my letters to the post office at Everglades City and we will so value the knowledge that you receive our love and news of our well being."

I got up from the table, poured the last of the coffee and stepped outside onto the small landing at the top of the stairs. Up through the trees I could see a quarter moon pinned to the sky like a pewter brooch, a film of cloud giving it a dull, unfocused shine. The backlit leaves were black, and below the treeline it was darker still. It had taken some time for my eyes to adjust to the darkness out here after a lifetime in the city, where one is never without some source of electric glow. But now I can pick up the glint of pale moonlight caught by the water below, make out varied shades of darkness, or distinguish a solid tree trunk from a thick stand of common fern. I have stood listening to the unique hum of night insects and the occasional movement of predators. At night I have paddled out into the endless acres of sawgrass and marsh of the flooded Everglades, where it is not unlike a trip to sea except that the thick heat is inescapable and the clouds of mosquitoes intolerable. In the 1920s, without the respite of cool, clean lodging or even a drop of cold water to drink, working in such conditions would quickly have grown exhausting. Was it enough to cause a mutiny of laborers like the Mayeses, despite their desperate need of work? Mayes's final letter raised too many possibilities and questions.

My Dearest Eleanor,

I do not wish to unduly alarm you my darling, but our situation here has become increasingly troubling. For now the boys and I are still in good health despite the hardships that I have written of earlier. Both Robert and Steven have in fact been my inspiration in all this, watching them outwork most of this crew and holding their deserved complaints for my ears only. Still, I sense both a fear in them and a rising anger. They are looking to me for answers and I too believe it has come time for drastic measures.

By my own rude calculation we are now the furthest point into the swamp from civilization at either end of this planned roadway. Our supply depot at Everglades City must now be thirty miles behind us. It is an impossible trek on foot for a man without supplies in the God forsaken heat and the constant natural dangers that abound. Still, three more men in the crew left late last night after the foreman again refused them any aid in abandoning their work and their so-called legal contract.

Steven has told me that the three had stolen fresh water bags and when he felt them raise the mosquito netting and heard them leave, he woke us and we lay listening for more than an hour. Then we heard Mr. Jefferson's rifle, three separate reports, echoing from some distance to the west. The sound put the fear of God in us and we prayed quietly together. This morning when one of the crew asked Mr. Jefferson if he were out gator hunting again in the night the silent man only nodded his head under the brim of his hat and climbed back up to his lookout perch. Like the few discouraged but brave work-men who have left on their own previously, we know that we will not see the three from last night again and we pray that they returned safely to civilization and their families.

I dream my darling wife, that these letters have reached your hand. We have been ten weeks now in this hell called the Everglades and we also dream that the wages that await us when our time here is done will give us all a way to the future. Our way is through persever-ance, but I do not know how much more strength we have.

Love from us all,
Cyrus

I went back inside the shack, turned out the lamp and peeled off my shirt. In the dark I lay in the bottom bunk, listening to the living Glades noises outside, staring into the blackness of the mattress above me and finding only my own visions of the glistening white yawn of poisonous snakes and the smell of sun-baked flesh.

CHAPTER 2

The stinging odor in my nose woke me. Or the rising sound of someone calling my name. When I came partially awake I could hear "Mr. Freeman! Mr. Freeman!" being shouted from a distance, a panic building behind the words. When my eyes finally cleared, the sight of white smoke curling and thickening in the ceiling made the panic my own. My house was on fire. I rolled out of bed onto one knee and caught a lungful of the acrid smell and coughed it back out. A weak light was making it through the windows, along with the shouting and the sound of a man splashing.

"Freeman!"

I crawled to the door, staying low, but glanced up in all four directions in search of flames. I pushed the door open and a wave of fresh air hit my face, which caused my mouth to involuntarily gasp open and my eyes to tear. Down in the canal, the park ranger was waist-deep in water. He was balancing a fire extinguisher on his shoulder with one hand and using the other to pull and stroke himself forward.

"Freeman! Are you OK?"

I stood with help from the handrail and nodded. My lungs were stinging with each breath but the oxygen was clearing them. The ranger made the dock and hoisted himself up and started up the stairs.

"You all right?"

"Yeah," I said. "Yeah." The second word was clearer than the first.

"The fire's on the backside, north corner," he said, pushing my door open wide with his dripping boot. "Maybe we can knock it down from the window ledges."

He pulled the pin on his boat extinguisher and then bent low and started in. I took as deep a breath as I could and followed. The ranger crab-walked across the room to the north window and I broke for the kitchen counter, where my own extinguisher was stored.

The ranger had already figured out the inside latch system by the time I got to the east window. We pulled open the hinged mosquito screens and pushed our heads out. The flames were crawling up the sides of the shack in an odd wave of blue and orange. They licked up over the edge of the roof but there were no eaves in the design to stop them and let them gain heat. This was a good thing. I saw a billow of white chemical spray fan out from around the corner, then stepped one leg through the window and straddled the casement. I pulled the pin on my canister and let loose a shot of spray, aiming down at the base of the flames. The fire retreated but then stubbornly reignited. It looked as though the tall piling itself was on fire. I leaned farther out to get a better angle and squeezed off another blast.

It may have been ten minutes, maybe thirty. The ranger's extinguisher ran dry before mine, but we had doused all the live flame we could see. When my can was empty, he helped me back in through the window and we both stumbled out the door and down the stairs. The wash of fresh air set us both coughing again, and when we reached the dock at the bottom the ranger sat with his feet in the water and retched between his knees. I lay down on the opposite side and cupped the river water in my hands and splashed it up into my face and eyes. It was several minutes before either of us could speak.

"You OK, Freeman?"

"OK," I said, realizing I had long forgotten the ranger's name.

"Griggs," he said. "Dan Griggs."

"Thanks, Griggs."

The eastern sky was lightening, though the sun was still too low to break through the tree canopy. In time we both sat up, leaning our backs into opposite posts at the end of the dock. I finally took a solid look at the guy. He was a good ten years younger than me, lean with sandy blond hair and skin too fair for his job in the Florida sun. His ranger uniform was soaked up to a dark line across his chest. His leather boots were oozing mud. He was still wearing his belt with a knife scabbard and a flashlight holder.

"You swim out here at dawn often?"

He grinned and shook his head without looking up.

"I'm usually on dawn patrol out on the main river," he said. "I've seen white smoke rising from your stovepipe before, but when I saw it was black, I knew something was wrong and motored up here."

"Couldn't get the Whaler in," I stated.

"Had to tie her up and wade in. But I could see the flames even from deep water."

"Guess I picked a bad morning to sleep in."

Griggs still hadn't looked up into my face.

"I figured you were here 'cause I could see that your canoe was gone from the landing."

"I appreciate you looking after me," I said. "The whole place might have gone up if you hadn't been here."

This time Griggs did look over at me. The irony was not lost on him. Several months ago it was Griggs who had to serve papers from the state informing me that the Attorney General's Office was attempting to break the ninety-nine-year lease that Billy held on the old research shack. Until then I'd been left alone and had even befriended the old, longtime ranger whom Griggs had replaced. But there had been a messy business. Blood had been spilled in these waters through a violence that didn't belong in this place. Many people blamed me, and it was a point of view I couldn't argue with. That was when the state began trying to toss me out. Billy had been fighting the eviction at my request, and he had kept them tied up in legal maneuvering ever since.

"I don't suppose you noticed any lightning while you were on dawn patrol?" I asked, finally making it to my feet and looking up under the base supports of the shack.

"Nope. And I'm sure you can rule out faulty wiring." He too had gotten to his feet. "But unless you reached out and doused the back wall with kerosene and lit the match yourself, I'd say you got an enemy."

The ranger was pointing to a small slick of rainbow-colored water that seemed to float independently on the surface of my channel. Some sort of petroleum-based accelerant had spread into the water.

"Whoever they are, they don't know much about Dade County pine," he said. "It'd take a whole lot more heat than that to do anything more than just scorch that tough old wood."

While Griggs used my canoe to retrieve a camera from

his Whaler, I went back inside. There had been no interior damage, and the smoke had mostly cleared, rising up through the ceiling cupola as the design had intended. Still, the place reeked of burnt oil and wood. I closed the screen frames and changed my clothes. I found my cell phone and started to call Billy, but put it off. I would need to stay at his place until the shack aired out, but the conversation I anticipated was better off held out of earshot of anyone else. I grabbed my still unpacked travel bag and rejoined Griggs below.

In the canoe we took a circle around the base of the shack. The back wall and northeast support pillar were blackened, but there was no apparent structural damage. We pushed up next to the pillar, where I used a knife to dig out a scarred piece of wood and put it into a plastic bag. Griggs had been right about the arsonist's ignorance of the pine's resistance, unless his intent was to be more psychologically than physically destructive. Maybe someone was more interested in scaring me out than burning me up.

When we finished gawking, we returned to the ranger's boat and tied a line to the canoe for towing. Griggs motored slowly down the narrow upper river, the sound of his engine sending most of the river animals I would normally see this early in the day into hiding. But just as he cleared the canopy and pushed the throttle up, I caught a glimpse of the long lazy wings of a blue heron, its yellow, sticklike legs not yet folded from its takeoff. I watched it keep time with us, then circle back toward the west and finally disappear into the distance.

CHAPTER 3

I waited until I was on the road in my truck before calling Billy on my cell.

"Jesus, Max," was his response when I filled him in on the morning's events. "Are you going to file a report?"

"What? And have cops crawling all over my stuff?" I knew the kinds of useless messes cops made. I'd made them myself.

"Besides, what good would it do? It's not like you're going to find footprints out there. And contrary to popular belief, the bad guys really don't leave torn pieces of their shirts on the thornbushes that often."

"So what you're saying is, you'll investigate on your own."

"Yeah, if waiting to see what happens next is investigating."

"Good. Then you've got two cases to work. You're pretty busy for a new businessman."

Several months ago, after sliding into two different sheriff's cases and pissing off the local law enforcement brass, I'd caved in to some not too subtle suggestions and applied for a Florida private investigator's license. My years on the Philadelphia force hadn't hurt, and even the street shooting didn't stop them from granting me a concealed weapons permit. Of course I was one of more than 300,000 such Florida residents so permitted, and how many lobotomies were included in that select group was anyone's guess. It also hadn't hurt to have a detective with the Broward Sheriff's Office vouch for me. She was, in fact, my next call as soon as I got off with Billy.

"So you're heading over to my place?" Billy asked.

"Not right now, but if that's an offer, I'd like to reserve it until the shack smoke clears, as they say."

"My place is your place, Max. Diane and I will be out at the Kravis Center for the philharmonic, but make yourself at home."

Diane McIntyre was another attorney, and one of the few women I'd met in South Florida who had enough class and moxie to keep up with Billy on several levels.

"By the way, I've set up another appointment with Mr. Mayes in my office on Thursday, and I'd like you to sit in."

"He's here?"

"He graduated from Emory and is considering an acceptance to the seminary at Luther Rice. I get the distinct feeling he's trying to clear this thing, Max, before he moves on."

"All right, Thursday. I'm heading out to southwest Dade now."

"Nate Brown?" Billy asked, guessing my moves, sometimes before I even made them. Nate Brown was an Everglades legend. He'd been born and raised in the swamp and if he was still alive, no one knew the stories or the topography of that vast place better than he. If men had died while the Tamiami Trail was being built, Brown would at least have heard the rumors and tales of their passing around the late-night campfires or early-morning fishing swaps.

"An excellent idea, tapping Brown if you can," Billy said. "I can't give the same approval to a trip to Loop Road, if that's where you're going. Should I have a cold compress and an auto-glass repairman standing by?"

My last trip to the sanctuary of the Everglades' denizens had not been altogether friendly.

"I'm going to be careful this time," I said. The other end of the connection stayed silent, but Billy's wry smile was in it.

"What?" I said. But the phone had softly clicked off.

Before I made the turn to the southbound ramp of I-95, I pulled over and made another call.

"You have reached the desk of Detective Sherry Richards of the Metropolitan Investigations Unit. I am either on the phone or . . ." I waited for the damned beep.

"Detective. I am presently on dry land and if at all possible would like to meet with you on that matter we discussed last Tuesday," I said. One never knew these days about who had access to office phone mail, especially at a cop shop.

"I am occupied on another case this afternoon, but could meet you at our usual drop-off point at 1930 hours. Call my cell if this is acceptable. Aloha."

I punched off the cell and wrinkled my forehead. "Aloha"? Where the hell did I get that? I pulled out onto the interstate, and any thoughts of misplaced levity quickly disappeared. In the few years I'd lived in South Florida I had never experienced I-95 when part of it was not under construction. And despite the constant presence of orange cones, disappearing lanes, ramp signs with burlap slung over them and the inevitable group of yellow-vested construction workers, I also have never experienced traffic doing less than sixty-five in a fifty-five-mile-per-hour zone. I eased into a spot in the middle lane and tried simply to keep pace.

An hour or so later I was in Miami; got off on Eighth Street heading west. The Spanish signage for everything from food markets to computer stores, dry cleaners to haircutters, restaurants to movie theaters, had lost its novelty for me. Miami-Dade County is now 54 percent Hispanic. Those who have danced to the luscious and lively beat of Afro-Cuban music in the street concerts or tasted a homemade *salteña* outside the American Airlines Arena, have no argument with multiculturalism. To think that Cuban- or South American–influenced politics is any more corrupt or two-faced than many homegrown administrations is to forget the good old boy history of Miami. I grew up in the days of Frank Rizzo's Philadelphia. To borrow from the NRA slogan, the linguistics and the melanin content of the skin don't devalue people; people devalue people.

I kept driving west through the typical Florida one-story commercial district, through the miles of three- and four-story apartment complexes, and finally through the construction zone of yet another expanding development of "town homes for luxurious country living starting in the low $90s to $120s." Then, in the span of a quarter mile, the road narrowed to a two-way macadam, and I rolled over the first of several water-control dams, through which man now decided how much flow was let loose into the lower Glades and on to Florida Bay. Eighth Street had turned into the Tamiami Trail. The vegetation crawled onto the side of the road and I could see the canal water on the north side, the ditch that the Moneghan dredge had originally dug. Beyond the ditch were acres and acres of land, some open and filled only with low sedge grasses and the occasional outcrop of cabbage palms, some grown thick with strangler fig and pond apple trees. The sun was directly overhead, and even though the temperature had climbed into the eighties, I rolled down the window and stuck my elbow out. Out of the city the air again felt worthy of letting in. Another thirty miles and I began looking for the turn to Loop Road.

Back in the early 1900s, an optimistic developer had laid out Loop Road as a hub of the future that would equal Coral Gables to the east. When the Trail project faltered during WWI, the long loop into the deeper Glades fell to whomever might use it. For the next few decades it became a jump-off point for illegal whiskey runners, gator poachers, small-time criminals or just societal dropouts looking to hide. The city to the east was where governments and laws were made. Out here in the wide-open Glades, those conventions were ignored.

Partway down the loop, I turned into the white-shelled parking lot of the Frontier Hotel. There were two old, mud-spattered four-by-four trucks pulled up near the entrance and a sun-faded Toyota sedan off to the side. Business was slow and it made me optimistic. My last trip here had included an ugly encounter with some young locals. It wasn't, and had never been, a place for outsiders. I pulled up next to the other trucks, rolled up the window and locked the doors before heading in.

Inside the entryway I had to stop and let my eyes adjust to the sudden dimness. I remembered the cramped "lobby," which gave up registering guests many decades ago, and I followed one of those long, rolled-out, industrial-strength carpet runners into the adjacent barroom. It was even darker in here. There was not a single window to the outside, and the electric sidelights glowed a dull yellow. Somewhere in the back a window air conditioner rumbled. A handsome mahogany bar ran the length of one wall, and two elderly men sat on stools at one end studying a cribbage board. I sat at the middle and watched the woman bartender ignore me at first, then cut her eyes my way too many times, like she was trying to remember an old one-night stand. Finally she moved my way, shuffling a wet bar rag from hand to hand.

"Can I get cha?" she said. She may have been the same woman from my last visit, but her hair color had been changed to a hue of red not known to nature. She was wearing a tight cotton pullover that formfitted her breasts and didn't make it down to the waistband of her jeans. Her other nod to contemporary fashion was a silver belly button ring, through which was looped a matching chain that circled her waist. The rolled skin of her flabby stomach was too soft and too pale for the look.

"Nate Brown," I said in answer to her question.

She narrowed her eyes and tilted her head just so.

"Thought I recognized you," she said. "You was in here just the other day. Gave them Brooker boys a ass-whippin'."

While she talked she reached down into the stainless cooler of ice, pulled out a longneck bottle of beer and opened it.

"Mr. Brown said you was all right."

"It was a couple of years ago," I said.

"Yeah?" she said, putting the cold bottle in front of me.

The two men at the end of the bar had turned their attention to us. I met their eyes and they both carefully, almost imperceptibly, nodded their respect, maybe to a man who Mr. Brown had said was all right or maybe to someone who could ass-whip the Brooker boys. They returned to their cards. I took a drink from the bottle.

"Have you seen Mr. Brown lately?" I asked the bartender. "I'm trying to get a message to him."

She straightened her look this time, being careful.

"Maybe," she said. "The other day."

Nate Brown had some kind of native status in the Glades. His ancestors were some of the first white people to settle here. No one seemed to know how old he was, but a logical guess put him in his mid-eighties. Still, I had personally been pole-ferried by him in a Glades skiff over a dozen miles or more of canals and water routes into the heart of the swamp. I had seen him appear from nowhere and then disappear into the emptiness of four thousand acres of sawgrass without so much as a compass.

"If I leave you a phone number, could you get it to Mr. Brown along with a message that Max Freeman needs to see him?" I said to the woman.

"Maybe," she said, glancing down to the cribbage players.

I took a bar napkin off a stack, used my own pen to write down my cell number and handed it to her.

"I appreciate it," I said, finishing the beer and putting a twenty-dollar bill next to it. As I turned to leave I gave the eleven-foot gator skin mounted on one wall a cursory look, but below it I noticed a pair of framed black-and-white photographs. I bent closer and could make out a group shot of a dozen men, standing stiff and posed before the raised iron neck of an ancient dredge that had the word NOREN painted on one side. The photo paper was dulled with age, but I could make out the thin figures of the men, dressed in dungarees and long-sleeved shirts. Some sported thick, handlebar mustaches; some showed dark hair pasted across their foreheads. There were old ink scratchings at the bottom of the picture, but the letters were indecipherable.

"Are these the old road builders?" I said.

"Don't know," the bartender said. "Them pictures been up there before that gator probably."

"Anybody out here have family in the photos?"

She looked at me oddly.

"They's just a bunch of old-timers," she said. "Nobody knows 'em."

CHAPTER 4

I kicked up the AC and was on the trail back to the city when my cell phone rang.

"Freeman," I said.

"Aloha? What the hell is Aloha?"

"Hey, I don't know, a guy tries to be humorous, sometimes it doesn't work."

"You're not a funny guy, Max—face it."

"You're right, Detective, I'm not."

"So don't try."

"All right then, seriously. Can I see you tonight?"

"Depends."

"On?"

"On whether I can get this case paperwork done on time and whether seeing means we can go see a movie or you just want to sleep with me."

"Oh, your turn to be funny," I said.

"I'm not laughing."

"In that case, how about I pick you up in the parking lot at seven? It'll give you more desk time. We'll eat at Canyons, then walk around to the movies at eight fifteen."

"What? No sleeping?"

"We'll have to see how the evening goes."

"You're a true man of mystery, Max."

"True," I said. "See you at seven."

"OK."

Jesus, I thought, and clicked off the cell.

Richards and I had met during an investigation of a series of child abductions that brought her task force to my river. I'd tried to avoid her. I had once been married to a cop. The romance had been short-lived. Richards had also been in a police marriage. Her husband was killed in the line of duty by a kid who wasn't old enough to grasp the true difference between pulling a real trigger versus the one in an arcade game. The kid was still in a Florida prison, a real one, doing a man's life sentence. My ex was still in Philly, and I had not talked with her since before I left.

Despite some effort to keep our distance, Richards and I had been seeing each other more and more often. The emotional distance was closing, but we were both carrying a lot of baggage. We were working at it, letting it come if it was going to.

In a few minutes my 7:00 P.M. promise was being broken. The only time traffic on I-95 isn't running ten miles over the speed limit is when it's locked up at five miles per hour and the bumper-to-bumper wall of commuters makes it physically impossible. It is a time when South Floridians collectively curse railroad baron Henry Flagler for bringing civilization to the subtropics in the first place and his friend Henry Ford for engineering cars that were cheap enough to let just about anyone pack up and drive on down.

The only advantage to a South Florida traffic jam during the evening rush hour was the chance to see the sunset. Because the state is as flat as a pool table and the interstate overpasses are often higher than the one-story buildings, you often get treated to a spectacular swirl of purple, orange and soft lavenders in a stubborn cobalt blue sky that hangs on to the late light. I thought of the Tamiami Trail workers eighty years ago who must have seen a similar sight lose its grandeur in their desperate daily labor. By the time I reached the Broward Boulevard exit to downtown Fort Lauderdale, the sun was bloodred, and from the top of the interchange I could see a necklace of bright, starlike lights strung out in its glow. They were the landing lights of airliners stacked up in their approaches to the international airport. More tourists and a returning business class flowing into paradise.

Three blocks off the interstate, I pulled into the sheriff's parking lot, fifteen minutes late but lucky enough to arrive during a shift change. I found a space near the front entrance and backed in. I watched the employees coming and going, mostly civilians with an occasional uniform of dark green trousers and a white, short-sleeved shirt. The men tended toward the thick-armed variety, their sleeves tight around the tops of their biceps and their chests expanded by the bulletproof vests under their shirts. Most of them looked young to me.

While I watched, my fingers unconsciously went to the side of my neck and found the small soft spot of scar tissue that the bullet had left after passing through skin and muscle and then smacking into the brick wall of a Philadelphia dry cleaner. My eyes were unfocused until I picked up the familiar movement of Richards's long-legged gait. She was halfway across the broad courtyard. Her hair was pinned up in the way of a good professional and she was dressed in a pair of slacks done in some light fabric, with a jacket to match. There was a bounce to her step, an unmistakable athleticism in the slight swing of narrow hips and the squared stillness of wide shoulders. I liked the look.

She almost made the curb, swung her head to scan the

lot for my truck and spotted me. I had the window halfway down to wave when something grabbed her attention. She spun on one heel and looked back toward the entrance at a deputy in uniform who was jogging to catch her. He was barely taller than she and had the biceps and the chest. He was also carrying a 9 mm on his hip and a radio microphone clipped to the epaulet on his right shoulder. Patrol cop.

I watched as he started the conversation in earnest, though they were too far away for me to overhear. When I saw Richards square her stance and cross her arms I knew it was no Sunday chat. I'd seen that body language before and it wasn't pretty. The tight knot of Richards's blond hair was bobbing on the back of her head as she spoke. The cop half turned away in one of those, "I don't have to listen to this shit" moves, but then he snapped back, putting his hands on both hips and leaning his chin into Richards's space. She never gave an inch and instead uncrossed her arms and raised a pointed finger, and this time I could read her lips saying "back off." The cop flattened out a hand and raised it, as though he was going to slap the finger out of his face. My instant reaction was to open the door of the truck, but Richards, always observant of movement around her, turned an open palm my way without looking around.

The sound of her voice caused the heads of two passersby to turn toward her, and the cop quickly put his hands out, palms to her, and took a step back. He was in midsentence when Richards turned on her heel and stepped off the curb, giving him her back. She walked directly toward my truck, with the dissed officer watching her and me, opened the passenger door and let herself in.

Her face and throat were flushed, and if she had looked me in the face, I knew I would have seen her eyes flashing that green color that always came when she was pissed.

"Hi, honey," I said. "How was your day?"

"Shut up, Max. You're not funny."

I pulled out and drove, sneaking a look at the pulsating artery in her neck, waiting for it to trip down a few beats before opening my mouth again. I drove east into the city, crossed Federal Highway and took the back way to Canyons, passing the park and the old Florida-style homes along the river. I parked in a lot behind a line of Sunrise Avenue stores and walked around to open Richards's door. She stepped out and into my extended arm and kissed me on the mouth without saying a word.

"Apology accepted," I said.

I closed the door and could see a grin come to the corner of her mouth before she turned away. We sat at the bar waiting for a table. I was drinking coffee, and she waited until she was well into her first margarita before she finally spoke.

"David McCrary. And I don't care what Lynn says, if he touches her again, he's canned." Her eyes had gone back to their bluish hue, but there was still some fire in them.

"McCrary's the cop in the courtyard?"

"Control freak," she said. "And all the shit that comes with it, including physical abuse."

"And Lynn is, who? A friend?"

"She's a good cop, a real sweetheart, and she's in love with this asshole."

I waited for Richards to take another couple of sips of her drink.

"She tell you he's hitting her?"

"Not in so many words, but she's just leaving that part out. All the signs are there. He calls her constantly on her cell, even when he's on duty. If she's with us at Brownies, he shows up and cuts her right out of the group like some damn sheepdog separating the flock. Hell, these days she'll rarely come out alone."

Control and ownership, I thought. The cornerstones of an abusive relationship. These days every cop gets the lessons, takes a class on dealing with domestic violence. Some of them don't pay attention. Some don't want to pay attention. Some can't see in themselves what they're trained to see in others.

"You want to talk about it?" I said.

"No," she said, but she did.

When we were seated at a window table, she talked about her friend between bites of black beans and rice and a mesquite-grilled snapper. I had a wood-grilled filet—I liked to take advantage of steak when I was off the river. We split a bottle of chardonnay and I ate slowly, mostly listening while she argued with herself over reporting the cop to internal affairs.

"You realize your friend is the one who's going to have to file a complaint," I finally said.

"Yeah."

"Tough thing to do, being part of the blue crew and all."

Every cop knew that if a wife or girlfriend filed a domestic assault charge against him, his head would be on the block. If the charge was upheld, forget it. A conviction meant you could never carry a weapon again. Your career was over. It was a tough decision, holding a fellow officer's career in your hand. It's why so many incidents got swept under the rug, or dealt with internally and off the books.

"I warned him if I ever saw a mark on her that's exactly what I'd do," Richards said.

"And?"

"He denied he ever touched her. Said Lynn was upset. Said he loved her and wouldn't hurt her."

"They all do," I said, finishing the wine.

"Voice of experience?" she said, raising an eyebrow.

"I'll tell you about my father sometime," I said, getting the waiter's attention. "You ready to hit the movies?"

"I don't think so. How about if you just take me home and let me jump your scrawny bones," she said, taking me by the arm.

"I really didn't have any such thing in mind," I said, leaving a tip.

"Liar," she said, pushing me toward the door.

We made love in the hammock on her back porch, surrounded by the nighttime arboretum of oaks and transplanted palms and birds of paradise that lined her city yard. The breath of night-blooming jasmine was in the air, and the aqua light from her swimming pool danced in the tree leaves above. In the wake of our dinner conversation I tried to be tender, but she was having none of it. We ended up on the wooden planks of the patio deck and then in the chlorine-scented water. We were in her bed when I automatically woke at dawn. I rolled onto one shoulder and watched her sleeping. She hated it when I stared at her. I had not brought up the subject of my shack fire or the new investigation Billy had me on. Both were too tentative and given her mood, not worth the interruption. I knew it would come back on me, that I wasn't sharing.

I brushed a strand of hair off her face with my fingertips, then got up quietly and went to the kitchen to start the coffeemaker. I got through one cup and then took a shower. I was dressed and finishing my third cup on the patio when she stepped out to join me. The sky had lightened and she was dressed for work. She put a hand on my shoulder and looked up into the oak at the sound of a trill made by a Florida scrub jay.

"You sleep all right?"

"Not much," I said, kissing the back of her hand.

"You wanna go to Lester's for breakfast and tell me about it?"

I didn't respond, so she added, "About whatever you wanted to talk about when you called yesterday. It's your turn."

I shook my head and smiled. This intuition thing. It was one of the things about women that always amazed and befuddled me.

"Let's go," I said.

After breakfast in a booth at Lester's, after I told her about the fire and the long-shot speculation that at least a few eighty-year-old disappearances in the Glades might be suspicious, I dropped her at work. She had listened, like a good investigator. I've found that most people in conversation listen only to the voice of the person they're talking to, waiting for it to stop so they can throw out their own thoughts and speculations. Richards listened to my words and then weighed them before answering. She pointed out that finding evidence of a homicide in the Glades, if that's what Mr. Mayes was talking about, would be close to impossible. Criminals had been dumping bodies in the lonely stretches of muck and sawgrass for a hundred years. Her own unit worked the disappearance of a young prostitute last month whose dismembered body was found in a Glades canal by an unlucky fisherman. Nature had a way of eating up evidence out there.

She was more concerned about the fire. Who knew what wacky environmentalist or mouth-breathing Glades cracker might want him out of there.

"Maybe it's time to move back into the civilized world, Freeman," she said as she got out of the truck in front of the sheriff's office. It wasn't the first time she or Billy had brought up the suggestion.

"Maybe," was now my standard reply.

"Bullshit," she said, and waved as she walked away, always getting the last word.

I drove north to Billy's building, where the concierge with the fake English accent greeted me formally and then electronically buzzed me into the penthouse elevator. The doors opened upstairs onto a private foyer with no other entrances but the one to the apartment. I always left some clothes and a pair of running shoes in the guest suite. My old faded Temple University T-shirt had been pressed by Billy's laundry service. I put on a pair of shorts and laced up the shoes. I went back down, waved at the doorman, passed the pool out back and walked out to the beach. I sat on my towel in the hard sand below the high-tide mark and stretched my hamstrings, then left the towel as a motivating finish line and started jogging south. The first fifteen minutes I took it easy, pulling the sea air deep into my lungs, judging if there had been any real damage from the smoke I'd inhaled during the fire. Then I opened up my stride a bit, staying down on the hard-pack and occasionally getting caught by a high, running wave. After thirty minutes I turned around and pushed it. I had to dodge a couple of shell gatherers but kept a steady pace. I couldn't help stealing glances at Billy's growing building, trying to judge the distance. My heart was banging and the blood was pulsing in my ears when I saw the towel and started sprinting. I squeezed my eyes shut over the last ten yards and pulled up only when I felt my foot hit the terry cloth. I jogged to a stop and felt a rasp at the end of each exhalation; could taste the acidic smoke in the top of my mouth. I pulled off my shirt, kicked off the shoes and waded into the surf, letting the breakers wash over my head and the water leach away my body heat. I stood facing east, at the rumpled line of the horizon. I was preparing for something that I did not want to catch me flat-footed, or out of breath, or weak. I couldn't see it yet in my head, but it was there, a tingle of violence that vibrated low in my spine. Something was coming, and even though I could not name it, I knew I would not welcome it.

I shook the sand out of the towel and mopped myself off before attempting to get back into Billy's building. I even slipped my shoes back on. The concierge nevertheless gave me one of those closed-eyes, shake-your-head gestures that says, "Riffraff these days. What can you do?" Upstairs I showered and dressed in a clean pair of canvas pants and a white polo shirt. I drank one more cup of coffee while standing at the rail outside and watched the wind set down a corduroy pattern across the Atlantic. I knew why Billy loved it up here. He had been born and raised in the ghetto of north Philadelphia. By the strength of his own intelligence and his mother's refusal to accept any preset station in life, he had risen. Captain of his public school chess team, a group of black kids who annually kicked ass in national competitions. Top of his class at Temple Law School and the same when he took an advanced degree in business at Wharton. The only thing that kept him from being one of the finest trial lawyers in the East was his inescapable stutter. His background had also turned him into a staunch capitalist. He was never going to settle for academia. Instead he left Philly and came here. He quickly built a client base and a range of contacts that was enormous. He got rich and moved high above the streets into the fresh ocean air and sunlight, determined never to live below the horizon again.

With his shrewd business sense, Billy had invested my disability buyout from the police department and created for me a sizable portfolio. Last year he'd counseled me to leave the shack. "Hiding" he now called it, and he wasn't completely wrong. Maybe I had even considered it, but not now. I drained my cup, grabbed my keys and the plastic bag in which I'd placed a charred sliver of wood from the cabin piling. If I left my river, it wasn't going to be because I had been forced. If someone was trying to scare me out, I'd find out who.

CHAPTER 5

I drove south on Dixie Highway, and at a section of commercial buildings between coastal cities, I turned off and pulled into a warehouse complex near the Florida East Coast Railway tracks. I rolled down in front of a long, corrugated steel building lined with garage-style doors and simple entrances. Some had trucks backed up to open garage bays. Others were unmarked and shuttered. I found a space in front of a door with a small unobtrusive sign that read GLOBAL FORENSICS INC.

I stepped out into the midday heat that reflected off the concrete and the steel walls. Across the way some kind of rap music was thumping out of an open bay. A low-ride Honda Civic with those little toy-sized wheels was jacked up outside, with a pair of skinny legs sticking out from under the front end. Inside the bay two young guys wearing either real long shorts or real short pants were bent halfway into the open hood of an old Pontiac GTO. Three inches of underwear was showing above their belt loops, and both had black and blue tattoos on their lower legs, the details of which I couldn't see from here.

I locked my doors. Riffraff these days. What can you do?

The door to Global Forensics was open, and I stepped into a small reception area that was devoid of any clutter, dust or human presence, and that was freezing cold. When I entered I heard a muffled buzzer ring somewhere behind another inside door, and thirty seconds later a baritone voice sounded over a small white speaker mounted high in one corner: "Hey, give me a minute. I'll be right with you. Have a seat."

There wasn't a chair in the room, just a single metal desk with nothing on its surface. There were no pictures on the pale walls. No calendar. No license. I was sitting on the corner of the desk, dangling one leg, when I heard a gunshot ring out from behind the inside walls. It was a heavy report, large caliber. I'd jumped at the initial crack, but stayed seated. I knew what kind of business went on here.

A minute or so later the inside door opened and the large head of a whiskered man appeared. He was wearing a pair of safety glasses and had a set of protective earmuffs pulled down around his thick neck.

"Well, Max Freeman," he said. "Come on in, boy. What can I do for you?"

William Lott is a big lout of a man with opinions on everything but a true knowledge and specialty in only one: forensics science. At one time, despite his irascible personality and love of good Scotch, he was one of the best in his field at the FBI labs at Quantico. He says that he quit just before the media exposed the myriad problems and botched cases of that unit. He said he had ducked out so that his own "sterling reputation" wouldn't be sullied by the government administration "hacks" and management "drones" who left the true scientists "hung out to dry." He opted to set up his own private forensics lab in Florida. It would amaze you, he said, how many people mistrusted the government and the cops. Since O. J. his practice was booming with clients wanting independent DNA tests, chemical analysis and crime-scene reanalysis of evidence gathered against defendants. "And you don't even wanna know how many sheet samples I get in here from the wives or the husbands in Palm Beach and East Boca," he was fond of telling me. He was also quick to add, "All I do is the science. What they do with the results is their gig." Lott was one of Billy's many acquaintances, and on that recommendation alone he would have prospered. Billy had introduced us at lunch one day, and I sat humorously amazed while the scientist downed three dozen hot chicken wings and a six-pack of Old Milwaukee and never lost a beat in conversation.

"Let me put this old cannon away, Max," he said, and I followed him inside. As we passed a dimly lit room off to the right, I could smell the stink of cordite drifting out. Lott was carrying a military .45 loosely in his right hand, and his white, long-sleeved glove meant he was capturing blow-back residue from firing the weapon. We entered a large white room that looked like a cross between an industrial kitchen and the biology lab I had in high school. Glass-fronted cabinets, sinks with long, swan-necked faucets, hooded workstations and three different microscopes set up against one wall, along with rows of numbered drawers.

Lott was a big man, as tall as me at six feet two but carrying sixty more pounds than my 205. Still, he moved about the place with a grace that came from familiarity and a perhaps unconscious efficiency. He laid the gun on a countertop and then carefully took off the glove and placed it under one of the lighted hoods. He then unlocked one of the drawers, placed the gun inside and relocked it.

"OK, Max," he finally said, taking my hand in his big palm and shaking it. "What's our boy Billy got you on now?"

"Nothing, yet," I said. "But he will. You know Billy."

"Yeah. Smart little bastard, ain't he? Sweet move you getting in with him, Freeman. Got ethics up to his eyeballs. Not like them other scum-sucking lawyers out to line their own damn pockets creatin' a fuckin' crisis a minute that, of course, only they and their own brethren can solve at three hundred dollars an hour plus expenses."

I nodded, fully prepared to let Lott go on even though I'd heard his line before. But he stopped on his own accord.

"Gettin' on to lunchtime here, Max. What can I do for you, unless you wanna join me over to Pure Platinum, where they have got the finest little buffet and boobs lunch special goin' on. They is a little honey from one of them daytime soaps struttin' her stuff you would not believe...."

"No thanks, Bill," I said, pulling the plastic bag with the charred wood sliver from my pocket. "This one's for me. A matter of accelerant, I believe."

Lott took the sample, his eyes and demeanor instantly changing with the challenge. He turned the bag in the light, then opened it and took a careful smell, like some fine-wine connoisseur.

"Gasoline," he said. "But with an additive."

He turned and walked over to another hooded workstation, sat down on a metal stool and opened a drawer. I knew enough to stay where I was. Bill Lott was not the kind of guy who let someone look over his shoulder while he worked. It took him only five minutes.

"Marine fuel," he said, getting up and bringing the sample back to me. "Mixture of gas and oil. The kind you use in outboard motors on small boats. Impossible to tell what brand 'cause you can buy regular gas and mix it yourself."

I took the sample back from him.

"Piece of old hardwood there, Max."

"Piling," I said, not elaborating.

Lott nodded and smiled.

"All I do is the science," he said.

I was headed back to Billy's when I turned off into the parking lot of a convenience store and called him on the cell. I left a message that I'd been there during the day but was going back to the shack to spend the night. I would call to confirm our meeting with Mayes in the morning. After punching off, I went into the store and bought a pre-wrapped sandwich, a cheap Styrofoam cooler, a bag of ice and a six pack of Rolling Rock, and headed for the river.

I'd finished the sandwich by the time I pulled into the landing parking lot. I flipped my canoe and set the cooler of iced beer in the center. The wind had died, and in the high sun the surface of the water looked like a sheet of hot glass. The ranger's boat was cleated hard against the dock, and I noted the red, five-gallon auxiliary fuel tank stored in one corner of the well. I floated the canoe, put my right foot on the center line inside, and with both hands on either gunwale, pushed off and glided, balancing, onto my river.

I paddled in a slow rhythm: reach, pull through, and a little kick-out at the end. The river's banks were still. I watched the high clouds in the west sit like smeared white paint on the sky. An osprey seemed frozen at the frondless top of a dead cypress tree. The raptor's white head did not move; its yellow eye was locked on something below in the water. I shipped the paddle and let the canoe glide in the sun. I popped a cold beer and sat back to watch the bird. The osprey is a true hunting bird, an animal with magnificent patience and aerobatic skill. And unlike the bald eagle—which has all the public relations but nowhere near the same hunting pride—he will take only live prey. The eagle will eat another's carrion and will also get his ass kicked in flight by an osprey. I kept as motionless as my sipping would allow. I was on my second beer when the bird lifted off its perch and made a strong, graceful swing to the south, then looped back. The aluminum against my palm was cold, but I didn't change my grip as I watched the osprey come hard and fast back to the north. The bird seemed to lay back its wings as it increased its speed and tilt at a steep angle to the glassed-out water. It looked like a suicide run, but at the last second I watched his talons stretch open as he pulled them forward into the attack position. The movement stalled his air speed just inches above the water, and then, in a flash of tendon and muscle and the light splash of sun-brilliant water, he struck deep. His body lurched slightly forward from the instant water drag, but with two strong flaps of his wings he climbed up with a small, silver-sided snook in his grasp, the fish's tail vibrating in a death throe. The bird soared out over the tree canopy and disappeared, and as I watched I switched the beer can into my other hand and pressed the cold of my palm against the small of my back, where the tingle of something waiting to drive me off my river had started on the beach.

When I finally got back to the shack I didn't bother to paddle around to look at the black smear on the north wall, but I did take extra care to look for prints on the stairway. If an arsonist had wanted to harm me, why wouldn't he have set the staircase leading to my door aflame? It would at least have forced me to jump. I tied up the canoe and went up. The air had cleared some of the burnt stench from the shack but there was still an odor inside. I coughed on the first lungful, almost as though it had tripped a memory. I started coffee and then stripped naked and stepped back out on the landing, where I showered off under my jury-rigged rain barrel. The barrel was mounted just below the roofline, and the gutter system refilled it with fresh rainwater. A rubber hose clipped above a perfrated garden nozzle gave me enough flow to rinse off a film of sweat. I heard the low grunt of an anhinga but couldn't see it hiding back in the foliage. I dressed, but my clean T-shirt had taken on the smoke smell. I tried to ignore it while I moved one of my straight-backed chairs over to the window, where an early evening breeze was sifting in. I don't remember finishing the coffee or falling asleep. But I remember the light change and then the burnt odor too, and then the sight of a young woman sitting in a Philadelphia hotel room chair, a pillow held tightly in her arms. The look on her face made her appear both quiet and terrified at the same time. I even asked her a question before I realized she was dead.

My partner, Scott Erb, and I were working Center City on the two-to-eleven shift and got a dispatch call at 10:45. The security manager had requested our presence at the Wyndham Hotel ASAP. We both winced at the language, and then the dispatcher added her own sardonic, "He reports that discretion is advised." We were only a few blocks away and had no calls holding. The security guy met us in the lobby, introduced himself and led us straight to the elevators. He waited until the doors closed before saying, "I think we've got a murder-suicide, and you're not going to like the shooter." We looked at each other while he punched in a code and lit a floor button near the top. Scott took out a pad, checked his watch, and started scratching in notes. The hallway was empty when the doors opened on the eighteenth floor. It was a nice place, less than ten years old and pricey. There were fresh flowers in the foyer, even at 11:00 P.M. The security man led us to the end of the hall.

"Honeymoon suite," he said, unlocking the door. "Guy took it for one night only. A special getaway rate."

He pushed the door open and let us go in first. The odor was of cordite and of something else burned. The entry opened onto a large room, the decor ruined by a man's body in the middle of the floor, a stain growing in the carpet by his head. I stepped over the man's legs and bent to look at the 9 mm Glock on the floor inches from his hand.

"Max," Scott said, and when I looked up, my partner was staring at the coffee table, where a department-issue black leather holster lay empty.

"I already checked the I.D.," said the security man, reading our eyes. "He's one of yours."

I stood and stepped farther into the room and started to say, "and where's the . . . ," when I saw her in the darkened corner, sitting, her head up against the back of the high Queen Anne chair, her eyes in shadow. I said "Excuse me miss but . . . ," before I realized I was talking to a dead woman. Her hands were crossed over a white pillow that she was holding tight to her chest. Only close up could you see the small hole in the material where the 9 mm had entered.

"They registered as Mr. and Mrs.," the security guy said. "The door was locked from the inside. I had to snap the security chain to get in."

"Yeah, thanks. We'll call it in to homicide," Scott said, ushering the guy back out.

"Phil Broderick," Scott said after closing the door.

"You knew him?"

"Worked the Twenty-second. Hung with Tommy Mason and those guys."

"That his wife?"

Scott stepped across the room. He had stopped taking notes. He looked into the dead woman's face for only a second.

"Yeah," he said, but there was an unusual tone in his voice.

"What?" I said, watching his eyes.

"You know, locker-room shit," he said, turning away. "Guys said he was using her for a punching bag."

"And let me guess. Nobody reported it."

We both went quiet and I stepped back over to the woman. There was a half-burned photo of a couple in their wedding clothes on the floor next to her. The smell of the burned acetate was still in the air.

"Maybe he was trying to make it up to her," Scott said, "with all this."

"Yeah. Make it up," I said.

I crossed the room back over to the body and knelt down into the deep carpet and turned the officer's head and looked into the dead face. At first it looked familiar, the low trim of the long sideburns, the oil in the hair, and then the dream turned on me and I could see the face of my father.

I was startled awake by the feeling of falling and struck my heels hard against the plank floor to keep myself from sliding out of the straight-backed chair. The room was dark and thick with humidity, and I could feel the sheen of sweat on my back and under my thighs. The mix of dream and memory had left me shaking. I moved with habit and got a gallon of fresh water from my makeshift cooler and drank for several seconds from the plastic bottle. As I stood in the night, shaking, the first few drops of rain began to ping against the tin roof and patter in the leaves of the canopy outside, and I knew there would be no more sleep before dawn.

CHAPTER 6

I stopped at a roadside place on the way into town that was popular with truckers and local farmers, and I joined a handful of them with hash browns soaked in gravy, collard greens and strong, black coffee. The middle-aged black waitress looked at me twice, and winked at me when I left her a large tip. It was still before 7:00 A.M.

Once in the city, I parked in the same lot I always used off Clematis Street, near the county courthouse. The old man who ran the lot put me close to a space next to his payment shack and touched the fender of the truck after giving me the ticket.

"I take care of her, Mr. Max."

"I know you will," I said, and walked south. The streets of West Palm Beach were busy with cars, but the sidewalks could never match them the way they did in the big northeast cities. People here parked close to their offices, and newer towers were built with parking inside on the first few floors. You rarely found yourself mobbed up at a crosswalk with other pedestrians unless it was lunch hour or after hours on the more popular restaurant and club strips. The early morning rain had wrung out the clouds and the sky had gone clear and blue with the southeast breeze. The walk was worth it—I was disappointed when I got to Billy's building and had to go inside.

Billy was behind his broad desk with piles of stacked

folders and the flat-screen computer monitor holding his attention.

"M-Max," he said in greeting, without looking up. "You are l-looking w-well."

I knew not to break his concentration and crossed the room to the floor-to-ceiling windows that formed the southwest corner. From up here you could see the southern parts of the city of Palm Beach to the east, the line of office buildings and condos along Lake Worth to the south, and the horizon in a cloudy fog to the west. Billy and his views.

"A little last-minute cramming for Mayes," I finally said.

"No. F-For you," he said, tapping something on the keyboard and getting up.

"County c-codes would restrict you from r-rebuilding any part of the original st-structure of the research station even if it was to b-become uninhabitable due to any cause, n-natural or m-man-made."

Billy had not dismissed my news of the fire.

"Despite the ninety-nine-year lease?"

"Categorically."

"Shit."

"My s-sentiments exactly."

Billy's secretary, Allie, came in with coffee and placed the service on a table in front of the couch with a view. She had included two china cups and a large mug. She smiled at me when Billy thanked her.

"So whoever tried to torch the place gets two jumps at once. He either scares me out, or messes the place up enough for the county to close it."

"You said R-Ranger G-Griggs was right there when it started?"

"Yeah."

"C-Convenient."

I took the mug and blew over the rim, rippling the top layer.

"He's there to m-make sure you're awake and g-get out safely and t-to make sure the fire doesn't sp-spread into his forest."

"Why, Billy, I'm stunned at your lack of belief in the sincerity of your fellow man."

"Sh-Shit."

"My sentiments, exactly."

Allie's voice on the intercom stopped our speculations.

"Mr. Mayes is here, Mr. Manchester."

Billy crossed back to his desk and answered. Allie ushered in a young man, maybe early twenties, dressed uncomfortably in a suit and looking somewhat sheepish in his surroundings.

"Mr. Mayes," Billy said, grasping the young man's hand. He held Billy's eyes with a practiced politeness despite his obvious jitters. "And this is M-Max Freeman, a p-private investigator who w-works with me."

I took Mayes's hand. Again the polite eyes. He was good-looking, freshly shaved, with short dark hair that probably had some kind of gel in it recently but not this morning. He was Billy's height and shape, lean and anxious. I thought of a college student on his first day of a law internship. Billy motioned for us to sit on the couch, and I watched Mayes take the opportunity to sweep the room, taking in the wall of law books, the spotlit oil paintings and pieces of expensive sculptures and artwork that Billy always surrounded himself with. He sat on the edge of the leather couch and glanced at the view through the tall windows either in admiration, or as a means of escape. He accepted the offer of coffee and Billy began.

"Mr. Freeman has f-field experience in law enforcement," Billy said as a way of introduction. "He has also w-worked before in the d-deep Everglades and w-would know the areas we're talking about much better than I."

Mayes looked at me and held my eyes for a moment. The look came off as respectful, but I could tell he was also reading me. He was not just a kid who accepted words on face value.

"You would go out there, to look for them, I mean, their bodies?" he said to me. "I mean, if they're out there."

Now I was holding his eyes, clear, intelligent, but with an ache that I had seen before, maybe in my own mirror. The look said he was searching for answers in his past that were connected to his future. In that way he was not unlike the young cop I had once been, trying to judge my steps by the way my family had walked them before me. We held the look a few seconds too long, and broke away at the same time. I felt the flush of embarrassment on my throat and ears. He rubbed at his own neck while turning away.

"Max has had the opportunity to r-read your letters, Mr. Mayes, and he's as intrigued as I," Billy interrupted. "But p-perhaps some of the background that w-we have discussed is better coming from you."

"Uhh, just Mark, please, Mr. Manchester," Mayes said.

I was trying to read his reaction to Billy's stutter. Before I came to Florida, I had talked with Billy several times on the phone but never face-to-face. But Mayes was either overwhelmed by his own nervousness or too polite to show that he even noticed the stutter. He turned to me and took a deep breath.

"Well, sir, it started when my mother passed away about eighteen months ago," he began. "When she died, I was really the last one in the family left in a line going way back."

While we sat drinking coffee we let Mayes tell his story yet again, its familiarity making him comfortable and our attentiveness bringing out detail. His own grandfather had been the youngest of Cyrus Mayes's three sons, too young to join the others in their attempt in the early part of the century to find work and earn their family a way out of the poverty of the recovering South. Stories told by his grandmother and subsequently by his own mother depicted homes dominated by women. Little, he recalled, was ever revealed of the habits or working talents of the men of the Mayes clan. Even his own reticent father, the lone male son of the lone male survivor of the Mayes family, had died of a heart attack at the relatively early age of forty-eight.

Mayes repeated Billy's explanation of his great-grandmother's hope chest, found in the attic of the family home in Atlanta after she had died. A young man who'd never been told the history of the men in his family now had a handful of history before him—but it was filled with more questions than answers.

"So, you've seen the letters, what do you think?" Mayes said. The directness of the question was the boldest statement he'd made since first coming through the door. "What do you think happened? All of a sudden, I've got this religious grandfather trying to do right by his family and then what? Did they die out there in the Everglades? By accident? Did they just give up? What can I take away from what the letters say about them, if I don't know what happened?"

There was desperation in the kid's voice, and it made both Billy and me hesitate.

"Like I told you, Mr. Manchester, I'm not even sure where to look to find out. I did some library searches up at Emory. I even came down to Tampa and looked at some old microfiche of the newspapers at the time for names or some story of the men who worked on the roadway. Professor Martin up at school was able to get some Florida state records from the Department of Transportation, but this all happened before the state took over the Tamiami Trail project. He said that if I needed to see corporate records from the private companies that worked on the roadway, forget it. That's why he gave me your name, Mr. Manchester. He said you were the best."

I watched Billy's face. Professor Martin had been a client. Billy had helped him through a Florida stock swindle that he said had probably saved the guy's university tenure. But the compliment had passed completely over his head. He was concentrating on something more important to him.

"Corporate r-responsibility can follow a company around for a l-long time," Billy finally said. "Even the h-hint that your great-grandfather's l-letters seemed to indicate that workers d-died unaccountably or w-were forced like slaves to s-stay on the job would not be something any corporation would l-like to see come back from the p-past."

Though the words seemed to be rhetorical, I watched the uneasy effect they had on the young Mayes. His eyes had gone off to some point beyond the glass, and I watched his fingers go to a necklace just inside of his collar.

"Well, sir, I already wrote to a couple of them," he said. "After I met with you and you seemed, you know, to believe me. I was just asking, you know, if there were any employee records from the time."

"And?" Billy said.

"They sent sort of a form letter back, saying it was private information and I'd have to contact their legal department."

"And?" Billy said again. I could tell this was new information, and not exactly welcomed.

"I, uh, told them we'd get back to them."

"We?"

"Uh, you, sir. You."

Billy stood and stepped across to the window, his profile stark against the bright light of the sky. Mayes looked at me and I tried to keep my face neutral. He still had his hand unconsciously at his throat, the same kind of gesture I'd long tried to break after the Philadelphia bullet had left its scar on me. Finally Billy turned.

"Mark. M-Maybe we'd better go over some of these n-names and resources you've already got," he said, heading over to his computer. "And the entities you've already c-contacted."

"Uh, yes, sir," the kid said, standing.

I stood, shook the young man's hand and took the opportunity to check the necklace. Hanging high on a silver chain was a simple religious cross that had settled into the shallow indent of flesh where his collar bones met.

"M-Max," Billy said. "S-Shall I c-call you later?"

I just nodded and started out. It was not a question.

I went home and spent the next two mornings fishing, working the edges of the mangroves in the open, slightly salty middle river, trying to entice a tarpon or snook to hit just for the thrill of the fight. There were rarely more than a few boats on the water during the week. Most of them were small boaters who lingered along the edges, occasionally waving as though we were club members, a brotherhood of fishermen. One of them passed and asked about the fly I was using. On both days a thirty-two-foot cabin cruiser with twin inboard screws hung in the middle channel downriver. I could make out at least two men working poles, but it was a poor place to anchor. It was unusual for a boat that size to stay put. Downstream the river opened onto an inlet to the ocean, and most of the bigger boats moved out to sea to take on the wider challenge of true saltwater fishing. I shrugged it off. Money and boats, I thought. Sometimes people just had it to have it so they could show it.

I spent both afternoons sitting out on my top landing—where the hot sun kept some of the mosquitoes at bay—reading and rereading books that Billy had given me. I tried not to stray far from the shack, wondering when I had become so protective of the place. On the second night, the moon was near full, and I took advantage and paddled my canoe hard upstream late into the darkness, working up a full sweat in the humid air and feeling the burn of oxygen-depleted muscle in my shoulders and arms. In an hour I reached the small man-made dam and had to get out and yank the canoe over the concrete abutment and refloat it on the upper river. The water was black and the sound it made as it plunged over the four-foot drop seemed far too loud as it ripped and then boiled into the reflected moonlight and spun quickly away. This upper section went south for another two miles, fed by the accumulation of rainwater in hundreds of acres of low-lying slough in the Everglades. It was a section of the river where I had physically punished myself for many months after I had arrived here, letting the face of a dead boy chase me. I climbed back into the canoe, set myself and judged the curve of the river by the dull silver reflection of moonlight, and began again, paddling and grinding. I had talked with Billy by cell phone earlier in the day. He had gone over the contacts that Mark Mayes had made and had double-checked some of his requests for information. I could tell by his voice that he'd been impressed by the boy's resourcefulness but was pissed that his name had been dropped without his knowledge or permission.

"But our Mr. Mayes may be correct about one of those companies," Billy said. "PalmCo has a long development history in the state, and we've already tracked corporate officers and previous owners all the way back to the 1930s. Before that it gets difficult because of the crash of 1929, when a lot of businesses went under, including most of South Florida's development speculators. When they came back, it was under different names, even though the people and the source of the money were the same."

Billy and I had already talked about the coincidence of Cyrus Mayes's reference to the name Noren and the photo of the road workers on the wall of the bar in the Frontier. I'd wondered if the name was that of the dredge manufacturer or the construction company. Billy had already done an Internet search and had not found any dredge manufacturers by that name in the twenties or thirties, and he was moving on the assumption that the contractor's name had been affixed to the dredge boom. "That's the one I'm working on, but the name might be buried in old archives," Billy said. I was always impressed by his abilities to paper-chase. It was a skill for which I had little talent and less patience. Still, I had to hand it to Mayes. Even if it had been unintentional, he'd pushed Billy's buttons, got him on a chase I could tell he wasn't going to give up on easily.

The kid had more going on in his head than just curiosity about his great-grandfather and uncles. He was putting most of his grandmother's inheritance on the line to find answers. But maybe his real questions had more to do with what he had inherited from the men he never knew. That icon around his neck wasn't there as a style statement. Something was chewing at the young man. I didn't know what, but I could almost feel his need for the truth. Maybe he was pushing my buttons, too.

CHAPTER 7

Early the next morning I heard the "thunk" of wood on wood before I felt the shiver in the foundation. My physical sense of touch has always been less sensitive than my sense of smell or taste or even hearing. *Thunk.* But still, it was the vibration that finally popped my eyes open. From my bed I looked to the east window and could tell that it was not much after dawn. *Thunk.* Someone was on my dock. The unexpected visitor. I rolled off my mattress onto all fours and instantly the ache in my shoulders from last night's paddling almost caused me to cry out. I thought about the 9 mm stashed in the armoire, still wrapped tight in oilskin since it had last been fired in anger and then recovered from the river bottom. I'd tried to put it out of my head, the feel of it in my hand, the violence of it. But still it was there. I hadn't thrown it out, despite what it represented in me. Leave it, I thought, and then stood and moved quietly to the door. *Thunk.*

I held the knob and eased pressure up into the old hinges to keep them from squeaking and opened the door enough to see. Down on the landing, sitting with one foot in his wooden skiff and his hands working a small line in the water was Nate Brown. He moved his leg and the skiff banged lightly against the dock piling. *Thunk.*

"Mornin', Mr. Freeman," he said in a slow drawl that was pure dirt Georgia. "Your memory is 'preciated."

He was dressed in a long-sleeved, light-colored work

shirt and denim overalls. His steel gray hair was cut short to a scalp that was as tanned as the rest of his skin. His wiry build seemed folded and angled and delicate, but I knew better. He diverted his eyes from the water and looked up the stairs.

"I heard y'all was lookin' for me?"

I made morning coffee and brought two large tin cups with me and sat on the bottom steps. Nate nodded a thanks for the coffee and took a deep draw from the cup without flinching from its steaming heat. I blew air across mine.

"How's the river running this morning?" I said, attempting small talk and knowing better.

"Prolly high, what with that rain yestiday," he said. "Don't rightly know. I come in from the west."

I looked into the homemade flats skiff, a workmanship long forgotten from a time when the Gladesmen used the small boats and hand-shaved poles to push themselves over miles of channels and shallow, grass-filled water. There was a single small bundle tucked in one corner and a long, canvas-wrapped object I knew would be Brown's old Winchester rifle.

"Just out on a little hunting trip?" I said, making my mistake twice. I had not seen the man in two years, the last time being when he had saved my life.

"No, sir," he said, his clear eyes working into mine from over the rim of the coffee cup. "I heard you was lookin' for me."

After that I talked for an hour, telling Mayes's story while the old man listened to each word, looking up from his fishing line to judge my face when I hesitated or to correct my assumptions of the years or the locations of the road-building project that had ripped the land he and his family had known all their lives.

"So, I thought you might have some ideas, some recollection or knowledge of what happened to these men," I finished.

Brown's eyes came up from the water and took in the cover of foliage above us. The sunlight was now spackling the oak leaves and ferns with spots of leaking light.

"My daddy an' his brothers mostly tol' them stories," he said, not looking at me. "Was before my time, but we heard about them days whilst sittin' round the buttonwood fires out on coon hunts and such.

"Folks then wasn't too welcomin' on the idea, bringing a road through some of the finest huntin' pieces in the Glades. But they was payin' money and it was tough times then. The construction boys brought bidness down to Everglades City, an' the locals didn't seem to mind when they got they pockets full.

"Even Daddy's brother, Mitchell, went out an' worked on the dredge rig with some other local men, but not for long. He tol' stories 'bout how miserable them city boys was with the swamp angels, what we call mosquitoes, an' the heat and all. He said some of them boys like to abandon ship after just a couple of days, and some of 'em did.

"Mitchell and them finally just walked away—course they knew them Glades since they was kids, so's it was easy for them."

Brown stopped and searched the water again, tickling the line, weighing his words.

"Wasn't till later, after they'd pushed 'er out near Shark Valley that Daddy said they heard stories 'bout men goin' out on the job and not comin' back in.

"Mitchell would tell a story 'bout a dead man's island where they buried them quittin' boys up to they necks in muck an' marked the spot with a Christ cross, but us kids thought he was just tryin' to scare us round the campfire."

"And nobody ever said anything?" I asked. "No sheriff or any authority?"

Brown let a wry grin pull at the corner of his mouth.

"Hell, weren't never no law out there to speak of. Besides, Daddy always said them boys didn't have no bidness comin' into our country anyways, an' what happened to 'em weren't none of our bidness either. Daddy said the Glades weren't never meant to have no road over it anyways."

I went back upstairs for fresh coffee and came back with Mayes's letters. When I offered them to Brown, he cut his eyes away, and I felt a flush of embarrassment at my own assumption that he could read warm my throat and ears. When I read the pages, Brown listened without interruption. When I was done, both of us went quiet and the old man rewrapped his line. When he got to the end, I noticed that the barbless hook was bare.

"So, what do you think? Just a fireside tale? Or are there bodies out there?" I said while he stood, preparing, I knew, to leave. He stepped into his skiff and took up the long pole.

"Y'all come down and meet me at the hotel," he said.

"When? Tomorrow?"

"Gon' take me a couple days, son. Might even do a little huntin' on the way," he said, and pushed off to the west.

I was too anxious to spend another day fishing. I have a vision of truth in my head and it is a smooth, logical, ethical stone that occupies my brain. But the chunk there now was growing more and more jagged despite my chronic grinding, and it was just about to sprout another flawed edge.

I had just gotten off the cell with Billy when I spotted the guys following me. White van, dark lettering on the side. I'd first noticed the van back at the on-ramp in West Palm, and I didn't pay any more attention than I usually did in traffic. I was on my way to Richards's house in Lauderdale to pick her up for a Diana Krall concert and dinner at our favorite Cajun place, just to forget about swamps and fires and the unmarked graves of tired men for a while. When I saw the van take the same off-ramp, I got more interested. I'd just finished filling Billy in on my conversation with Nate Brown, and that I'd planned to meet up with him in two days.

"Does Brown think any of this is feasible?" Billy said.

"He's hard to read."

"Do you think it's possible?"

"I think it's going to take more than old letters and fire-side ghost stories," I said.

"That's why I'm record-hunting, Max. We might not even be able to prove the great-grandfather and his sons were even out there."

I punched off with Billy and saw the white van speed up to catch a light with me. Maybe I was paranoid, nervous about leaving the shack. Maybe it wasn't even the same van. God knows how many white vans are on the road—just ask the sniper task force up in D.C. and suburban Virginia. Still I did a figure-eight through the tight blocks of Victoria Park before finally backing into Richards's driveway. I watched both ways for ten minutes and had just reached for the door handle when a sharp rap sounded on the passenger side window and made me jump. Richards opened the door and pushed her head in. Her eyes glowed blue and her hair was down.

"Forget the stakeout, Freeman, the neighbors already know," she said, sliding into the seat.

"Know what?"

"Know the nice policeman's widow next door is seeing some unemployed swamp guy with a pickup truck," she said.

We drove through her quaint neighborhood and into what had over many years comfortably become the downtown area of Fort Lauderdale—small one- and two-story condos and side streets of old, motel-style apartments whose days were now numbered by the rising value of the land they sat on. For the last fifty years the population flood into South Florida had surged west off the beach and into the drained swamp to create suburbia. But somehow a barrier—both political and environmental—had been raised, and the new and supposedly final boundary of the Everglades established. Now, like a wave started at one end of a pan of water, the still-growing number of new arrivals was sloshing back toward the sea. The only place left to go was vertical. Turning west on Las Olas Boulevard, the city's venerable shopping lane, we were soon surrounded by high-rises.

"Are we being followed, Freeman?" Richards suddenly asked.

Her question caught me off guard, but shouldn't have.

"You've been checking the rearview since we left the house," she said. "Bad form for a cop not to let his partner in on the game."

"Sorry," I said. "I thought I picked up somebody on the way down. White van. But I could be wrong."

"The fire starter? Or this other thing you've got going with Billy?" she asked, using the remote control on her own rearview side mirror to take a glance behind.

"Maybe I'm just skittish these days," I said.

"So what kind of car does this park ranger drive?"

"You know, I don't know why I'm not more suspicious of him," I said, stopping for yet another red light. "It's way too easy, him being there, his access to marine fuel, the state trying to roust me. It doesn't feel right."

Richards reached over and put her hand flat on my thigh. "Stop grinding, Max. Let's go out and have a good time."

I leaned over and kissed her, got distracted by the smell of her perfume and the touch of her lips, and the guy behind me popped his horn.

"Green light," she murmured.

We rolled on. But before we got to the old post office parking lot on Second Street, I'd caught her checking her rearview mirror twice. Always a cop. 24/7.

Richards had great seats at the Broward Center. The jazz was superior and the piano riffs were still in my head afterward as we walked down Second Street, holding hands and debating which of Krall's talents was better, the interestingly malleable voice, or the equally eclectic keyboard work. The street was in its late-night lively mode. With restaurants and clubs on either side, the concept of a crosswalk was long forgotten. One of the corner bars had stainless coolers filled with iced beer for sale right out on the sidewalk. Cocktail chatter floated on the warm night air, and somewhere a saxophone wailed. All along the way, patrons stood with one foot in the street and the other up on the curb, as though it were a bar rail.

We crossed to the other side and were a door away from Creolina's when Richards was greeted by a pair of guys with brown beer bottles in hand. I tried to read them, but the signals were mixed. The clear eyes and expectant demeanor said friends. The longer-than-regulation hair and comfort in street clothes said maybe cops, maybe not.

"Hi, Sherry," the tall, better-looking one said.

"Hey," she responded, and stepped forward to give him a kiss on the cheek. "How're you doing?"

I could read a slight hesitation in her voice, and automatically watched the eyes of the other one, who was doing the same to me. I nodded. He nodded back.

"You're not working?" Richards asked, using an innocuous tone in the question like it could have been posed to anyone.

"No, no, I'm sorry. No, we just finished a job over in the isles. Just stopping off," the friendly one said. Richards relaxed.

"Dennis Gavalier, Max Freeman," she said in introduction. I shook his hand.

"The P.I. from the Eddie Baines case? Pleasure. This is Russ Parks, transferred in from robbery last month," Gavalier said, bringing the other guy in. "Sherry Richards from MIU."

The guy smiled one of those twenty-five-year-old "glad to have you meet me" smiles. Richards asked about the job. Gavalier was vague but obviously pleased. The conversation stopped and the four of us shuffled our feet.

"We were just heading in for dinner," Richards finally said.

"Hey, good to see you, enjoy," Gavalier said. "Good to meet you, Max."

I nodded. "You too."

We stepped away in different directions. "Dennis is narcotics, probably one of the best undercover guys in the country," Richards said. "I've never seen him in uniform, and you never know how to say hello to the guy because he might be working something."

"Partner's nice," I said.

She just looked at me, then shook her head.

"What?"

She shook her head again. I opened the door to the restaurant.

"You guys and your alpha-male thing. You all get the same hydrant out there?"

I just smiled. What could I say?

Rosa put us at the corner table, by the front window with the wall at our backs.

"Mr. Max. You out with this fine young lady again? You keep this up, baby, I'm a get jealous you cheatin' on me."

Rosa is a big, joyful, teasingly profane woman. She is a special spice at Creolina's, and you let her have her way.

"Ms. Rosa, I would never take the chance of hurting you and be denied your gumbo," I said.

"It's all right, honey," she stage-whispered to Richards. "All the mens lovvve my gumbo."

Richards laughed with her and ordered the étouffée. I got the jambalaya. We opened a bottle of wine. Richards took a sip and I caught her thinking.

"Guy with Dennis," she said.

"Yeah, Parks?"

"I think he's a friend of McCrary's."

"Your friend's control freak?" I said, digging the name out of my head. "How's that going, anyway?"

Rosa brought out our plates. The smell of andouille sausage and spice rose in the steam. Richards waited until after her first bite of the thick étouffée.

"She's pissed that I confronted him," she finally answered.

"He come back on her?"

"Not that she would admit. No. She said he apologized and told her again how much he cared about her and couldn't she see that."

It was my turn to finish a bite. I tasted the wine.

"There's nothing so romantic as a contrite lover," I said. "And he's apologized for caring about her so many times. It's a hard face to look into and not be suckered."

"That's why they stay?"

"That's what the domestic violence folks say," I said, but my eyes were focused out the window, across the street.

"I'm not sure I like your vast knowledge on this subject, Freeman," she said, but I was no longer paying attention.

"You know these two guys across the street? The one in blue and his buddy leaning against the light pole?"

She checked them for a full minute. They were older than the rest of the crowd, both thick in the shoulders and waist. One was taller, the other more nervous. I could see the silver in the hair of the bigger one.

"No. Don't think so."

"They've been there since we came in. Beer bottles in hand, but neither one has taken a drink."

"Did they get dropped off by a white van?" she said, and even though it bugged me, she was right about my paranoia.

"How about you watch to see if they pull out their guns and come running across the street while I eat," I said.

"How about we both eat?" she said, this time with that smile of hers.

"Deal," I said, and put my hand flat on her thigh under the table. I kept my eyes off the street through dinner.

"Get your hands up on the table where's I can see them!" announced Rosa when she brought the bill, her big, dark face full of mischief. "Now don't be bringin' no more young ladies in here, Mr. Max," she said as we got up to leave. I looked to see Richards's reaction.

"Oh, she OK, baby. Just no others, hear?"

"Good night, Rosa," I said, leaving her a twenty-dollar tip.

When we stepped out onto the sidewalk Richards said, "They're gone." I looked across the street.

"I hadn't noticed," I said.

"Liar."

She made coffee when we got to her house and spiked it with a crème rum that turned it sweet and light brown. I didn't object. She climbed into the big hammock with me and her movement set it lightly swinging.

"You comfortable, Freeman?"

"Very," I said. She had turned out the porch lights, so the only light was the soft iridescent blue from the pool.

"What am I going to do about my friend, Max?"

I knew what was eating at her. I knew how it could.

"Listen to her," I said. "Suggest some counseling. You know the PBA has programs for this. Maybe she can get him to go before it gets too far. If it hasn't already."

She was quiet. Thinking quiet. Running the scene

through her internal eye as a good investigator does.

"I'm not sure she'd go for that," she said. "And I doubt seriously that he would."

We both sipped our coffee and watched a breeze ripple the pool water and set its light flickering.

"And if she admits he's been hitting her? What do you do?"

"You gather the evidence and arrest his ass. It's a crime," I said, though it came out harsher than I expected.

She sat her coffee cup on the deck and stretched out next to me, her head on my chest. The smell of her hair was in my nose, and I was afraid she was listening to the elevated race of my heartbeat.

"Will you tell me about your father someday, Max?"

I ran the scene through my own internal eye.

"Yes," I said.

Later, when she was asleep, I lay staring up into the trees. I would use my left hand on occasion to push off the near railing and set the hammock swinging, because I did not want to close my eyes and did not want to dream.

I could never hear my mother's voice, no words of anger or fear or even begging to make him stop. I would lie in bed, the covers up to my neck and—forgive me, God—I would listen. The rough slam of the front door woke me. I counted the heavy steps past the staircase and down the hall to the kitchen. Eighteen. I heard the soft suction of the refrigerator opening, the clinking sound of glass against glass. A plate on the wooden table, a scrape of a chair being pulled back. Maybe he would stay down there tonight. Maybe he would fall asleep in front of the television and his hard snoring would be welcome music. But not this night. Not in this dream.

I heard each step up the stairs, the creak of old wood when he stopped and grabbed the smooth oak ball at the top of the banister to steady himself. I could feel him looking at my door, and then he went the other way, to their bedroom, and it would start. I tried, in the head of a thirteen-year-old boy, to make it another man's voice, the harsh, spitting curses. He was clapping his own hands together to make a point, I would lie to myself at the sound of skin slapping skin. A thump against the wall vibrated through the house. The sound of something porcelain from my mother's bureau shattering on the floor. And then, quiet. No sobbing. No gentle, conciliatory words. Just a long and empty silence.

In the morning I stayed upstairs as long as I could, listening for him to leave. I brushed my teeth, twice. I packed and repacked my football cleats and jersey. But the time forced me down and he was sitting at the kitchen table, his dark hair slicked back with Brylcreem, his shoes polished and shining, his blue policeman's uniform pressed and starched by my mother's hand.

"Running late again, Maxey?" he said, grinning, his eyes only slightly bloodshot from drink.

"Yeah, gotta run," I said, snatching something from the fridge, standing up close to my mother, who stood clearing the stovetop and no longer said anything to me about skipping breakfast.

I kissed her on the cheek and she turned halfway to accept it. "Have a great day at school, Maxey," she said. "And here, take your lunch." Then a car horn sounded out front.

"You got a game tonight?" my father asked.

"Yes, sir. Rafferty."

"OK, I'll be there, son," he would lie. "Good luck. And tell your uncle I'll be out in a minute."

Out on the street a black-and-white police cruiser was double-parked on Mifflin in front of the house. When I came down the steps, my uncle Keith called out from inside.

"Yo, Maxey."

"Hey," I answered, stopping to greet him through the open passenger's window. He too was in uniform. He and my father had the coveted day shift.

"How you doin', kid?"

"OK."

"St. Rafferty's tonight, eh?"

"Yeah."

"Go get 'em, kid. An' give that pussy quarterback of their's a shot for me, eh?"

"OK, see ya," I said, and walked away, refusing to look back, even at the sound of my front door opening.

The ringing telephone woke her, and Richards's movement pulled me out of my own fitful sleep.

"You want to let it go?" I said.

"I would," she groaned, getting up, "if it had stopped on the ninth damn ring."

She went inside. I blinked the haze out of my eyes and tried to judge the hour by the lightening sky to the east that swayed back and forth above me with the rock of the hammock. Twenty seconds later Richards returned with her portable in hand and an unpleasant look in her face.

"It's for you, and the asshole won't I.D. himself or leave a message," she said, then pressed her palm over the mouthpiece. "And I don't think I appreciate you giving out this number as a place to reach you, either."

She pushed the phone at me, spun, and walked back inside.

"Who is this?" I said into the phone, Richards's anger quickly transferring into me. The line was silent, but open.

"Hello!"

"Stay out of this Noren issue, Mr. Freeman," a man's voice said. "It's ancient history, and believe me, you're better off without it."

I tried to process the words, tried to come up with something to keep the guy talking. But before I could, the line went dead.

CHAPTER 8

"I've been bribed before. Asked to st-stay away from a case for p-political reasons. Hell, every criminal case c-comes down to a plea bargain offer at s-some point." Billy did not resort to swearing easily, so I knew he was pissed, or frustrated, or both.

When I got to his office at eight he was already working the phone. Allie served me my big mug of coffee at her desk in the reception room before showing me in. Billy had actually sounded congenial until I told him about the phone call to Richards's home two hours earlier. The information seemed to click things into focus for him. He started pacing the carpet in front of his windows, ignoring the view outside.

"These were corporate lawyers. I expected they w-would stonewall, say how impossible it would b-be to find any detailed records from all the way b-back in the twenties."

Billy had done a thorough job of tracking the name of the eighty-year-old corporate owners of Noren. Linking them, like a family tree, he had found the names and then the spin-off companies that the people behind the names had formed over the years. When he got into the sixties, he'd narrowed the list to a handful of real estate firms, independent contractors and a couple of large home-building enterprises. He went to the biggest of the group first, PalmCo, one of the largest and best-known development names in all of Florida. From the suburban tracks to the beachfront high-rises, to the shopping malls and now the business castles that were spiking up in every major city along the coast, PalmCo had a hand in the recreation of a one-time soggy seaside landscape. Billy had asked for, and with some hard pushing, been granted a meeting with PalmCo's legal representatives. It was held in the office of a private firm in West Palm Beach. Billy's reputation would precede him. Knowing this, he was astounded by the clear message the attorneys delivered.

"I even expected th-them to deny that they even hired itinerant workers on the old t-trail p-project. But they all b-but flat-out tried to buy me off. 'This historical matter would all b-be better off left in the p-past. It was a d-different time when business was so m-much less, uh, businesslike,'" Billy said, mocking the "boys will be boys" tone of the lawyers.

"Then he blows me a lot of sm-smoke about my reputation and wouldn't my time be much, much more valuable working on some big money eminent domain cases they c-could steer my way."

Big mistake, I thought to myself, being condescending to a prideful man who spent his life proving to himself and the world that nobody needed to hand Billy Manchester anything.

"And now this, this, amateurish th-threat against you."

He stopped pacing and stared outside. He could have been watching the dark bruised clouds to the west as they built over the Glades and marched east with a guarantee of showers. He never looked down. Billy never did.

"So what do you make of it?" I asked, to bring him back.

"They're scared."

"Hell, scared of what?"

"What we know."

"They don't know what we know. The damn little bit we do know."

"Sure they d-do. They know everything, Max. Even where you go to d-dinner. Even Sherry's phone n-number."

I didn't know how to respond.

"C-Corporate information gathering, Max. No big company s-survives without it. You're thinking l-like a cop instead of a P.I."

"Yeah?"

"First thing you'll have t-to do is get your truck swept for a tr-tracking device." I was still just staring at him. "Then, get r-rid of the cell phone you've b-been using. I'll get you a c-clean one."

By 11:00 A.M. I was back down at Global Forensics on Billy's suggestion. As a Philadelphia street cop, and even during my short and less than stellar stint in the detective bureau, I had little experience in electronic surveillance. We'd strapped up a couple of waiters and a shop steward with body wires while trying to work a South Philly mob case. I'd stood around watching a tech from the auto theft squad pull a LoJack unit after we followed a stolen Mercedes with a kilo of cocaine in the trunk for thirty miles into Jersey. None of that seemed to impress Billy, or William Lott.

"Nobody uses body bugs anymore, Max. These days you wire up a microphone to the inside of your cell phone. Everybody uses the damn things now, it's like wearing a fuckin' tie, you're considered naked without it.

"Your partners dial up your phone before you go into a meeting, they can hear every damn thing that's said and record it. Shit, they can monitor the thing from fuckin' Langley without ever having to get off their asses."

Lott was dressed in ratty, kneeless Levi's and a white doctor's lab coat with splatters of some reddish brown across the left chest and sleeve, the origin of which I was not about to ask. We briefly discussed Billy's, and now my, suspicion that somehow my movements were being tracked and my phone conversations were being intercepted.

"Goddamn government," Lott said. "You see that story about the medical chips? Surgically slip them under your skin and *voilà!* Your own doctor can monitor your heart 'and several other serious medical conditions so that you'll be worry free.' How long before one of them comes with every fuckin' social security number, eh?"

I tried to keep my face as neutral as possible while the big man raised an eyebrow with his rhetorical rant.

"Uh, bugs, William?" I finally said.

He nodded in approval, maybe giving me more credit than I was due for my silence.

"Never can be too careful, Max," he said, continuing to wipe his thick fingers, and moving to the doorway that led back outside to the parking area.

"I don't do the work myself," he was saying over his shoulder as I followed him past my truck. "But I will personally refer you to the best in the business."

We were halfway across the access road, heading for the warehouse door on the other side, when Lott called out: *"Ramón! Mira, Ramón!"*

"These cats are not early risers," he said over his shoulder. I looked at my watch. We were headed for the open door where I had seen the young group of Hispanic kids working on the tricked-out Honda.

"Ramón! I got business for you, dude!"

Before we reached the door, a young man poked his head out from the garage bay and then stepped out, still fastening the snaps on his calf-length shorts.

"Hey, Mr. Lott. What up?"

They greeted each other with extended fists, barely touching knuckles. Ramón appeared to be in his mid-twenties, dark, almost black eyes, a thin line of a mustache, and a collection of sparse beard under his chin. His hair was shaved to the top of his ears all around his head and then it was long and slicked back to a braided ponytail. He was assessing me as sure as I was him.

"This is my friend, Max Freeman," Lott said. "He's got some bug problems with his truck that maybe you could help him out with."

I extended my hand in a more traditional manner and Ramón shook it.

"You look like a cop, Mr. Freeman," he said without the slightest tone of accusation or disrespect.

"I used to be," I replied, trying to match his composure. I looked at the tattoo on his right arm, impressive artwork of the Virgin Mary, much higher quality than prison ink work.

"He's a P.I. now," Lott said, cutting in. "He works mostly for Billy Manchester."

Ramón's placid eyes reacted immediately to Billy's name, as though absorbing the glint of light. A smile came to his face.

"OK," he said, the flat wariness gone. "Wheel it over, man. My friends and I will take a look."

Lott and I walked back to my truck and parted in front of his lab.

"No questions asked, and believe me," he said, "these kids know more about the electronics of this shit than any FBI tech I ever met."

When I backed my F-150 into his garage, Ramón explained his work terms. "One hundred in cash and we keep whatever hardware we find. You don't get it for no evidence in some courtroom," he said, then changed the seriousness in his voice and winked. "But you do get to drive around free."

For the next hour I sat in the shade in a cheap lounge chair listening to an odd form of Cuban rap while Ramón and two of his boys crawled in and under my truck with a variety of tools and sensors and voltmeters. I was lost trying to eavesdrop on their conversations, which were carried out in some form of hip Spanglish peppered with street slang. When they were finished, Ramón walked me outside holding two chunks of electronics. One was the size of a cigar box. The other, a single cigarette pack.

"Both of these are tracking devices, Mr. Freeman. Whoever is keeping the leash on you, man, they ain't taking no chances. This one is a real-time vehicle tracking device. They had it plugged into your battery so it could run constantly. It's got a modem so they can access it from a PC and map exactly where you been and for how long. It's long-range and very expensive, man. The local law can't usually afford them, even when they're trying to follow the stolen car shipments to the islands.

"And since the serial numbers are gone," he said, pointing to a rough acid burn on the metal casing, "I'd say it was a private enterprise doing the installation."

He looked in my face for reaction. I didn't give him any and he shrugged it off.

"This other is more run of the mill. Works like a LoJack. Once we unhooked them, they're deactivated and your friends are going to know, *claro?*"

"*Sí. Pero es no use por tu?*" I answered, bringing a smile to Ramón's serious face.

"We have our uses for them—and a market, my friend."

"I'll bet you do," I said, peeling off five twenty-dollar bills. "No listening bugs?"

"*Nada.* But that's not so much anymore," Ramón said. "It's hard for the transmitters in a car. Too much noise, and now with cell phones, man, they just use an intercept."

"A cell phone intercept?"

"Yeah, sure. Someone with the money for something like these would probably use a Strikefisher. It's compact enough, they can carry it around. It's got plenty of range. They can pick up your cell frequency and hear everything you're saying, no problem."

I was thinking about the white van, the thirty-five-foot fishing boat on the river near my shack, any place I'd made a call to Billy.

"Thing about these private guys, they don't need no warrants, man. It's all fair game, dude."

"So how do I avoid it?"

Ramón smiled. "Stay off the phone, man. Do business face-to-face," he said, pointing his finger at me and then back at himself. "It's old school. But it's safe."

I shook Ramón's hand and got in the truck.

"Good doing business with you, Mr. Max. And tell Billy Manchester ciao for me, eh?"

CHAPTER 9

"Ciao," I said to Billy, and he gave me one of those quizzical looks that when held long enough by an intelligent man makes you feel stupid enough to ruin your attempt at humor.

"Ramón and his electronics crew down in Forest Hills," I said.

"Ahh. Ramón Esquivil. How is m-my young inventor friend?"

My turn to look quizzical. Billy was pouring a boiling pot of angel hair pasta into a colander at his sink and waiting for the billowing cloud of steam to rise to the ceiling.

"I represented him in a patent c-case. Some b-big electronics company trying to claim the r-rights to a pneumatic bypass switch that Mr. Esquivil had invented in his g-garage."

"And?" said Diane McIntyre, Billy's attorney friend who was standing at the counter sipping chardonnay and watching him cook.

"And w-we were quite successful," he said, shaking the colander and flopping the pasta into a bowl. "And so is Mr. Esquivil, if I r-recall correctly that the c-contracts he eventually signed were worth over seven figures."

I took a long drink of beer and filled Billy in on the discovery of the tracking devices on my truck and Ramón's guess that we were probably dealing with civilians.

"S-So. Your suspicions of the van and the c-call to Ms. Richards?"

"And your attempted buyout."

"That's why our f-folks at PalmCo are very, very n-nervous," Billy said, stirring a saucepan of sautéed bacon, scallions and garlic into the pasta.

"Sounds like you boys have your fingers into something nasty again," McIntyre said, scooping up the bowl and taking it to the table. She was dressed in the conservative suit she'd probably worn in court that day. And as was her habit, she'd kicked off her shoes at the door and was padding about in her stocking feet. She smoothly shrugged out of her jacket, laying it carefully on the back of the sofa, and then sat herself in front of one of the places she'd set.

"Please, gentlemen," she said, her fingers splayed out in invitation. "Sit and tell me all about it. I am freakin' starving."

Between bites and compliments to the chef and several glasses of wine, we hashed through the discovery by young Mr. Mayes of his great-grandfather's letters and their allusion that extraordinary means had been used to keep the laborers on the brutal job in the Glades. Billy had as much luck as Mayes finding death certificates, employment tax records or any public notice of even a pauper's gravesite.

"PalmCo is big, Billy," McIntyre said. "They could stonewall you forever, even if you did file suit."

"At this point we don't have anything t-to file about," he said. "But if we f-find proof that Cyrus Mayes was indeed there, and that he and his s-sons and other workers were trapped out in the Glades by Noren or their representatives, and that they d-died out there eighty years ago and were n-never accounted for, then we've g-got a wrongful death suit, and a possible payday for our young Mr. Mayes."

"And that'll hold up?" I asked. "Even after eighty years?"

"Corporate ties," said McIntyre. "All the advantages and all the liabilities follow."

She raised her half-drunk glass. "Sins of the fathers," she said. Neither Billy nor I looked up from our plates, and McIntyre quickly read the reaction and gathered herself. "But you're saying you haven't got any of those pieces together yet."

"Which begs the question. Why w-would these PalmCo people be tailing and snooping and tossing out b-bribes to cover something no one can p-prove, even if it is t-true?"

"Hedging against the possibility of a multimillion-dollar suit," McIntyre said. "Remember the Rosewood survivors v. the state?"

Billy had schooled me on the case. In 1923 in the northwest part of the state, an entire town had been burned to the ground and many of its black residents killed in a racist attack that was essentially ignored by local and state law enforcement. The shame and bloodletting had been buried by the years and the dream-soaked fears of those who survived. The story had remained untold, whispered only by a handful of the old like a secret nightmare, until a group of historians and journalists revived and proved its truth nearly seventy years later. The state had broken its essential promise to all of its citizens of a lawful protection.

"The state legislature finally paid two million in compensation to the survivors and the heirs of those people who died," McIntyre said. "But the public relations hit was the worst of it. Imagine that happening to a private company. That's why PalmCo wants to nip this thing early.

How about a new slogan: 'We built Florida on the bones of our workers.' "

Billy and I looked at each other while McIntyre looked with dark, innocent eyes over the rim of her wineglass.

"Have you ever considered a career in t-tabloid journalism, m-my dear?"

She did that thing she does with one eyebrow.

"Possibly."

We triple-teamed the dishes and then moved out to the patio. The wind was nonexistent, and even from this height you could hear the slight shore break brushing the sand in rhythm. The sky was moonless and the ocean black and vast, with only a few scattered flickers of light from overnight fishermen out on the shallow swells.

"The Everglades is like this, black and silent, late at night, isn't it, Max?"

McIntyre was sitting on the chaise, her back propped up against Billy's knees and shins as he sat back with a brandy.

"If you're far enough in it, yeah," I said. "And most of the time even quieter."

"I can't imagine those men out there, not knowing quite where they were or what the next day was going to bring."

"I can," I said, sipping the cold bottle in my hand. "More of the same. Day after day until they got desperate."

Then we were quiet. Maybe all three of us were looking out on the blackness and trying to visualize what desperation looked like. After a time, Diane got up and made her apologies to leave. "Court again at eight."

She and Billy walked back inside. I stood up at the railing and found one of the boat lights out on the blackness, and as I watched it flicker I tried to put myself into the head of a man in the hot, choking and foreign Glades, his sons next to him, working through his hope of money and the stability it might bring his family as the only motivation to push back his fear. The light in the distance would fade and then come back again. I knew it was the rise and fall of the swells. Sometimes it would disappear completely, but then come back. It didn't move north or south. The captain must have her anchored, I thought. Maybe over one of his favorite night spots. A place he felt lucky or comfortable.

I heard the foyer door close and a minute later Billy came back out and the aroma of coffee came with him. He set a cup on the small glass-topped table beside me and leaned his elbows on the railing, his own cup in both hands, extended out over the empty one hundred feet to the pool below. He may have been watching the same floating light I was.

"You tell any of this to Mayes?" I asked.

Billy nodded. "He r-reacted very quietly. Not w-what I had expected."

"You tell him it was going to be a long haul?"

He nodded again. "I told him it c-could eventually l-lead to a civil suit. But I'm not s-sure our Mr. M-Mayes wants to s-see this through," Billy said. "He has t-told me that he is d-debating whether to enter the s-seminary in Georgia. He s-seems quite at odds with the p-proposition."

The cross at his neck, I thought.

"Can't make up his mind until he finds out what happened," I said, guessing.

"No. I b-believe he is looking for something m-more than that," Billy said. "Something about m-motivation."

The surf was like a soft broom below. We both listened for some time.

"You ever think about your father?" I finally said. "I mean, I know he wasn't there when you were growing up. But, you've got him in you."

Although I had not met Billy until we were grown men, our mothers—a white Irish Catholic from South Philly and a black Baptist from the north side—had cemented our friendship.

"He p-played chess when he was young," Billy said. My question did not unnerve or offend him. "My mother said it was one of the th-things that attracted her when they m-met in high school. Once, without her knowing, I l-looked up his picture in an old school yearbook. He hadn't m-made the official photos, b-but he was in the back row of the chess team picture."

I was quiet and let him look out at the darkness, and the picture.

"I think of him w-when I feel anger, M-Max. The uselessness of it."

I sat and picked up the coffee.

"You're m-meeting with your Mr. Brown tomorrow?" Billy said, moving to the door.

"Noon," I said.

"I h-hope he is helpful. Good night, m-my friend."

I remember the uniforms. Men, all lined up in a row, all with the same dark blue uniforms. They all seemed tall to me, as an eight-year-old sitting on a folded chair trying, at first, to pry my mother's hand from mine and then forgetting and letting her hold it as the line of men took their places on the small stage. My father was the third man on the right, his own uniform brushed and creased, the buttons polished and shoes buffed to a gloss by my mother late into the preceding night. I remember being fascinated by the lights from the television crews gleaming off the brass buttons and bars and yellow gold stripes on some of the men's sleeves. They were all wearing their hats, what my father called his lid, even though we were inside and my mother would have called it impolite. I remember the man at the microphone beginning to speak and my father looking out to find us, and under the brim of his lid he winked at me. The man at the microphone told the story that I had already heard so many times, though he did not include the harsh laughter and cussing that my uncle and my father's other policemen friends used in the backyard when they were drinking beer. The man used my father's full name and when he was finally called to the podium, he dipped his head and the man draped a gold, shining medal around my father's neck and everyone clapped and I looked at my mother's face to see her reaction and saw a single tear that she caught halfway down her cheek with a gloved finger, and I did not know as a child whether she was too proud or too sad.

For years afterward I would secretly seek out that piece of gold with the red-striped ribbon. I would wait until the house was empty and go into my parents' bedroom and open the bottom drawer of the bureau and find the dark blue case pushed hard against the back corner, buried under the old Arnold Palmer sweaters that I never saw my father wear. I would take out the case and lay it in my lap and open it and stare at the thick carved gold that seemed to grow richer in color over time. Then I would again unfold the newspaper clipping that showed the uniformed men in a line and I would read the story.

Philadelphia police yesterday awarded the medal of valor to one of their own in a ceremony to honor the officer credited with killing the celebrated Mifflin Square Molester in a shootout last spring.

Anthony M. Freeman, 28, a six-year veteran of the department and the son of another decorated officer, was wounded in the gun battle with Roland Previo after Previo was confronted with evidence that he was the man who had brutally raped and killed four young girls in his own South Philadelphia neighborhood three years ago.

Freeman, assigned to the detective unit just days before the discovery of the first victim in the killings, had "tirelessly pursued the case with the dogged determination of a true veteran," read Det. Commander Tom Schmidt.

Although the case had run dry of leads and legal evidence, Freeman's superiors said the young detective developed his own information over two years. While confronting Previo with newly discovered stained clothing that tied the ex-convict to two of the slayings, "Freeman, acting without regard to his own safety, attempted to make an arrest and was twice wounded by his suspect before returning fire and mortally wounding his assailant," Schmidt read during the ceremony.

When asked later for his reaction, Freeman said he did not consider his actions to be heroic and that his determination to find the killer had been a simple pursuit of the truth.

"I just wanted the truth to come out. There were a lot of rumors and lies and legal bull—— being passed around over the years. But the families of those little girls deserved the truth," Freeman said.

Freeman's father, Argus, was also a decorated officer for

the department. He had been awarded a medal of distinction for his work as a street sergeant during the years of racial unrest in the late 1960s.

I would refold the clipping, pat it against the golden medal and return the box to its place tucked deep in the drawer, and wonder again why my father hid it there.

I was still sitting up in the patio chaise when I woke. The purple gray light of a dawn that was still an hour away glowed dusky and cold out past the horizon. My mouth was dry and my knees cramped. I rubbed my hand over my face and got to my feet, gathered a half-empty coffee cup, and placed it in the sink before making my way to Billy's guest room. I lay down on the bed with my clothes on and fell into a hard and dreamless sleep.

CHAPTER 10

The sun was high and hot and reflecting off the white-shell parking lot of the Frontier Hotel like heat off a stove. I cracked the truck windows before I got out and knew it would make little difference. I'd still be climbing into a hotbox when I got back. Inside the bar it appeared that the same two card players were still at the same game. The bartender appeared to have added an earring to the other seven. I sat on one of the stools and let my eyes adjust to the dark and the woman pulled a cold beer from the cooler and walked down to set it in front of me.

"You've got you some ugly enemies, Mr. Freeman. An' that's your business," were her opening words. No hello. No "Can I get cha?"

"But folks here don't like you draggin' 'em round behind you."

"Is there a message in there somewhere?" I said, not reaching for the beer.

"There was a couple of city boys come in after you left last week, askin' questions."

"Yeah?" I was trying to get the rhythm of the conversational rules here.

"They wanted to know who you were talkin' to and whether you were a regular." She was wiping her hands with the gray bar rag, looking first at my face and then at the untouched beer bottle like I'd sinned by leaving it there alone.

"And you told them what?"

"To fuck off," she said.

The cribbage boys sniggered down at the end, nodding their recollection of the conversation and their approval.

"Can you tell me what these two men looked like, other than ugly?"

"No, sir. Just that they didn't belong out here. They were from the city."

"Do you happen to know what they were driving?" I said, this time reaching into my shirt pocket and pulling out a fold of bills.

"A new, dark-colored Buick sedan when they come in. And a dark-colored Buick sedan with a busted out back window when they left," she said, and the boys chuckled their approval again. Rag woman knew I understood the distinction. I had experienced the parking lot etiquette myself in the past. I stayed quiet and put a ten-dollar bill next to the bottle and lifted it to my lips.

"We don't like visitors round here, Mr. Freeman. Y'all are here cause you got a friend," she said, this time tipping her head to the back of the room. I turned and the adjustment of my eyes allowed me to see the shape of Nate Brown sitting alone at a table in the corner.

"Thank you," I said to her, but she had already turned away with my money and was not bringing back change. I picked up the bottle and joined Brown. The old man stood when I approached and I shook his leathery hand.

"Nice girl, eh?" he said, nodding at the bar.

"A true charmer," I said, pulling out a wooden chair. The table was a polished raw mahogany like the bar. The wood was native to the hardwood hammocks of the Glades, but the early loggers had recognized its beauty and sales potential, so little of it was left in the wild these days. A fat, cut-glass tumbler of whiskey sat before Brown, soaking up the yellow light from a nearby wall fixture and holding the glow. Another sat next to it, empty.

"How much you wanna poke round in this here look at Mr. Mayes, Freeman?" he said after a few quiet seconds.

"Depends on what the poking tells me," I answered. "Why?"

I had forgotten Brown's penchant for abruptness. He was not a man who had survived in a rough wilderness for eighty years by being subtle. He had also not survived by being stupid. He reached down beside his chair and came up with a bottle and half-filled my glass. I thanked him and sipped some of the smoothest whiskey I had ever tasted.

"I'm trying to find the truth, Mr. Brown," I finally said.

My answer seemed to stop him, and an amusement came to his eye.

"The truth," he repeated. "The onliest truth is the sun comin' up and the ocean moving, son. I know y'all are smart enough to know that."

I let him watch me drink. I knew he was right, but such philosophy was not on my timetable yet.

"Do you think Cyrus Mayes and his boys died out here, Nate?" I said instead.

"More'n possible."

"Do you think they were killed?"

"They's a lot of scar out here, Mr. Freeman. Some of them deserve to be healed and some don't." It was not a question and I knew he did not expect an answer. I waited while he sipped his own drink. "That's why I asked you how much you want to find out."

The skin on his face was nearly as dark as the whiskey

and had captured some of the same glow.

"I consider what you done before with me was an honest collaboration. An' that might be the onliest way to do this one," he said. "I believe maybe I owe you. But it ain't just for you neither, just like before."

"So what do you suggest?" I said.

"Let's go."

As we walked to the door, the bartender called out, "Good afternoon, Mr. Brown," with more politeness than I would have thought she possessed. He waved and got the same response from the card players. As I passed the bar I looked for the old construction photograph but it was missing from the wall. When I turned and asked the bartender about it she looked past me at the clean, empty rectangle its removal had left on the wall and shrugged her shoulders. "I hadn't noticed," she said.

Outside we got into the truck and Brown directed me south. I had never seen the old Gladesman in anything other than a boat and he looked small and uncomfortable in the passenger seat. He rolled his window the rest of the way down and I half expected him to thrust his head out like a retriever. He was not a man for closed-in places. He soon had me pull off onto a dirt track and we bounced a quarter mile west into a thick stand of rimrock pines. When we ran out of trail I stopped and he simply said, "You might want to slip right there under them boughs. Keep her out of the sun some." I did as instructed and we got out. I could see no path or obvious opening beyond the trees, and when Brown started to move off I said, "Should I lock it up?"

"Suit yerself," he said, and kept walking. I had learned in

my last encounter with Nate that in his world, you were best off just to trust him. I locked the truck and followed.

He slipped into the trees, moving with a slow and steady grace that I could not match. I stepped where he did, ducked under the same limbs and avoided the same ankle-breaking ruts and holes, but with only some success. About fifty yards in, the pines thinned and the ground turned moist. We skirted a patch of cabbage palms and in seconds were calf-deep in standing water. I was about to break my silence when I spotted the white fiberglass of a boat hull. Nate had left his center console runabout floating along a wall of cattails in crotch-deep water. He clambered up over the stern and I followed. I watched as he wordlessly pulled in the anchor line and then used a pole to push the boat backward into some kind of natural channel. When he seemed satisfied with the depth, he stood at the console, cranked the starter, and at idle speed began to guide us along the snaking ribbon of water. Soaked to my waist and now completely lost I finally checked my patience.

"If you don't mind my asking, Nate, where the hell are we going?"

"We's headin' over to Everglades City, son," he said, not taking his eyes off the water, studying, I assumed, its depth and direction. "I got you a man you need to talk with."

I could tell from the sun's position that we were moving generally to the southwest, even though the serpentine route of the water sometimes spun us in near circles before turning and heading again toward the end of the Florida peninsula. The cattails soon gave way to sawgrass that often sprouted six feet tall from the water. Tucked down in the brownish green maze it was airless and hot. The only breeze was from our own movement, and the air held the sweet, earthy odor of wet decay and new growth like some freshly cut vegetable just dug from a rain-soaked row.

At times the water became so shallow that both of us would have to pole the boat forward. Other times Brown was able to use the electric motor tilt to raise the propeller blades until they were barely churning and spitting the water. When it deepened again he would lower them back and we would gain speed, and the breeze it created was a luxury.

Above, a bowl of blue sky covered us from horizon to horizon, and while the sun traveled across it, Brown told me the story of John Dawkins.

"He was the colored man that was in them letters," he said. "The one that trucked the dynamite out there on the trail 'cause there weren't another man alive out here could have done it."

John Dawkins might have been from the Caribbean Islands or from New Orleans, but he and his family's blackness made them unique. But there were few enough families living in the Glades in the early 1900s, and those who had made it their home and braved its harshness knew one another as community.

"My daddy and John Dawkins was friends 'cause they needed to be. Out here, the onliest way a man got judged was by his work, and Mr. Dawkins was judged high on that account," Brown said.

Slope-shouldered and thick in the chest, with legs "like a full growth oak," Dawkins never turned down a job for which he would be paid with money or trade and was often called when the strength of other men flagged.

"Onliest time the man wouldn't work was on the Lord's

day, and Daddy said everbody knowed that. Said Mr. Dawkins had a contract with God."

I waited for the story to continue as Brown pushed up the throttle in the now widening creek. The sawgrass fields were beginning to change.

"We're comin' on to Lost Man's River," he said as the stands of spidery-legged mangroves began to appear. With his own bearings set, he continued.

"I remember Daddy's stories 'bout John Dawkins bein' the man that hauled dynamite. He knowed the country as well as any and he had them oxen. I member ridin' in that there cart with his kids and ours comin' up with loads of mullet from the docks."

"So this Mr. Dawkins has relatives who are still living?" I said, hoping he was finally getting to his point.

"He got a son still livin'."

"And this son might have some recollection of his father transporting mail for Cyrus Mayes?"

"Don't know," Brown answered. "You gon' have to ask him yourself."

Now the river had widened and so had the sky. Brown pushed up the throttle and it was impossible to talk without shouting. We cleared a point of high mangroves and the water opened up onto Florida Bay. I settled back onto the gunwales and breathed in the stiff salt wind, while Brown remained standing, guiding the boat north through what was known as the Ten Thousand Islands region along Florida's southwest coast. The name comes from the uncountable patches of mangroves. From the air or at a distance they look like thick, green lumps of land, but up close there is little if any dry soil around the mass of roots that support and feed the leaves. The semiprotected water that flows through the green islands is a perfect breeding ground for fish. But the area has no beaches, no hard sandy shores on which to build. It is not the stuff of Florida post-cards. And the few people who have chosen to live here over the past century like it that way.

Farther north, Brown swung the boat into what he called the Chatham River and again began spinning his way through thin waterways and around piles of man-groves. Again there were times he would have to use the electric motor tilt to skirt over sandbars that were hidden to an untrained eye. The old Gladesman would look back on occasion; I thought it was to check his trailing wake until he called out to me.

"Them those enemies the gal at the hotel was warning you on?"

I instinctively looked back at the water behind us, but saw no sign of another boat. When I turned back to Brown he was pointing one finger to the sky. High behind us a helicopter hung in the sky. It kept a distance but swayed back and forth to keep its line of sight and our V-shaped wake in view. It was too far away for me to make out the number on its belly or tail.

"It ain't the park service or the sheriff," Brown yelled above the whine of the outboard.

"Some kind of tourist ride?" I said. He shook his head.

"I know 'em all."

He pushed the throttle up another notch and seemed to take a line that cut much closer to the mangrove walls.

"It ain't the DEA neither," he said, and I'd heard enough of his reputation to believe he knew what he was saying. Brown jacked the engine to a higher pitch and I squatted down and got a firmer handhold on the rail.

White water was cutting deep off the prop wash. The old man banked the boat into the next turn, sending our wake surging into the mangroves, and I watched the chopper slide into the same movement. At this speed the green walls beside us were blurring and I couldn't make out the turns ahead. Suddenly Brown turned his head and yelled: "Hold on!"

I had just shifted my weight when he cut the wheel to the right and killed the engine. The instant silence might have been peaceful, but for the sleek glide that was sending us into a mass of mangrove. Brown leaned his weight hard into the starboard gunwale and said "Duck," and the boat seemed to buck against its own wake then slide to the right onto a partial water path and plow into the outcrop. When she hit the thick roots the bow made a fingernails-on-chalkboard screech and I tumbled forward. Brown kept his feet.

I lay still for several seconds, not as stunned by the crash as by the change. One minute we'd been just short of flying across sunlit water in front of a screaming, full-bore outboard, and the next we were stock-still in a dark, silent cocoon of tangled leaves and roots.

"Y'all OK?" Brown said, still crouched on the balls of his feet.

"Yeah," I said, sitting up and pushing my back against the console.

The old man looked up and specks of sunlight danced on his face.

"Let's just see if they was trackin' us or not."

We waited without speaking. I watched a family of spiders shaken from the mangrove branches scurry across the deck. Any birds or nearby gators would be long gone, scared the hell away. It took a few minutes, and then I could hear the patterned woofing of the helicopter blades. The sound grew but I couldn't see through the ceiling of green. The pilot had circled back but kept his altitude and never came close enough to stir the leaves with his downdraft. I swatted at a gang of mosquitoes on my face and checked my fingers for the smear of blood. We listened to the chopper circle and hover for maybe ten minutes, until it finally flew off to the northeast and did not return.

"Ain't nothin' bothers me more'n to have somebody follerin' me," Brown finally said.

He shifted his weight but could not stand up, and when I saw him slide one leg over the side to get out I copied him and went out the other side into the water and warm muck. It took us a few minutes of pushing and rocking to get the boat floated back out in deep water. We climbed back in, again soaked to the waist. I could see now that Brown had made a calculated turn into a passage that broke off the main river and looped around a small mangrove stand. From back out in the main channel the turn was nearly impossible to see. It had been a firsthand example of Brown's legendary knowledge and ability to slip the park rangers and anti-drug agents who had tried to catch him poaching gators and offloading marijuana trawlers from the Gulf to make deliveries inland. He'd done it for years. I was used to being the law, not running from it, and I knew if the chopper had been tracking us, it wasn't the law doing it this time.

"Slick move, Nate," I said, truly impressed.

He restarted the engine and turned us south onto what he called the Lopez River.

"Them boys in the helicopter got anything to do with what you're lookin' for?"

As he pushed up the throttle and we eased farther out into the channel, I told him about my discovery of the tracking devices on my truck.

"If any of this bothers you, you don't owe me, Nate. I don't want to get you involved in something you would rather stay out of."

He did not answer at first. His eyes, hard-creased from years of squinting into the sun, stayed focused ahead.

"You ain't," he finally said.

CHAPTER 11

We motored up Chokoloskee Bay and for the first time since leaving the loop, other boats came into sight. We passed some low-slung utility buildings, and as the ground elevation got higher, some warehouses and marinas. Tall, invasive Australian pines rose up in spots along the water where the shore had been dug out for dockage or access ramps, but it was essentially a low, flat land and I wondered about its ability to take a heavy storm out of the Gulf. The Calusa Indians had created most of the land that was high enough to be habitable in the Ten Thousand Islands. The indigenous tribe had, by hand, piled up acre after acre of shells. For hundreds of years the habitual toil had built the shell middens that were the foundation. Gradually, the dirt and detritus carried by the wind and tides and trapped by the shells became its soil. Seeds eventually took root, plants grew, and the Calusa farmed. A civilization thrived where before had only been water. No matter how many times I'd read about it and seen its proof, it was an accomplishment that was hard to conceive.

Brown cut back the engine and idled up to a series of docks set against a bulkhead. Two commercial fishing trawlers were tied up against the wall. Old and steel-hulled, with similar cabins built forward, they were each fifty feet long and had a large, motor-driven winch mounted on the stern deck. Brown eased up to the dock ladder and slipped the engine into neutral, and a young boy jogged up and caught a line the old man tossed him. Brown tipped his hat and the boy did the same; then he cleated the line and left without a word.

When the boat was tied off we climbed up onto the dock. On a broad crescent of land stood a bare, tire-worn lot that served the two fishing boats and that buzzed with activity. Two men were aboard each vessel and another worked with the boy on the small wharf. A sixth man was driving a forklift from a corrugated shack nearby, moving pallets loaded with wooden crab traps. When he set the pile next to the near boat, the men jumped to and began a brigade line, passing the big, awkward traps down to a hand in the open aft deck, who would then stack it forward. While they worked the pile, the fork driver went back for another.

They were all similarly dressed in high rubber boots, faded jeans and either T-shirts or flannel rolled up at the sleeves, and they paid no attention to us as we approached. That is, all but one on the deck of the near boat. He was a black man with skin so dark that at a distance, I thought he was wearing a black T-shirt under his yellow bib overalls. When we got closer I could see he was shirtless. He also seemed to be the only one speaking, giving directions and keeping the work moving. When we got close enough, he stopped moving, tilted the bill of his cap up and smiled.

"Afternoon, Mr. Nate," he said, slipping off a thick canvas glove.

"Captain Dawkins," Brown said, and reached out over the water to shake the big man's hand. I noticed that the younger men had all stopped at the mention of Brown's name. Even the crew at the next boat was staring. It was like Ted Williams had stopped in for a visit. I saw one man lean down to whisper in the boy's ear and the kid's eyes went big.

"This here's the feller I was tellin' you about," Brown said, and I stepped forward.

"Max Freeman," I said. When I took his hand I could see four distinct lines of raised scar that lay nearly parallel across his forearm. They were smooth and pink and wrapped like pale worms over his black and nearly hairless skin.

"Johnny Dawkins the third," he said with a smoothness that let me know he always introduced himself that way.

"I'll leave you to it," Brown suddenly said. "I'm a walk up to the café for some coffee."

I swallowed, and when he turned to go I swear the old coot winked at me.

"So, Mr. Nate says you wanted to talk about my grandfather," Dawkins said, pulling my attention back, getting straight to it.

I lost a beat, now realizing who the old man had brought me to.

"Yes. I, uh, I've come across some letters written in the 1920s by the relative of a client. Mr. Brown said your grandfather might have had something to do with delivering them," I said, not knowing how much Brown might have told him.

"Client, huh?" Dawkins said, pulling his glove back on. "But you ain't a lawyer?"

He moved his eyes over me, my mud-caked boots, the white streaks of salt stain on my now-dried jeans.

"No, sir. Just a private investigator, looking for some truth."

"Well, Mr. Freeman, I don't mind talkin' 'bout my

granddaddy's stories. And God above knows they're true. But I'm down a man here an' we got traps to load. So if y'all want to listen an' work, we got an extra pair of gloves."

The men in the other boat had already begun to move. The forklift operator gunned the engine. There was still a smile on Captain Dawkins's face.

"OK," I said. "Where do you want me?"

My height dictated that I catch and stack down on the boat deck with Dawkins. The boxlike stone crab traps were made of slatted wood and wire. In their bottoms was a two-inch-thick slab of poured cement to keep them down on the ocean floor. They weighed about forty pounds apiece. I learned quickly how to grip the top edge from the man passing the trap down and then use the weight of the box to swing it down and up and catch it with the other hand. While we worked the deck together, Dawkins told stories.

"My granddaddy was the first to come down here. He was a deck hand on a merchant ship that made the trip from New Orleans to Key West and then north up the Gulf Stream to the Eastern Shore and New York. His own daddy had done the same all the way back to the days of sails and schooners.

"He was a God-fearing man, Mr. Freeman, and loved to fish. God, my grandmother Emma May an' fishin', them was his priorities."

Dawkins looked up at his crew and winked. We were falling into a rhythm now and even if they'd all heard it before, the story was like a nip of soothing whiskey on the brain while the muscles strained.

"It was here that he met my grandmother, right over at Smallwood's Store, and she anchored him. They said he could unload mullet on these docks like a machine. He'd get done with a day's work and go home, dig up the rows in the little garden they had out back and then spend the night hand-fixin' catch nets."

"And he had oxen?" I said, trying to lead the story without putting any spin on it.

Dawkins never wavered, just kept stacking and talking and I was grateful not to have to waste my own breath, which was in short supply.

"He got the oxen from some freight captain in 1918. Daddy said grandpa figured that captain had to have been drunk to agree to take the animal in the first place. He was supposed to ship it to Key West, but when he stopped here for a load of fish, the animal had already gone crazy tearin' up the hold and he was beggin' somebody to take it off his hands.

"Was a mean sumbitch and Daddy said nobody but Grandpa would dare go near it. He took and hand-built him a cart and then used 'em both to haul fish from the smaller boats from the docks up to the fish house."

"So when the road crews came in to work the trail to Miami, your grandfather used that cart to haul dynamite for blasting?" I said. My arms and shoulders were aching, the lactic acid building up as I tried to keep pace with Dawkins. Each row of traps we stacked as high as the wheelhouse, and pressing the forty pounds up onto that six-foot top row was soon going to be impossible for me.

"They say there was plenty of work around Everglades City when the road crews were working. But Daddy used to say it was on and off, and the local folks didn't take too kindly to outsiders coming in to a place they didn't know or give a damn about.

113

"But Grandpa just wanted the work, and when they said they needed somebody to take the dynamite out there on the roadway to the dredge site, he took 'em up on it.

"Hell, most of the locals didn't know dynamite 'cept to use a quarter stick to stun a school of fish once in awhile. An' most of them company boys was scared to be out in the Glades at night. So Grandpa, he just loaded up the cart and he and the ox made the trip by themselves. Sometimes Daddy said it would take him days to get out and back when the rains turned the trail into nothin' but slop mud."

"And it was on these trips that your grandfather picked up mail?" I said.

Dawkins tossed up one more trap and whistled sharp and hard through his teeth.

"Y'all take a break now, fellas. Jordie, go on get us some water."

The boy ran off and the men found places to sit in the shade. Dawkins picked up a small towel from the gunwale and mopped the sweat from his face and neck. I sat, exhausted, on one of the short rows of traps, trying to hide my heavy breathing.

"That was Ms. Emma's story," Dawkins said, letting his voice go softer as he sat against the gunwale. "Only Grandma would tell it."

I said nothing and waited on him.

"When Grandpa hauled the dynamite out there, the foreman in Everglades City would have him deliver some kind of pouch to the job boss at the end of the line. Grandpa had never learned to read so he didn't know what the stuff was, but he did take a look-see, men bein' natural nosey, and they was only papers and documents and maps and such.

"Sometimes out at the dredge site, if it was late, he would stay overnight and he was allowed to eat with the workers. They was a raggedy bunch. Most of 'em down and out. Some runnin' from the law, but that wasn't unusual out here.

"Granddaddy wasn't much for ungodly men, so when he met a fellow out there prayin' before mealtime with his sons, they struck a friendship. He's the one who would give granddaddy the letters, and as soon as he got back, he'd go an' mail 'em out from the post office at Smallwood's, kind of secret-like."

When Dawkins took a pause, I interrupted, the possibility too close.

"Was the man's name Mayes?" I asked. "Cyrus Mayes?"

"Granddaddy wasn't much on names, Mr. Freeman. Like I said, he didn't read."

I sat for a beat, thinking about another identifying mark, some way to tie Cyrus Mayes with Dawkins.

"There was mention in one of the letters of a gold watch," I said.

"He gave it back," Dawkins said, and his tone was suddenly defiant and defensive at the same time. The captain's tone stopped the young boy in his tracks as he was approaching with the water. Dawkins stood up and smiled at the boy and took the two spouted coolers from him.

"Thanks, Jordan." He handed me one of coolers and I could feel the ice bumping inside it.

"Ms. Emma told the story of the day Grandpa come back from a trip to the road crew and set down to show her a big gold pocket watch. Said the man who had him deliverin' the letters gave it to him in payment.

"Them were tough times, and it didn't bother Ms.

Emma till she opened the watch. Inside the place for a little picture was empty but there was an inscription. Grandpa couldn't read it, but when Ms. Emma saw it was scripture and engraved to a man's son, she told him he had to give it back lest the Lord take it as a sin."

Dawkins took a long drink of his water. There was a look in his eyes and I waited until he had enjoyed the memory of his family.

"These were stories, you know?" he said. "Just stories of the old times told around the fire at night to us kids. Granddaddy tol' 'em. My daddy tol' 'em. I tell them to my own kids. They ain't written down."

Dawkins stood up and let loose his whistle and the crews got up again and moved to their positions. As the lift driver rolled up with another pallet, I pulled on my own gloves.

"Captain Dawkins. There was one name that did appear in these letters. He might have been a local, name of Jefferson. That mean anything to you?"

For the first time, a darkness clouded the big man's face and he did not look at me when he spoke.

"I don't mind tellin' my family stories, Mr. Freeman, because they're mine. But other folk's families, those are their stories. If others are tellin' 'em, it's just rumor and I ain't gonna hurt nobody with rumor."

While we finished the stacking, Dawkins engaged us with the story of the day Al Capone came to Everglades City on a fishing trip and stayed at the Rod & Gun Club, and the embarrassment of the staff when they realized they'd put the famous mobster in the same room earlier occupied by President Truman. He chuckled and we all sweated and chuckled with him.

When the loading job was finally finished, the captain thanked me for my help and asked if I wouldn't mind spending the next thirty-six hours with the crews as they went to sea and dropped the traps for the first true and legal night of stone crab season. I declined.

"Well then, you can come back next week when we start pullin' 'em up," he said, smiling again. "Then you'll see the real work. And the payoff."

"I'll see the payoff at a restaurant in Fort Lauderdale," I said.

"Then pray for a high price, Mr. Freeman, and maybe we'll break even this year," he said, and shook my hand.

As I walked away, the forklift driver was just pulling up with a load of frozen chicken parts and trash fish. Dawkins took up an ax, and the sound of his chopping blade faded behind me.

The captain had given me directions to the café. It was a fifteen-minute walk, and even though I'd taken only three or four steps at a time back and forth across Dawkins's boat deck, my legs felt rubbery and my hamstrings tight from the two hours of work. My arms and shoulders ached like I'd rowed the fifty-footer to Key West and back. When I got to the café, Nate Brown was sitting out front on a pinewood patio in the shade. He'd already eaten and had his heels up on a small wooden keg with a huge bowl of ice cream in his lap. I sat down at a table near him without a word. Within a few seconds, a middle-aged woman came out with a large ceramic cup of hot coffee and when I smiled up at her she said, "Mr. Brown said ya'll would be coming. Can I get you something to eat, sir?"

I ordered a fresh grouper sandwich and when she left I

watched Nate working his bowl of vanilla like a careful child who'd been warned it would be his last if he wasn't polite. From the cream-colored pile in his bowl the old man carved off a spoonful and then took only parts of it into his mouth at a time, sanding off the lump with his cracked lips three or four times before it was gone.

"You an' Captain Dawkins have a talk?" he finally said between his sculpting.

"He work that hard all the time?" I said.

"Yep," Brown said. "All his life. Ain't no other way for a man like him to git a two-boat operation like that and keep her goin'."

If there was a racial implication in the "man like him" statement, I couldn't hear it.

"His daddy was like that and his granddaddy before that. Handed it down just like the name."

I asked him about the scars, the scrolled lines of damaged flesh on the captain's forearm.

"From the trap lines," he said. "When they start to pullin' them traps, they got the trap line on that power winch an' she don't never slow down. A man got to hook the trap when she comes up from the bottom, snatch out the crab, throw the new bait in, lock it down an' dump her over agin, just in time to hook the next trap. Got to do it like clockwork, and it goes on for hours.

"You get your glove or your movin' hands caught in that line, it'll wrap on you and pull your arm off. Every stone crabber takes that chance."

I took another deep sip of my coffee and silently chastised myself for whining about sore muscles.

"He wasn't willing to talk about this Jefferson character Mr. Mayes mentioned in the letter," I said. "But it sounded like he might have known the family."

"Oh, everybody knowed of the family," Brown said, and went quiet, concentrating on his spoon. Across the road a half-dozen pure white ibis worked a low patch of grass. A heron let loose a high "quark" somewhere behind us.

"First time I seen ice cream I was eighteen years old," Brown said, staring at a new lump on his spoon. "It's still like a miracle to me."

Brown kicked the throttle up, heading out through Chokoloskee Pass. The Gulf was green in the late afternoon light, and out to the southwest low clouds were scudding just above the horizon.

"We'll take her on the outside an' beat that line a squall," Brown said, looking out in the same direction. "Course, a bit of rain never hurt. An' it'll maybe keep them folks in the helicopter out of the air."

His words made me look back and scan the sky. It was empty except for a line of pelicans, their crooked wings fanned out as they cruised north over a long lump of mangroves. Brown swung us toward the east and pushed the boat up on plane and we began slapping over the light chop. I stood up next to him, gripping the console, and asked him why he had not told me that he recognized Jefferson's name when I'd first read him the Mayes letters.

"I was thinkin' on it," he said.

The old Gladesman kept his eyes fixed ahead and seemed to squint them down even though the sun was mostly to our backs. He was looking back, and then started putting words to what he remembered.

"He was a small, mean fella. Least that was what folks said, and that's what they believed. Even my own.

"It wasn't easy to avoid people out this way back in them days. But my daddy always said he stayed clear of the Jeffersons. Fact was, Mr. Jefferson was about the same age as my daddy, and the talk that gets told is that the two of them was the best shots with rifles that there ever was in these parts.

"Now, I seen my daddy shoot the eye out of a racoon at fifty yards. Seen him drop a squawk on the wing out of the sky at more 'n that. An' you know how boys are. We'd ask him if Mr. Jefferson could match him, an' he'd go quiet on us. Never said yep. Never said no."

Brown looked back over his shoulder and I did the same. The cloud line had darkened and massed up into a curtain that was soon going to shut out the sunset. It was another twelve miles or so to the entrance of Lost Man's.

"So the rumors just kept on a growin'. Some said Jefferson learnt to shoot as a criminal, others that he'd been a hired gun and come out this way to lay low. Then there was some killin's. A game warden who watched over the plume hunters was found shot out in the rookery. A state revenue agent workin' the illegal stills come up missing. Course, we'd hear the men, speculatin' around the fires at night and Jefferson's name would come up, him havin' the talent and all."

"So no one would have been surprised to hear that this Mr. Jefferson signed on with the road-building crew to be the company sharpshooter to clear the way of alligators or panthers so the men could work?" I said, watching Brown's face for a reaction. He let the sound of the outboard and the erratic smacking of the hull on water fill the silence.

"To some, like Daddy, it just made sense to put a man with a gun out there. But to others it just hardened up the rumor. They said Jefferson was a hired gun who'd shoot anything for money, an' that's just the job the road company hired him for."

"Captain Dawkins said something about family that Jefferson had. Are there relatives still around?" I asked.

"Long gone," Brown said. "They lived in a place on the Chatham River an' left it. His one son was in the war and when he got back he stayed a bit until the old man passed and they sold out. They was a grandson and rumor had it that he moved north up by the lake and become a preacher. That one must have been about the same age as Captain Dawkins, but I ain't never seen him."

The western sky had turned a pearl gray by the time we made the river entrance and we headed north onto a winding path. As the light continued to fade, I watched as hundreds of white egrets came in and thickened the sky like a noisy cloud and began their nightly spinning and dancing above the tall mangroves. The squawking rose to a crescendo as the birds picked out a roosting spot for the night, and within minutes they had settled in the branches. Brown cut back on the throttle to match their noises and we watched the last of the day's light get caught in the globs of white feather and the trees take on the look of tall cotton rows in a darkening field. To my city-bred eyes it was an unreal display. But even the old Gladesman seemed momentarily transfixed. We slid on through the growing shadows and did not share another word for some time. After an hour or so, Brown shut down the motor and the boat glided into a patch of cattails. From inside the console, he reached down and came out with a flashlight. He flipped on the beam and pointed it out ahead. I was surprised to see it reflect off something chrome.

"Yonder is your truck, Mr. Freeman. 'Bout twenty yard or so," he said, handing me the light.

Again I eased myself over the gunwale and into the thigh-deep water.

"How do I get in touch with you?" I said.

"When you're ready, son, y'all let the girl at the hotel know. They'll get me the word."

I never heard him crank the motor back to life, and by the time I got to my truck a light rain was falling. I used the flashlight to find the door lock, and it wasn't until the interior lights came on and I slid in behind the wheel that I noticed the bullet hole.

A single shot had been fired into the windshield, face high on the driver's side. A spray of spidery cracks webbed out from the hole. I stared through the opening and my fingers went involuntarily to the scar on my neck and stayed there.

CHAPTER 12

It was nearly ten when I got back to Lauderdale. There had been no other damage to the truck and I had not bothered to report the incident to the local police. It would have been written off to rural vandalism, the sort visited on stop signs, or even a hunter's stray round. And it could have been just that, but I didn't believe it.

I pulled over for gas and made a call to Richards from a pay phone. Maybe she could hear the exhaustion in my voice. Maybe she was intrigued by the short description of my day.

"I'll start some coffee and a hot bath, Freeman," she said before I could gracefully invite myself.

When I arrived she was able to keep any look of disgust out of her face but directed me to the outside shower by the pool. Under a steady spray I peeled off the salt-caked clothes and waterlogged boots and washed some of the Glades stink off my skin. I was standing naked on the pool deck when she came back out with a steaming mug of coffee.

"Shall I just burn these, nature boy?" she said, picking at the pile of wet clothes with her toe. I was too tired to think of anything clever.

"OK. Into the bath then, Freeman."

After an hour of soaking in water as hot as I could stand it, I finally got out and dressed in a pair of canvas shorts and a T-shirt I'd left on a previous visit. Richards had cooked up a plate of scrambled eggs with ranchero sauce. She poured more coffee and we sat at the kitchen table. I ate and talked and she listened until I was through.

"Your truck has been bugged and shot. You've been followed by vans and a helicopter. You've been warned off and Billy's been offered a bribe. And you still don't have anything more to go on but a few old letters and a bunch of old Everglades campfire stories," she said, trying to rake it together.

"I'd offer some advice, Max. But imagine spilling out that missing-person's case onto a detective squad's table: 'Well, sir. We think we've got an eighty-year-old murder case going here in which a multibillion-dollar development corporation is trying to cover up the forced labor and assassination of its own reluctant workers. All we need to do is find the remains of one of these bodies somewhere along the sixty miles of road that cuts through the middle of the Glades and hope he's got a pay stub in his pocket and a detailed note identifying his killer.'"

"It might still be premature to call in any official inquiry," I said.

My legs and arms were rubbery from fatigue. My head was equally spent. I'd like to say I remembered getting up and making it to her bed. I'd like to say I remember lying with her, curled up like spoons under a single sheet in the soft breeze of the ceiling fan. I'd like to say I was aroused by the smell and touch of her warm skin. But I fell asleep, stone asleep, and did not wake until nearly noon the next day, by which time she had long ago left for work. She'd left me a note saying she'd call a detective friend in Collier County on the west coast where the other side of the Tamiami Trail first enters the great swamp. She described him as an "old-timer who might have collected some rumors of his own." I dressed and went outside. The sun was already warm in the trees and when I opened the truck cab the huff and odor of sweat and salt and tracked muck spilled out. In the daylight I could see the sprinkle of glass on my front seat and without too much trouble I found the flattened slug that had passed through the windshield and probably ricocheted off the back cab wall and ended up on the floor behind my seat. It was misshapen, and I had to guess that the caliber was anything from a .38 to a .45. Not hunting rifle material. I picked it up with a paper towel and put it into a plastic Baggie from my glove box and stored it away. I then drove over to Federal Highway with the windows rolled down to make a call to Billy on a pay phone. I no longer trusted the cell and refused to use Richards's home phone again. Inside a convenience store I got Billy at his office and told him I would stop at his apartment and then meet him for dinner at Arturo's on Atlantic about eight. He said I might be getting too paranoid, and I might have believed him, but out of the store's plate-glass window I watched a squad car pull up behind my truck and stop, blocking my way out.

"I'll see you at eight, or call you from jail," I said to Billy, and before he could ask, I hung up. I bought a large coffee and a box of plain doughnuts and went outside.

Both officers were out of the car. One was leaning his rump against the trunk, while the other was checking the contents of my truck through the driver's-side window. I walked up and unlocked the passenger side and leaned in, making eye contact with the younger one through the glass. I was smiling. He was not.

"You Mr. Freeman?" he asked. I slid back out and we

reestablished the sight line over the hood. His right hand was now on the butt of his holstered 9 mm.

"Yes," I said. "How you doin'?" I set the doughnuts on the hood, halfway across. He stared at them for a couple of beats and his face got grumpy.

"You the owner of this vehicle, Mr. Freeman?"

"Sure. Isn't that what the tag check came back with?"

The other cop, the older one, was now on his feet. He had a black enameled riot stick in a metal loop on his belt. I'd recognized him even before he took off his sunglasses. It was the patrol cop who'd confronted Richards in the parking lot, the one I knew was slapping Richard's friend around, even if she hadn't admitted it yet.

"Can I see your license and registration, Mr. Freeman?" the young one asked. I fished out the paperwork and put it on top of the doughnut box.

"This windshield damage," he said, looking at the license and deliberately not finishing his question, expecting me to take it up and be defensive. I stayed quiet and he finally looked up, his eyebrows raised. I raised my own.

"Do you know what caused it?"

"Hunting accident," I said.

The wife-beater had taken up another position on my side, leaning against the truck bed, but his feet were planted firm on the parking lot macadam.

"Anybody hurt?" said the younger one.

"Not that I know of."

The kid had had enough of my attitude. I probably would have, too.

"Well, Mr. Freeman. It's a violation to be driving this vehicle in this condition," he said, taking out his ticket book.

"I could write you a summons and have the truck impounded, if that's . . ."

He stopped when he realized I wasn't paying any attention to him. I was looking at the partner, who was wearing one of those smirks we used to snap off the faces of the football players who used to walk into O'Hara's Gym in South Philly. Most of them had never seen a professional jab thrown by someone who knew what they were doing. This guy hadn't either, I was willing to bet.

"Mr. Freeman knows it's a violation, Jimmy," the older one said, not willing to be stared down. "Mr. Freeman was a cop up north. One of the Philly brotherhood, right Mr. Freeman?"

Again I stayed silent and held his eyes. It's the one thing a true street cop can't stand, some asshole trying to lock on to his face, cut his attention off from what was going on around him. But this guy's macho was overriding even that.

"Hell, Mr. Freeman was probably on his way to get this fixed, and we don't give out tickets to our fellow officers, do we, Jimmy? Even former officers."

Out of the corner of my eye I saw Jimmy put his book away. I lowered my voice: "You following me, McCrary?"

The truck cab was now between us and the partner, a bad move on the kid's part.

"Why would I be following you, Freeman? What you do is none of my business," McCrary said, matching my volume. "And what I do is none of yours."

The statement made me think too long and McCrary turned on his heel, giving his partner a jerk of his head and giving me his back as they both moved back to the squad car. I watched them pull away, and the emblem and motto emblazoned on the door just below McCrary's profile stuck in my head: TO PROTECT AND SERVE.

On Atlantic Boulevard they were just beginning to come out. The young women were dressed in the kind of casual clothes that at a glance seemed simple and comfortable from thirty feet. But close up you could see the tightness across the ass of the jeans, the waistband designed to sling so low that one would surely have to shave to stay within the limits of obscene. The cotton tops were at least a size too small and stretched over cinched up breasts to accent the curves. There wasn't a heelless shoe on the sidewalk, and even accounting for the Florida sun, nearly every woman, regardless of age, had streaked her hair, and a good minority of the young men had matched them.

I got to Arturo's a half hour early, and when I asked for Billy's reservation, Arturo himself came out and seated me at a sidewalk table that I knew was one of the most sought after on a Saturday night. I asked for my usual, and the waiter brought me two bottles of Rolling Rock stuck in an ice-filled champagne bucket. I leaned back, sipped the cold beer and listened to a burst of female laughter across the avenue, the voice of some miked-up emcee down the block that rose and fell on the breeze, the sharp wolf whistle of a kid hawking girls from the window of his car, and the bubbles of different brands of music that floated out the doors of the nearby clubs and burst out into the street.

Billy arrived exactly at eight. He was dressed in an off-white linen suit and oxblood loafers, and I distinctly saw three women of two different generations turn to watch him as he passed by. Arturo greeted him with a flourish and before he was settled in his chair enough to cross his legs there was a stylish flute of champagne placed in front of him.

"M-Max, you are l-looking well."

It was his standard greeting and had almost become a joke between us. Billy sat back, took a sweep of the crowd and a lungful of air.

"To subtropical evenings and g-good friends," he said, raising his glass. I touched the lip of my bottle to his fine glassware.

"Long as you're not up to your subtropical ass in mosquito-infested muck," I said, smiling.

"T-Tell me about your t-trip, Max."

While we dined on Cuban-style yellowtail snapper and black beans and rice, I described the unknowns who may have stolen the Noren photo off the wall of the Frontier Hotel, the boat ride to Everglades City, and our helicopter escort. Billy nodded at the appropriate times without comment. He would be filing the info away, sliding it into a spot in his revolving carousel of fact and possibilities, building in his head a legal slide-show that might eventually be flashed before a judge.

But I could see a different level of interest in his face when I described Capt. Johnny Dawkins III and tried to convey his story. Billy leaned in and did not take a drink during my retelling of the captain's tale. I finished and he sat back. The waiter saw his head turn and was immediately at his elbow. While he ordered more wine and a beer for me, I scrolled the street again. No one had occupied the same spot across the way for more than a couple of minutes. No white van had dared compete with the Mercedes, BMWs or shined-up low-ride toy cars parked near us. Any sight lines from the high buildings across from us were obscured by the decorative white lights strung through the trees, and in the swirl of street noise and conversation on the sidewalk, it would be difficult for a directional microphone to cut through. Maybe I was taking this whole P.I. thing too seriously. When my beer came I took a long drink.

"I've b-been running as much of a computer record ch-check as I can but there's so m-much missing," Billy said. "At the state and l-local historical archives, we've got some genuine material on the early Tamiami Trail, mostly p-progress of the road building through old newspaper stories on m-microfilm.

"I was also able to f-find a copy of a rough history of the p-project written just after the road was finished in 1928. N-No names of workers, but an extraordinary admission that an unknown n-number of men lost their lives."

"Why extraordinary?"

"Because b-by the end, the State of Florida's road board was in on the construction. M-Money from a Collier County b-bond issue was being used. And men were still dying."

Billy stopped and looked down the boulevard, seeing something that was focusing only inside his own head.

"Does that mean there's state liability?" I asked, trying to make a lawyer's logic work.

"Possibly."

"Does our client know about this?"

It was Billy's turn to take a long drink of his wine.

"Our young Mr. Mayes seems to b-be the rare client who d-doesn't care about the monetary gain.

"He honestly s-seems to be motivated only b-by the question of what happened to his g-great-grandfather."

"All the more reason," I said, gaining my partner's eyes, "to find him some answers."

While we finished I told Billy of the vague recollections of the man named Jefferson in the letters. His past was as loose and improvable as anything else in the Glades. A possible grandson in the state who may or may not be a minister. Not much, but it was something.

"We can t-track the birth records, if they b-bothered," Billy said. "There are clergy listings that are fairly c-comprehensive because of the tax-exempt r-regulations for churches. We could narrow it b-by staying south of, say, Orlando to b-begin with.

"If we st-start with the assumption of a B-Baptist connection, which was p-popular in that area, we could g-get lucky, though Jefferson is not exactly a unique n-name."

Billy was getting cranked, his head moving hard with research possibilities. It was contagious.

"Your home office clear tomorrow?" I asked.

"I've g-got to see clients."

"I'll come in from the river about ten. You can guide me on the searches from your office." He didn't even try to dissuade me from going home to the shack anymore.

Arturo escorted us to the sidewalk and Billy was generous with his praise and his tip. I let a tourist couple pass and caught their double take of the handsome black man in the thousand-dollar suit.

"C-Call me if you need computer help," Billy said as we shook hands.

"I'll definitely call you," I said, and headed for my truck.

CHAPTER 13

It was nearly midnight when I got to the river. A slice of the new moon lay crooked in the field of stars and reflected in flashes of erratic light on the water. I took my time paddling up into the canopy. The air was warm with a southeast breeze, and along with the envelope of darkness in the forest tunnel came a slight change in humidity. After so much time spent here, I could pick up the most subtle differences. When I first moved into the shack, my years in the Philadelphia streets had honed my senses to the noise of the traffic and voices and things metallic, the smells of food aromas and man-made rot and the constant perfume of exhaust and the night sight of ever-present electric light. I'd been as lost as a kid with a canvas bag over his head when I got out here. Now I could taste the slightest change of humidity in my mouth.

I tied my canoe and unloaded supplies onto the dock, then used a small pen flashlight to check for footprints on the stairs. Inside I lit the oil lamp and made a pot of coffee with rainwater from my barrel reservoir. I changed into fresh clothes and then sifted through the printouts of Cyrus Mayes's letters. His schoolteacher's old-style prose was leading us in our search for truth for the great-grandson he had never even dreamed about. I'd been hooked by the mission. But I wasn't confident that there was a string to follow that could take us there. I selected one of his early reports and then sat at the table with my heels up. The dull light painted my oversized shadow onto the pine wall as it read with me:

My Dearest Eleanor,

We are two weeks into our labors and the experience has been both exhausting and unique. You would be so proud of the boys. Steven seems to have become a master of knots and is actually in demand when the crew is at the task of lashing the huge poles together to create a floating platform for our dredge work. The depth of the water and muck here has caught our foremen off guard and we all have had to improvise. Often the company's machinery sinks into the earth like a quicksand has swallowed it and by pure muscle we all must raise it with lines or it is lost and the demeanor of the engineer becomes blacker.

I recently considered forming a prayer group among the men but held off until I had a sense of them all. They are a rough lot and many have lost their way. One fellow, attracted by our daily prayers before eating, seemed friendly but later developed a rough coughing and a pallor that someone likened to malaria. He was quickly isolated by the foremen and one morning we saw him loaded into a rail cart headed back west, we assumed, to Everglades City. Later, the armed one called Jefferson made it a point to warn us of what he called swamp fever, saying he'd seen it consume an entire town of Florida settlers who "picked up the bug while they was collectin' the gossip of they neighbors."

Steven has, I believe, an inordinate fear of this rifleman and has confided that he sees the devil's eyes in him. I have dissuaded him of the notion and tried to guide him through prayer. I could not admit that in my own heart, I see a grain of truth in his fear.

Forgive me my darling if I sound suspicious and maudlin. Your son Robert, your dreamer, has found the beauty in our midst. We gain strength from his fascination with the flocks of white birds that move above us at times like huge snow white clouds. His discovery of a vast army of colorful snails on the sawgrass kept him in awe for days. On a day last week when the dredge had been silenced by repair, he was the first to call all our attention to a feeding flock of birds of which none of us had ever seen. These creatures glowed with a pink color that was a fascination to the eye with the incredible contrast of the unbroken acres of brown and green grasses around them. Even the hard-driving foremen could not keep their eyes from the sight. Robert seemed mesmerized watching the flock feeding in an open pool of water, looking from a distance like a soft pile of pink cotton.

He is, as you would imagine, the one whose eyes seem to cloud over in the glory of God's creation at sunset when the hues of purple, red and orange spread above the horizon. In only three weeks we will be finished with our tour of labor and we shall gather our pay and make our way back to you.

Love from your family men,
Cyrus

I folded the letter and sat in silence. I sipped at the coffee and watched the low flame of the lamp play with the wall shadow. Outside it was dead still until I heard the distinct, guttural "kwock" of a night heron. I thought back to the first time I'd seen one feeding along the river. It was stubbornly territorial but let me paddle within fifteen feet. He then turned his white crown away to show his marked cheek and fix me with one intense, deep-red eye.

I turned down the lamp wick to snuff the flame, and by memory moved through the lightless room. I set my empty cup on the drain board and checked the small propane stove valve to be sure it was off. Then I stripped to my shorts and lay in the bunk with only a sheet pulled over me. Sometime in my sleep, the eye of my heron turned into the eye of Arthur Johnson, whom I had not dreamed of in years, but whose look had been the closest to pure evil I ever wanted to see.

I was still with the Center City Detective Squad, not yet officially assigned and traveling on thin ice after strongly disagreeing with the arrest of a feeble-minded city maintenance worker for a woman jogger's murder along Boathouse Row. I was still just a probationer and the lesson that case clearance was placed above all else was still a concept that tasted like ash in my mouth. But my family history kept me on the administration's track and my own ability to take a figurative or literal shot in the mouth and not have it bother me much kept me from really giving a damn. I was working a late shift when we caught a DOA in the subway between the Speedline stop and City Hall. It was one of the cold months, January or February. But down below the streets on the subway platform at Locust Street, you couldn't see the steam of your breath like you could on the sidewalk. I was teamed with a veteran named Edgerton, and he bent over the dropoff to the tracks and looked up the tunnel leading north.

"How far?" he asked the transit cop who had called it in.

"Fifty, sixty yards. Up in a maintenance alcove," he said,

shaking his head and bunching his shoulders as though the thought of it made him colder. "Nasty."

Edgerton looked down at his loafers.

"Shit," he said, and the expletive led to me.

"Go on down there and take a look, Freeman. I'll get the particulars from the sergeant here and the PATCO types. My guess is it ain't gonna be much different than the others."

I borrowed a flashlight from the transit sergeant and climbed down to the tracks on a ladder at the end of the platform. Cold grease and black dirt coated every surface. At least I was smart enough to still be wearing the same polished combat boots I'd been known for on the street patrol. I'd purposely bought my pleated Dockers an inch too long and with the cuffs settled down on the glossed leather of the boots, the brass never noticed. I waved the flashlight beam down the tunnel and a smaller version waved back at me.

Fifty yards into the darkness a transit worker bundled in a winter jacket kept his hands in his pockets. "Yo. How you doin'?" he asked, like he didn't know my answer.

"Cold," I said.

The guy pulled out one hand and trained his beam on a recessed rectangle in the wall and the three metal rungs that led up to it. I pulled on a standard-issue pair of surgical gloves and started climbing. When my head cleared the floor of the platform, the stench hit me and I turned to inhale better air before going on. I flipped on my flashlight. The odor of garbage, urine and death was packed into a four-foot-by-four-foot space that was barely more than six feet tall, and when I stood I had to keep my head bent. A locked metal door took up the rear wall. Bunched on the floor was a pile of dark rags and musty wool that had no doubt covered a body. I squatted down and directed the beam onto one end and peeled back a coat flap. The light fell on a mat of dull, brittle hair, and I had to reach in and find a jawbone to grip before I could turn the head and confirm what Edgerton had already guessed. Two blackened holes looked up at me, the blood around them and the torn gristle deep in the sockets as dark as the skin of bruised plum. I felt the bile rise in my throat but dropped my circle of light quickly to the victim's chin. I pulled the rigor-rusted jaw up enough to expose the crescent-shaped gash across the throat. As if the missing eyes weren't confirmation enough.

I was doing a cursory check for any identification, when the transit worker said, "Jesus Christ." The guy was still on the tracks, staring pointedly down the tunnel. "Those assholes," he said, and started waving his flashlight beam to the north. Then I could hear it, the rumble of heavy metal on metal, and it was growing. I leaned out and could see the shine of light against a curved wall down the track, and then picked up a familiar clacking sound. The transit guy was still waving, but he had already taken two long steps toward the ladder.

"They was supposed to shut down traffic while we was down here," he said, fumbling for his radio under the back of his jacket. The clacking rhythm continued to grow.

"Fourteen to control. Fourteen to control," he barked into the mouthpiece. Now he had a hand on one rung, his eyes catching the train's brightening light.

"Asleep at the fuckin' wheel," he said, stepping up as the roar built exponentially.

I reached out and got a fistful of his jacket sleeve and

yanked him up and in. We backed to the door and stood shoulder to shoulder and foot to corpse. I could feel the pressure in my ears change as the train pushed the air in front of it. I had to close my eyes as the litter and dust swirled into the cubicle, and I did not open them to watch the blur of train windows and the skin of the cars flash by. In several seconds the roar passed. The final car rushed by and the vacuum following it sucked the air and stench of death out of the recess, leaving a dull silence. The flashlight beams were already bouncing toward us when we climbed down. The sergeant was well ahead of Edgerton, and I thought of my partner's loafers.

An hour later a single crime-scene tech and an assistant medical examiner showed up. The coroner's body bag boys took the remains and grunted and groaned as they hoisted it over the turnstiles and up the stairs. No one was pleased to be out in the cold at 3:00 A.M. The M.E. was as detached as Edgerton.

"Same as the other two. Cause of death was the slashed throat. A race between asphyxiation and bleedout, since he got the carotid.

"Male Caucasian. Probably in his early thirties, though it's tough to tell with these homeless guys. No I.D. that I could find. Might get some kind of tattoo or distinguishing mark when we cut the clothes off on the table."

The guy wasn't reading from any notes, if he'd bothered to take any.

"The eyes?" Edgerton said.

"Same. Removed postmortem with something blunt, like a spoon."

"Christ. Three in six weeks," Edgerton said. "This sick fuck is gonna ruin our clearance rate all by himself."

We worked the case for three days before Edgerton got bored and was able to slide off onto the double homicide of a Cherry Hill couple in the parking lot of Bookbinders that was stirring up press. They let me go it alone for five days. I started walking the deep subway corridors from eight to eleven at night, when I had a chance to interview stragglers from work who used the trains late. I went down again from five until sunrise when the tiled corridors were nearly empty except for the echo of the trains and the occasional skitter of rat claws over the concrete. I had used the subway since I was old enough to walk but never knew you could start at City Hall and stay underground all the way to Locust Street. I talked with the rag men, the homeless who sneaked down from the steam grates on the sidewalks when their clothes got too wet and they risked freezing to death. I looked in their eyes and felt their fetid breath and heard little more than psychotic babble.

A woman struggled with the burden of extra clothing wrapped in a plastic garbage bag. I tried to help her but she snatched the bag away and looked into my face with wet blue eyes and said, "Mercy!"

Other than her voice, her sex was revealed only by the tiny size of her white boots with the daisy on the strap, and I wondered about that single scrap of female vanity. I left her alone.

The lieutenant of the unit pulled me after the first week. "Got other cases, Freeman. Priorities, son." But on the weekend I walked the perimeters of the downtown stations, looking above ground for someone who would go down in the dark to kill human beings and steal their eyes. The second week I walked the corridors on my way to the roundhouse for the beginning of the shift, and again on the way back. I started getting the derisive smirks and "bulldog" jokes from the other detectives. Edgerton pulled me aside and thought he was counseling me when he tried to tell me I wasn't my father.

"It doesn't work that way these days, Max. Obsession ain't a positive trait in this business," he said. "Beside, this isn't a series of innocent kids you're talking about and . . ." He stopped himself, leaving out the "Look where it got your old man" that would have finished his opinion. The skepticism continued until the following Friday night.

It began to sleet at ten, frozen rain that looked like snow in the streetlights but stung when it hit your skin and then turned quickly to water. It drove everyone for cover. The subway cars had been packed during rush hour, but the corridors had cleared out as usual—until the sleet came and the Friday night clubbers and the half-frozen homeless started going underground. By now I knew a few of the regulars and could identify them by their individual stoops and shuffles. I assessed the new ones. Past midnight a tall man in a ragged peacoat slid past me at a concourse near Market Street. His long neck curved down like a garden hose, his shoulders wrapped around his sunken chest like it had been punched by a mighty blow and never recovered. By two o'clock the platforms and corridors were empty; those who were down here had found their hiding spots. I was working my way through a tunnel north of Chestnut when I turned a corner and scared the hell out of a young woman walking south. She was wearing duck shoes and a ski jacket and was carrying a backpack over one shoulder. She gasped when she saw me and I immediately showed her my badge and said, "I'm a cop. It's OK." I watched some of the alarm move off her face, and she was about to speak when we both heard an agonizing howl that was instantly cut short.

The woman's eyes went huge and she took a step in the direction away from the noise as I took one toward it.

"I'm Detective Freeman," I said. "Go up top."

She looked the other way and seemed to hesitate with panic, so I yelled, "Go up top! Just go." The echo of her running footfalls followed her and I went the other way. Before the next blind turn I had my radio and my 9 mm Glock in my hands. I turned the radio volume low and reported to dispatch my location and a possible subway assault. Then I clicked off the set. Fifty more feet and I heard a deep-throated groan that vibrated and carried off the graffiti-covered tiles. I knew there was an alcove up ahead that was sealed by a chain-link gate that had long been breached at one corner with a pair of wire cutters. I replaced the radio with my flashlight and moved on.

At the gate I stopped and listened. The growing roar of a train arriving at the City Hall station momentarily blocked out any other sound. I waited, and as the cars pulled out I used the noise to move through the bent corner of the gate. There was a stack of stored barricades against one dark wall and racks of metal scaffolding leaning against the other. A passageway between them was just wide enough for a man to get through. Farther in, the weak light from the corridor was lost and the shadows were black. I crouched to avoid being backlit and again tried to listen. After a few minutes of silence, I heard movement. The scrape of boot leather on concrete. A shifting of something heavy and soft. Then a noise, like the tearing of wet cardboard and the distinct sound of a watery suction. The sight of the empty eye sockets flashed in my head. I slapped the flashlight next to the barrel of my 9 mm, snapped on the beam and rushed forward.

"Police!" I yelled, jerking the light from shadow to shadow.

"Police!" I kept barking and then the beam caught movement and my fingers tightened on the Glock. I steadied the beam on his head as he rose, the white skin of his face illuminated in the light. I focused on his eyes and they did not seem to flinch in the brightness, and like a bad photograph I saw them glow red and fearless.

"Hands up and away from your body!" I yelled again, forcing my attention away from his eyes to the movement of his arms. He was tall and dressed in dark material, and he shuffled one step forward.

"Fucking freeze!" I yelled again, the adrenaline taking my voice.

He was ten feet away and I shifted the light and saw a flash of blade in his left hand and the dull metal of a spoon in his right. When I moved the beam back to the knife the light picked up the form of a body behind him. It lay still and I could see a patch of pale skin and then the light found a rubber daisy dangling on a small, white boot.

The man took one more step and I refocused on his eyes and shot him. I aimed low into his hip and did not care whether the round drifted in or not. He went down with a yelp of pain and I closed the distance between us before he hit one knee. I half skipped my last step and then swung my right leg and drop-kicked him in the chest with the toe of my polished combat boot. He was on his back, staring up into the flashlight beam, and the animal look of his red eyes had not changed. I stepped hard on the wrist of his left arm and watched the fingers uncurl from the handle of a six-inch butterfly blade.

"The suspect was armed and in fear of my life this officer determined that the use of force was required to subdue said suspect," I whispered aloud as I felt the ligaments in the man's arm pop under my shifting weight.

I reached down and swatted the knife out of his reach and then pointed the barrel of the Glock into his left eye.

"Roll over and put your hands behind your back."

I cuffed him and then moved my light to the woman. She was dead, and the sharp acid smell of fresh blood rose off her like heat. I rolled her and she stared up at me. One eye still glistened with a curved wound to one side. Her throat had already been cut. I got on the radio and was told a squad car was already up at the subway entrance. The man on the floor was crying now from the pain of the bullet wound but I turned away and let the rumble of the arriving train drown out the sound of his keening.

I woke with the sound of screeching metal train brakes in my ears and came up shivering in my bunk. The shack was still dark, and I swung my heels to the wooden floor and rubbed my eyes with the heels of my hands and half expected to see my breath steaming in the air.

I got up and this time tossed some kindling into the wood-burning stove and started it. I watched the flames dance and build and then set my coffeepot over an open port on top. I stepped outside while the water heated and drew in the night air to wash the remembered smell of subway rot from my nose. For several days after the slasher's arrest the other detectives gave me the razz.

"Yo, you Freemans ought to start a Mounties' division. 'We always get our man,' eh, Max?"

"Chip off the old block, eh?"

"Or off the old bottle," one stage-whispered.

By then my father was existing on the good ol' boy network. His alcoholism was being covered by friends in the department. His abusiveness was kept in the family. His reputation was now the fodder of jokes, but never to his face. I heard the rattle of the coffeepot and went back inside.

By nine I was at Billy's, sitting in his immaculate study, surrounded by floor-to-ceiling bookcases filled with law volumes, history and nonfiction collections as diverse at the owner. I was facing two computer screens and was using Billy's hookup to the Internet and LexisNexis to run through religious listings and church locations throughout South Florida. We were banking on Nate Brown's recollection that Jefferson's grandson had become a minister and hoping that he'd stayed in his home state. I was also hoping that his isolated, rural upbringing would have kept him from taking a position in a big city like Tampa or Orlando. By e-mail, Billy was coordinating with me from his office and guiding me to Web sites while he worked his own independent sources.

At noon I took a break from the air-conditioning and stood out on the patio. Out on the ocean I watched a sailboat at the horizon as it moved south, heeled over on a windward tack, its genoa sail pulled tight and its rails dipping into blue water. Before I loaded my canoe at sunrise I'd sat at my table in the weak light and cleaned my 9 mm. The gun had been wrapped carefully in oilcloth and stashed in the false bottom of one of the armoires. There were spots of brownish rust showing along the barrel and the trigger guard where the humid river air had gotten through. I found my cleaning kit and broke the weapon down on the table and meticulously rubbed and oiled each piece. I did not search for a motivation for what I was doing. The fire, the tracking devices, the helicopter, the blown-out windshield or even the psychotic eyes of the subway killer. There was something moving in my veins when I slid the parts back together, snapped the fifteen-round clip into place and dry-fired the piece one time before stowing it in my bag to bring with me. I'd left the bag locked in my truck when I came up, knowing that Billy would detest its presence in his home, but the thought of it somehow gave me comfort. I left the patio, poured another cup, and returned to my work.

By the end of the day we'd come up with eleven possibilities. Billy had found clergymen with the last name of Jefferson in six towns around Lake Okeechobee and in the south central part of the state. I'd found two each in Miami and Tampa and another in Placid City. We had eliminated several others by running their names through Billy's link with the Florida Department of Transportation's driver's license database. Using their dates of birth, we kept only those between the ages of forty and sixty, giving ourselves some guessing room. Without access to the software that would have displayed photo I.D.s, we couldn't winnow the list by race. Instead, we split the list and started making phone calls.

"Yes, this is Reverend Jefferson, what can I do to help you?"

"Thanks for your time, Reverend. My name is Max Freeman and I'm working with the law office of Billy Manchester in West Palm Beach on an inheritance matter. I was hoping, sir, that you might be the man we are searching for."

A slightly skeptical silence followed.

"Yes, Mr. Freeman. If this isn't a sales call, please, go on."

"Well, sir, our only information is that our Mr. Jefferson may be a member of the clergy in Florida and grew up with a family in the southwestern part of the state."

A slight chuckle sounded from the deep baritone on the other end of the line.

"Well, Mr. Freeman, you have eliminated me, sir. I am a native New Yorker, and my extended family is deeply ensconced in the Fishkill area. I only took on this congregation five years ago, quite frankly in an effort to leave the winters behind."

"Then I've taken your time unduly, Reverend. Forgive me. But can I ask if you might have come across another clergyman who shares your last name, sir?"

So the conversations went. We had no luck with our leads in the cities, which did not surprise me. When I was able to speak directly to the pastors, the lack of accent alone was a giveaway. You did not grow up as a native in the deep corner of southwest Florida in the forties and fifties without forever holding that slow, Southern speech. My sense of the man we were looking for was someone in a small, rural setting. An escape from the isolated world of the Everglades, if that's what it was, wouldn't have taken him into a place of high-rises and concrete.

I got a map of Florida up on one of the computer screens and looked it over, the remaining list of Jeffersons in my head. Plant City was just outside of Tampa on the I-4 corridor to Orlando. The interstate had become so commercial and crowded that it almost rivaled the I-95 strip to Miami. Harlem was a small agricultural town along the southern edge of the lake. It was a possibility, but when

I made the call to Pastor Jefferson at the Harlem Baptist Church, he too fell off the list.

"I am truly sorry, Mr. Freeman, but my family, we've been here and here alone for most of the last one hundred years. My own father led this church before he moved on to join the Lord and his father before him.

"But y'all might call up to Placid City. There is a minister name of Jefferson up that way. A fine man, though I can't say I know too much about where his people are from."

Placid City was represented by a small black dot on the map. It was just off U.S. 27 northeast of the big lake and south of Sebring. There were splotches of blue around it, representing small, landlocked lakes. But most of the area around it on the screen was stark, empty white. I circled the number of Rev. William Jefferson of the First Church of God on North Sylvan Street and dialed it.

"Yes, this is Pastor Jefferson's number, but he's not in right now. Can I take a message for him, please?"

The woman's voice was warm and personable, certainly not that of a secretary.

"When might you expect him back?" I said.

"Well, sir, he is out visiting with Ms. Thompson out to Lorida. She's gone sick and I do expect he will be late," she said. "This is his wife, Margery. Can I help you?"

I went into my spiel and she listened without interruption.

"You say this is an inheritance matter, Mr. Freeman? I'm not sure what you mean."

"Having to do with family that the Mr. Jefferson we are looking for would have had in the Everglades City area, ma'am. Can you tell me, ma'am, if your husband is from that part of the state?"

Again there was silence.

"That was a very long time ago, Mr. Freeman, and I can't imagine that my husband would have any kind of inheritance matters, as you call them, from that time. That part of the family has long since been passed on."

"Yes, ma'am, I understand. We may very well have the wrong person, but may I call again, Mrs. Jefferson, when your husband is available?"

"Certainly. Please give me your number, Mr. Freeman, and I will make sure he gets the message."

After I hung up I leaned back in Billy's chair and looked again at the small black dot of Placid City. It was the most solid lead yet, and the quiet, not wholly forthcoming quality of Mrs. Jefferson's voice slipped under my skin. "That part of the family has *been* passed on." It was not the usual use of the phrase, and the wording formed a small jagged rock in my head that I began to grind.

CHAPTER 14

I spent the next day on the beach with Richards. It was her day off and she'd called me with a request to do absolutely nothing, and I could think of no better venue. Billy's own Jefferson search had gained little except a couple of flat-out eliminations and the promise of some callbacks. We agreed that Placid City was the best bet so far, and I ditched my paranoia over the possible intercepts of my cell phone and brought it with me in case the Reverend William should call. I picked Sherry up at ten, and we cruised up A1A to the north end of Lauderdale's open beach and struck our umbrella into a plot of sand like Oklahoma land-rush settlers claiming our forty acres. We unfolded a couple of low chairs, made sure the cooler I'd packed was guarded by the umbrella's shade, and then sat. I heard a sigh of pleasure come from Richards as she stretched out her long legs and crossed her ankles in the warm sand.

"No cases. No cop talk. No dissection of investigations, Freeman," she said, her eyes hidden by her dark-tinted sunglasses. "Gonna be like normal folk, kicking back without a worry in the world."

"Since when have there been normal folk without a worry in the world?" I said, matching her stretched-out pose. The sky was clear and the water blue-green. A flock of some dozen white-bellied sanderlings was scattered at the tide mark, pecking at the backwash. When the next wave arrived, their black legs skittered like an old silent film at ridiculously high speed to keep ahead of it.

"You know what I mean, Max," she said, cranking the chair back so her face angled up into the sun.

She was wearing an aqua green one-piece made of some kind of Lycra that competitive swimmers wear. She was not the kind of woman who had to cover any part of her figure, but I'd never seen her in a bikini. Her hair was brushed back into a ponytail that she'd slipped through the adjustable back of her Robicheaux's Dock & Bait Shop cap. I was content to sit and watch her, occasionally shift my attention to a lonely cloud scudding across the blue sky, and then shift back to watch more of her. She was quiet for a few minutes, then pulled a tube of suntan lotion out of her bag and started on her legs. Once covered, she again reclined. I watched a woman in a straw hat and varicose veins work her way slowly south, picking through shells. I had great practice being silent. I knew I could wait Richards out.

"All right, Max," she said after twenty minutes. "You win."

"What?"

"Yeah, what. What's going on with your search for the trail workers, and what about the tracers?"

I didn't gloat. I just launched into what Billy and I had come up with, the list of clergy and my instinct on the Placid City minister.

"How about the tail?" she said. "No more white vans?"

"Not that I've noticed."

"You guys ever trace the numbers on that helicopter?"

"Could never really make them out. Just a private job was all we could tell."

"You check with the local airports? Takeoffs of private

choppers during that time frame?"

"You're talking like a cop, Richards. I'm not so sure the towers are going to be so forthcoming to a P.I., but no, I didn't check. Good catch, Detective."

She smiled and leaned back farther in her chair.

"I could do an NCIC on your reverend," she said. "If he pans out and you get a DOB on the father, we could go into the archives."

I knew the National Crime Information Center could be accessed only by government and law enforcement agencies. "Isn't that against policy, Officer? Using a government database for private reasons?" I said.

She finally turned her head and lowered her sunglasses to the tip of her nose. "Yeah, it is," she said, a smile behind the look. "But something tells me that with your track record, Freeman, this isn't going to stay a private matter for long."

We sat back for awhile, letting our skin soak in the sun. She pulled a paperback out of her bag and read and I watched the movement of the ocean, the curl and boil of the waves and the catch of spray in the southeast wind. The visibility was a good ten miles and to the south I could see the gray hulk of a freighter anchored out at sea, off the inlet to Port Everglades. The financial and manufacturing lifeblood of the South American hemisphere was now moving through southeast Florida and the ports that were dredged out of the coastal rivers over the last century. The infrastructure—railroads and highways—that moved the goods of that economic foundation were first built on the muscle and sacrifice of men like Cyrus Mayes and his sons. Was it any different with the men who dug the Panama Canal? Built the Transcontinental Railroad to California? Hell, some six hundred were killed by a hurricane that hit the middle Keys in 1935, many of them workers building Henry Flagler's impossible railway across the necklace of coral islands from the mainland to Key West. The barons and moguls and king's names always go down in the history books tied to such projects, while the names of the dead workers disappear or are scratched on some memorial long forgotten. It is the way of history. Was there any justice in it? Maybe not, but if nearly two generations of a family were killed for trying to walk away from such a project, wasn't some sort of justice or at least some amount of truth due? The sandy touch of her foot against mine brought my head around. I had outwaited Richards's nonstop energy again.

"Hey, before you go into a coma, you wanna take a run?" she said, folding her knees up. "Just an easy one?"

We stretched out on the hard pack at the water's edge, then started north at a loping pace. Richards had pulled on a T-shirt and was on my inside shoulder. She liked to be ankle-deep in the water as she ran. I admit I was the one who opened the conversation.

"How's your friend? The one with the patrolman problem?"

She waited about fifteen strides before answering.

"She came over to my place the other night."

"You made up?"

"She needs help, Max. I mean, she's bitching about this clown one minute, and defending him the next. She's confused as hell.

"I don't want to just tell her to dump the asshole and get out. I'll just end up pushing her away like I did last time, and she'll just fall back with him to prove she's not wrong."

Her frustration was in her pace. The angrier she got, the more energy went into her legs and the faster we both ran.

"But I can see the shit coming, Max. She was over for a couple of hours. We were out back and her cell phone must have rung twenty times. She just kept checking the callback number and not answering. I could tell it was him doing that control thing."

We were pushing now, fast enough so it was becoming hard to talk and keep our breathing steady at the same time. I let her gain a bit on me and watched her from behind, the bob and swish of her ponytail, the cabled lines of muscle in her calves. She finally eased up and drifted back to me.

"You ask any of the other guys on patrol about him? His partner maybe?" I said. I had not told her about the stop McCrary had made at the convenience store.

"I talked with his sergeant. He said he'd look into it. Give the guy the word," she snorted. "What word? Be careful when you're smacking your girlfriend around?"

She needed to blow this out. I let her grind on it for a few more strides and then challenged her to push it to the fishing pier that was coming up about three hundred yards away. We lengthened our strides and the effort stole any extra breath I had. My legs started to ache, and I think I caught a quick grin from her at the hundred-yard mark, when she caught me by surprise and opened up a sprint that put her at the wooden pillars of the pier. We pulled up in the shade underneath and circled each other, our lungs still grabbing air, our hands on our hips. When our breathing was back near normal, we turned south and she took my hand.

"Beat you," she said, and the smile had moved up into

her blue eyes. I said nothing and we walked together back to our chairs. We spent the rest of the afternoon in the shade of the umbrella, eating ham-and-tomato sandwiches and drinking iced tea while I fulfilled a promise to her and told her the story of my father.

She sat quietly, her legs crossed and shoulders turned close to me while I talked of the abuse that my cop dad had brought home on a regular basis from the time I was old enough to remember. I spoke of my own fear and shame at not having put an end to it myself. And I told her the secret that my mother and Billy's mother shared. How two women, unlikely friends of different races but of similar heart, had conspired and worked together to free my mother from a lifetime of control and humiliation. It was a story that I had not shared with any other person. Billy and I had even let the secret slip back into a past that neither of us wanted to revisit. When I finished, Richards took off her sunglasses and looked at me. Not a look of sorrow or of pity. She was studying me and I raised my eyebrows in question.

"What?"

"Thank you," she said, again taking my hand.

"For unloading?"

"No," she said. "For giving me a piece of you, Freeman."

I looked out again at the color of the water and the scatter of seabirds, then back at her.

"Fair enough," I said, and squeezed her fingers.

We packed away our beach things and walked up to the tiki bar and climbed the sandy ramp to the open-air restaurant. We ordered margaritas and conch fritters and watched the light of the day leak out behind us and turn the water a deep indigo and then a slate gray. My phone had not rung. I knew I would have to make the trip to Placid City to get answers, but tonight we were going to do nothing. No cop talk. No analyzing cases. We were going to be like normal people, without any worries.

CHAPTER 15

Early on a Sunday morning I packed up an overnight bag, folded a Florida map and started driving to church. Our list of clergy possibilities had been whittled by callbacks. I'd left two more messages for the pastor at the Church of God in Placid City that went unanswered. Billy and I had discussed the possibility that we might be on a fishing trip in a much larger sea. It had only been a rumor that the male descendent of our gunman Jefferson had become a preacher, and even then we were only guessing that he had stayed in the state. Billy expanded the search parameters into northern Florida and was talking about pushing it up into other Southern states. He'd even forwarded the idea that the grandson could have changed his name after leaving Everglades City in the 1970s and disappeared anywhere.

But Mrs. William Jefferson's accent and her affirmation that her husband had roots in southeast Florida made a visit imperative. Her single comment kept rolling in my head, the jagged edges refusing to nub down. "That part of the family has *been* passed on." The reticence in the voice of the wife of a country preacher pushed me on.

Southern Boulevard carried me through the urban sprawl of West Palm Beach, and twenty miles out, the land turned open and flat, with sugar-cane stalks, freshly tilled vegetable fields, and sod farms that lay as green and uniform as felt on a forty-acre billiard table. Route 441 took me nearly to Belle Glade, a farming town that has supported a migrant community of field-workers and seasonal pickers for more than half a century. The town sits at the southern curve of massive Lake Okeechobee, but I couldn't see the water. A huge earthen dyke had been constructed here by the U.S. government in 1930. It was their response to the hurricane of 1926, which brought more rain in its march from the tropics than anyone had seen or imagined in their worst nightmares. The storm twisted up waves on the lake that surpassed ocean swells and sent the power of tons of water surging over the southern banks and sweeping over the town of Moore Haven. Many of the 2,500 residents killed were never found, their bodies buried in churned black muck—all that was left of the rich soil that had made the region the world's green emerald of winter vegetable growing. In the wake of nature's disaster, man became determined to tame her. The dyke was built and the natural flow of fresh water to the Everglades, which runs from this point for more than a hundred miles to the end of the Florida peninsula, was forever changed—many say for the worse. The same charge was raised when the Tamiami Trail builders constructed their road, when Cyrus Mayes and his sons helped put down the first unnatural barrier to the flow of shallow water to Florida Bay. If one considers such evolution to be evil, then there was enough complicity to go around.

I cruised slowly through the sugar cane capital city of Clewiston and then northwest past a sign that read OUR SOIL IS OUR FUTURE. Then the highway opened back up. With every mile the elevation subtly changed. Pine lands, with individual, polelike tree trunks and green, tasseled tops, lined the road. The landscape was occasionally interrupted by carefully laid out orange groves, the rows running to the horizon and the close trees already showing gobs of the ripening fruit. I timed myself by the mileage signs along the way and made it into Placid City just after eight. There was little movement on the Sunday morning streets. I made two loops into commercial and residential areas that went no more than two blocks off the main highway. It was a narrow place of clapboard and red brick, pickup trucks and broom-swept sidewalks.

When I pulled into Mel's Placid Café, I turned off the engine and let the constant road noise of the trip leach away. There was a gray dust on the step up to the low porch of the restaurant and curtains on the windows. It was not until I reached for the door handle of the truck that I noticed a car parked across my back bumper. It took up the entire pane of my rearview mirror. "Jesus, Max," I whispered to myself. "You do attract them."

When I stepped out of the truck, there was a little man leaning up against the front bumper of a Crown Victoria. It was the kind of car a big man might drive, and he looked out of place next to it. I pretended I was counting out my change from my pocket while I measured him. He was dressed in khaki, but it looked more like a style than a uniform. There was no adornment on the shirt, no epaulets or insignia, only the one single gold star pinned over the left breast. I cut my eyes through the parking lot and saw no patrol cars or backup vehicles.

"Mornin'," he finally said, knowing that I was stalling. "One beautiful Sunday morning." He emphasized the observation by looking up at the treetops and sky. The man's head was bald and tan, and if he was more than five feet seven, I was being generous.

"You do have a gorgeous piece of country here, Sheriff," I said, guessing.

"And mighty quiet too, Mr. . . ." He bumped himself off my fender and reached out his hand.

"Freeman," I said, stepping forward to accept the small but firm handshake and thinking that little men in positions of power always had a habit of squeezing one's hand a bit more strongly than needed. "Max Freeman."

"Mr. Freeman," he said with a politician's smile. "I welcome you to Placid City. You came just for the delights of Mel's home cooking?"

"Not solely," I said. "Though I'm sure it will certainly be worth the trip, Sheriff, uh . . ."

"Wilson," he said. "O. J. Wilson."

It was difficult to judge his age. There were prominent crow's-feet at the corners of his eyes and three rows of worry lines across his forehead. But he was fit and there was an energy coming off him that belied an older man. He was looking up into my eyes, trying to hold them, and it did not please me. I'd done the same in street interrogations and didn't like being on the other side of the stare.

"You former law enforcement or military, Mr. Freeman?" he asked.

"You have a preference, Sheriff?"

"Sorry, just the way you carry yourself," he said. "No offense meant."

"None taken," I replied. I was actually intrigued by his slightly bulldog bearing. "I was a cop, up north. I'm working as a P.I. now, mostly out of West Palm and Lauderdale."

"You're on business then, up this way?"

"Just checking on an estate matter, for an attorney," I said.

He nodded as if he understood and reached out to touch the side of my truck.

"Nice truck," he said. "You a hunter, Mr. Freeman?"

"No, sir. Never have been."

"Then there wouldn't be any firearms back behind the seats there, correct?"

"I do have a permit for a concealed handgun, Sheriff. And that's in a bag behind the seat." I wasn't sure where this was going, but I did believe O. J. Wilson had his reasons and I really was in no mood to rile him.

"Would you like to take a look, Sheriff?" I said, and reopened the driver's-side door and folded up the seat.

"I would, thank you," he said, and bent in. He was short enough so that the floorboards were above his knees, and he reached in and gave my backpack and the sleeping bag I kept there a thorough going over. While he was bent inside, a couple parked their car and walked past us into the café. They did not so much as look back, as though the sight of the local constable going through a stranger's vehicle was as routine as the Sunday paper. When he was done he arranged the bags back the way they'd been.

"Thank you, Mr. Freeman. I appreciate your cooperation," he said, stepping back like some baggage security guard at the airport.

"Mind letting me in on what this is all about, Sheriff?" I said.

"Well, sir. I can't really," he said, dismissing me. "Let's just say it's a precaution and leave it at that if you don't mind, Mr. Freeman. Like you said, it's a beautiful and peaceful Sunday morning."

"No, sir. That was your description, Sheriff," I said, but the little man had already turned and headed into Mel's, leaving me to stand and simply wonder a bit before I finally climbed the stairs and went in to have my breakfast.

I was still frowning when a bell hanging on a curled piece of soft iron rang as I opened the door. The waitress actually said, "Howdy." A middle-aged man with a rough and mottled complexion tipped the bill of his John Deere cap as we passed and I nodded back. I sat at an empty table in the corner that was covered in a red and white checked cloth and decorated with a single plastic geranium. The waitress was dressed in jeans, with a string apron and a flowered western blouse. She smiled as if I were a friend.

"How you doin' today, sir? Can I get you some coffee to start?"

"You read my mind, ma'am," I said, and then asked about the special. When she came back I hooked my thumb at the front of the room and said, "Your sheriff always so attentive on Sunday mornings?"

She put a wrinkle in the side of her mouth and shook her head like a mother who was just told her son was teasing the girls again.

"Don't y'all worry about O. J.—he don't mean nothin' by it," she said. Then she lowered her voice to a conspiratorial whisper. "Truth is, he's like a protective daddy. The man got the worst luck with them gunshot killin's, and he thinks it's his fault they can't solve 'em."

"Killings?"

She smiled again and said, "You're not from around here, are you?"

"No ma'am."

"Well, sir," she began, her voice dropping even further, "we might be the smallest place in the state with a real-life serial killer out there." I could see John Deere pulling the brim of his hat farther down, and I guessed he'd heard the town gossip doing her thing before. "He's been knockin' off the bad boys of Highland County for more than fifteen years now. Every couple of years or so, another one drops, an' everyone gets themselves all in a fuss about how we ain't so far from the big city after all. Poor ol' Sheriff Wilson just took on the chore of finding him. Likes to frisk every stranger that comes through here."

"Annette?" John Deere had held off as long as he could. "Can we order over here, please?"

The waitress rolled her eyes and winked at me. I grinned back, friendly-like, and ordered the breakfast special—eggs over easy and biscuits with brown gravy.

I ate without interruption and gave the waitress's gossip little thought. Every little place has something, and violence doesn't have boundaries. Who isn't capable of it? You don't have to be a cop for long to find that answer: everybody. When Annette brought my check I asked if she could give me directions to Pastor Jefferson's Church of God.

"You really ain't from around here," she said. She told me the way in lefts and rights. I tipped her like a city boy at 20 percent and got a big thank-you in return.

The white-frame building was set well back off the road in a slight gully. There was no sign at the road entrance, but several cars and trucks were already parked on the brown grass to one side. I turned down the worn dirt drive and like the other early arrivals, parked in the shade of a stand of century-old oaks. The Reverend Jefferson's church reminded me of the plain, clapboard Quaker buildings in central Pennsylvania. The steeple was canopied and slatted at the top to vent hot air. The windows were tall and narrow, and none held the adornment of stained glass or anything more fanciful than simple double molding. I sat in the truck and watched folks arrive for the 10:00 A.M. service. They were a democratic group. A middle-aged white couple, he in a western string tie and tan sport coat, she in a patterned dress and a white embroidered sweater. A black family, the parents in clean, pressed white shirts and dark trousers and skirt, their three matching sons trailing behind, the top buttons at their necks done tight. A group of what I guessed were Seminole Indians climbing out of a big, club-cab pickup, the men in polished cowboy boots and the women in large, brightly colored skirts. Their hair was pulled back, black and glossy, and their stoic faces carried the classic flat and sharply angled forehead and nose.

I waited until near the hour and then got out and slipped on my navy sport coat and went in. I nodded and politely smiled as I found a seat in the back. The interior was as understated as the outside. The plain wooden pews were worn, the lacquer rubbed dull in some spots by years of wool and canvas, cotton and polyester. The ceiling was beamed and the highest windows let the morning sun streak through, illuminating lazy drifts of dust in the air. The altar was small and white and the expected dominant feature was a floor-to-ceiling cross behind it. The place looked like it could hold fifty congregants at most. There were some thirty-five this morning, and they all rose at some signal that I didn't see.

Pastor Jefferson looked young for fifty. His hair was dark, full and conservatively cut. He was slightly built and it was difficult to judge his height, but his face and shoulders were all angles and sharp corners.

"Good morning."

"Good morning, Reverend," the congregation returned.

"God be with you."

"And with you."

"Let us pray."

I was the only one who did not lower my head as Jefferson recited. As he scanned the room, he picked me up in a second, a tall stranger in the back pew of his church. His voice was clear but not strong. He depended on the words themselves and not his performance of them. He was as plain as the physical structure. I was too far away to discern the color of his eyes.

"Please, be seated."

The service was informal and simple. The pastor's sermon was personal and grassroots. He came across as patrician and neighborly at the same time. He kept the Southern drawl out of his diction during his readings, but let it slip through when he turned a phrase out of the Bible. I saw him stop his eyes on several of the congregants during the sermon, though he seemed to avoid mine. When the offering plate got to me I noted that it was filled with envelopes, all of which, I assumed, contained member tithes. I slipped a twenty under them.

When the service ended I stood watching until the last folks had filed out. Jefferson was outside at the bottom of the steps, clasping each hand and giving them a personal word. There was no one behind me when he looked up into my face and took my hand. His grip was soft and I could feel delicate bones through tight skin. He waited an extra few beats as the last true parishioner stepped out of earshot. His eyes were a dark blue that I had never encountered before.

"Mr. Freeman, the investigator, I presume," he said, a

professional smile on his face.

"Yes, Reverend," I said. He'd caught me off guard. "A fine cleric and a clairvoyant too?"

His laugh was less formal. "Yes, well, I knew you would be coming sometime. I suspect I've always known someone would."

An hour later we were alone at a picnic table under the oaks. Jefferson had made the rounds with his people, consoling, blessing, promising visits and agreeing to commitments later in the week. When it became awkward for him to simply keep introducing me as Mr. Freeman without elaboration, I wandered over to the open table and sat inspecting the sparse moss hanging in the oak limbs and trying to identify the birdsong coming out of a nearby field. With only a few cleanup volunteers on the grounds, the reverend had finally walked back to join me.

"You are originally from the Everglades City area. I don't have that wrong, do I, Reverend?" I said, cutting straight to it.

"That's correct."

"And your father and grandfather before him?"

"We left in 1962, Mr. Freeman. My parents moved to Naples the year my grandfather passed."

His face was calm and emotionless. I'd seen the look before, years ago, when I'd come to the home of a Germantown woman in North Philly who'd aborted her child. It had taken the squad and the M.E. several days to track her down and she'd been waiting for us when we arrived. Jefferson had the same resigned and haunted look, as though he were waiting for me to announce his arrest and cuff him.

"Reverend, I'm looking into the disappearance of three men. A father and his two sons. We have reason to believe that they may have been killed when they were at work on the Tamiami Trail in 1924."

Jefferson's eyes had closed when I mentioned the two sons, and he kept them closed.

"We came across some letters written by the missing father and he specifically mentions a marksman named Jefferson who, the letter indicates, watched over the laborers. Could that Jefferson have been your grandfather, Reverend?"

He opened his eyes and at first seemed to be focused on something far behind my left ear. I might have turned to look if I hadn't known that there was only a wide and knurled trunk of oak behind me. Then his eyes shifted back onto mine.

"If it had to do with killing and evil, Mr. Freeman, then it most likely did have my grandfather Jefferson's hand in it," he said in a flat and somewhat defeated tone.

"Sir?" I said. The bluntness of the statement had jarred me.

"You see, Mr. Freeman, John William Jefferson was an evil man. Some in that place and time may have thought of him as the devil himself."

With that the pastor crossed his arms over his chest, took a deep and brave breath and told me all he knew about his infamous relative.

John William had come to the Ten Thousand Islands sometime around 1920. He brought his wife and a sum of money that was unusual for the time. He bought a prime piece of land along the Turner River that was among the most elevated of the shell mounds in the area. It was consequently valuable since it had the potential to be farmed. But John William was not a farmer. He was a slight man, with delicate hands that his grandson would inherit, and he always wore a wide-brimmed hat that put his eyes in constant shade. The first rumor about him was that he was dumb and could not speak a word because it was so rare than anyone other than his wife ever heard his voice. Ted Smallwood down at his post office and store at Chokoloskee would eventually dispel that rumor. In his few dealings with John William, Smallwood knew that not only could the man speak, but he could also read and write and was highly proficient and meticulous in documenting his finances.

The second rumor was that the new arrival was, in fact, a criminal, a killer who had fled the law in Missouri and come to the virgin outpost of southwest Florida to hide. Unlike the other rumor, this one never died, and was in fact built upon throughout John William's life. Stories of his exploits held few if any provable facts. The only truly witnessed detail of the man was his prowess with a rifle. That ability was known by his family and those in the sparse and isolated community. But the speculation about that ability colored everything else he was.

He was not a lazy man, though his industry was the focus of many wagging tongues. On his river land he built one of the finest houses in the area, along with a stone cistern to gather fresh water and a solid barn that was considered ostentatious by his neighbors. But though his land was envied for its precious inches of rich topsoil, and his location next to the river for its easy access to the bay, John William did not farm or fish for profit. He was a hunter, and as the Reverend Jefferson's mother often said in her late night stories to him, he answered to no God or man other than himself.

John William made his living killing things. In the early years, when the fashion for ladies' hats in New York and the rest of the Northeast turned to outrageous displays of bird-feather designs, men with John William's talent were in demand. He knew the region, the nesting patterns of southeast Florida's pure white egrets and stunning pink flamingos, and being the finest marksman in the region, he became a hired "guide" for the acquisition arm of the distant hatmakers. Other locals in the same business would tell of coming upon hidden rookeries of the snowy egrets far from the more easily accessed nests around the islands. As the birds became sparse, they themselves spent days getting there by skiff, but if the wind was right, they could smell that they were too late. When they finally cleared the last curve of water they would spot the carnage—an acre of trees and the wet undergrowth covered with the mutilated and rotting carcasses of egrets. The larger ones had been killed with a single shot, the few valuable feathers plucked and the rest of the animal tossed away. Nearby a pod of fat gators would be rolling in the shallows or sunning themselves on mats of grass, lazy with the easy meals so plentiful that they could not begin to clear the area.

"It appears Mr. Jefferson gone an' beat us to it again, boys," would be the refrain, and another rumor would be piled onto the marksman's name. Later, with the rookeries all along Lake Okeechobee already wiped out by the plume hunters and southwest Florida facing the same eventual slaughter, the state banned the practice. But as long as there was a market, even an illegal one, the poaching continued. John William had long determined that it was his birthright to kill things for money. No government edict passed down from a capital city eight hundred miles away was going to stop him. It was less than two years later that the first Audubon officer sent to the Ten Thousand Islands area to enforce the law was found dead on a mangrove outcropping along the western edge of Chevalier Bay. The warden had been missing for a week when a group of fishermen found his body. From a distance they thought he was still alive. At first glance in the early morning light, he appeared to be standing on a solid clump of land, waving. It was only when they got closer that they realized the warden was sunk to his knees in the gelatinous muck at the base of the mangrove, his arm caught high in a limb, the wrist wedged in a V-notch. When they got closer they could see that he had been killed. A single gunshot had entered at the back of his neck and then exploded outward from his throat. The body had been left with no effort on the part of his assassin to hide it. Speculation in the community as to the identity of the killer settled in its usual place.

The sound of a screen door slapping shut stopped the reverend's recounting and we both looked up toward the church.

A woman carrying a tray with a pitcher and two glasses was walking toward us. She was dressed in a long printed dress and was tall even in the flat shoes that resembled black dancing slippers. Her honey-colored hair was up, and I could see touches of gray at the roots above her ears. Her eyes were red-rimmed and anxious, as though she had been both crying and angry at the same time.

"Ahh, thank you, Margery," Jefferson said. "Mr. Freeman, this is my wife, Margery. I believe you have spoken on the phone."

I stood up to greet her, but when she set the tray of lemonade on the table she did not offer her hand or look me in the eyes.

"Yes," she said, and then to her husband, "Are you all right, William?" The look in her eyes had changed to one of legitimate concern.

"Yes, Margery," he answered. "We'll be fine."

I could tell that "we'll" meant the both of them. She nodded and walked back to the church. When she had gone Jefferson poured the glasses. The coolness of the drink on my throat made me suddenly aware of the moist heat that was rising all around us in the canopy of shade. It was past noon and out in the sunlit meadow, grasshoppers were flying. I was about to ask Jefferson if he wanted to take a break, but held back. I had been in police interview rooms where you learned that once a guy started talking, you let him. The reverend was in his confessional; I bowed my head and listened.

"It was not an easy situation for my father and mother. The constant rumors. The fear," he said, looking out and seeming to find the grasshoppers himself.

His mother was a local girl from Everglades City, extremely religious. She knew the stories, the devil warnings about the Jeffersons who lived by the river. But Clinton Jefferson was her own age and they went to the only country school within fifty miles and the boy was polite and shy and nearly friendless. When she began coming by his house, she did not recall ever having heard Mr. Jefferson say a word. When she convinced Clinton to join her at Bible study, the father did not oppose it. When they were married at the age of eighteen, he did not attend the wedding. His wife excused him as being off on business. But

Clinton Jefferson would not leave his parents despite being tainted by his father's reputation. He could not leave his mother to bear it on her own and he moved his new wife into the river house. The two women grew close—the reverend's mother was the first to hear about the pent-up pain of the wife who'd shared her husband's strange isolation and odd justifications for so many years.

"My mother was the one who then shared the stories with me, doling them out little by little as I grew," Jefferson said. "She wove them in with lessons of God's plan and his forgiveness. It was the beginning of my religious education."

"And you moved away after your grandfather died?" I said. It was the first question that I had asked.

"Killed himself," Jefferson corrected me sharply, and the retort brought my head up. "My father found the body in the barn on a winter day in 1962. He had shot himself with his own rifle.

"My grandmother survived for only a few years afterward. I was twelve when we left and I remember my father locking the front door to the river house. We drove away with only what we could fit in the truck and never went back."

The reverend's eyes were still on the meadow when I asked him if his own father would remember any more of the details of John William's activities in 1924 and his work on the trail.

"I'm sure he would have, Mr. Freeman. I believe my father lived through, and was visited by, every suspicion and every true exploit that my grandfather performed or was quietly accused of performing. In a place like that, one wrestles with his own conscience alone and with only God to forgive."

"Is it possible for me to speak to him, just to see what he might recall?"

The reverend waited a long silent beat before answering.

"My father died by his own hand fifteen years ago, just after I took this church posting, Mr. Freeman."

He stood and picked up the tray his wife had delivered and started walking back toward the church. When I followed and stepped out into the sun, the brightness and sudden heat caused me to flinch, and the vision of Jefferson framed in the steeple shape of the church blurred and shimmered out of focus for a second and any words I might have offered were even further washed away. When he reached the back door he stepped inside without a word and I stopped and was considering my long drive home when he reappeared. His hands were empty and he had settled a light-colored straw hat on his head. He met my eyes and there was a look of determination on his face, like something had been settled.

"I need you to follow me, Mr. Freeman. If you would, sir, I have something for you."

I trailed his dark sedan through town and saw at least three people wave at him as he passed by the small hardware store, the barber shop with an actual working red-and-white-striped pole, and a sign outside a plain brick storefront that said HAIR AND TANNING SALON. Two miles later he turned off onto a side road going west. Two-story farmhouses sat back from green lawns, with stands of pines to either side. Another mile and he turned north on a dirt road; the dust boiled up behind his car and I backed farther off, out of the swirl. Finally I saw his brake lights flash and he pulled onto a two-track drive that led through a column of oaks and up to a white, clapboard house. There was a wide veranda across the front and an American flag flying from the corner post. He parked next to an older model van, and I stopped behind him and got out.

"This is my home, Mr. Freeman—excuse me for not inviting you in," he said with a voice of true apology, before leading me toward the back. Behind the house was a thriving garden that appeared to cover at least an acre, with more open land back to a windbreak of tall trees. The ruts of the two-track led up to the sliding front door of a small barn, and the reverend continued that way. He offered no comment, no expression of pride or information on his land, and I did not probe. He rolled the bare door all the way open, letting the sun pour in to illuminate the open bay and its array of tools propped against the walls, the workbench at the back, and the old iron tractor parked in the middle of it all. The smell was of dust and dry grass, gasoline and heat-cured, rough-cut wood. He went to the bench and took down a two-foot-long pry bar and then crossed to the base of a simple staircase. There he snapped on a light switch, but I couldn't tell where, or if, a bulb had gone on. I followed the line of stairs and saw that planks covered the back half of the barn's thick ceiling joists and served as an upstairs floor. The reverend started up and I followed. He waited for me at the top step, and when he moved to give me room, the plank creaked under his slight weight.

"Watch your head," he said, and I had to keep myself bent to fit under the low angle of the roof trusses. I could now see a single lit bulb hanging in the rafters.

"Back in the far corner there, Mr. Freeman, is a crate from my grandfather's river house," he said, nodding toward the northeast wall. "It is one of the few things that my father salvaged from that place."

I looked in his face, but he would not meet my eyes.

"You may take it with you, sir. And do with it what you must."

He handed me the pry bar and this time looked in my face and must have seen the questions. In his own face was a look of calm benevolence—and maybe a sense of relief.

"It is a new and scientific world, Mr. Freeman. Experts have broken down the double helix of life and snipped at individual strands of genetic material and told us they have the blueprint all mapped out."

He was using the voice of his pulpit now, and I looked over at the corner.

"But the sins of the father aren't chemicals and chromosomes, sir. And in the end we are all, each one of us, much more than just DNA."

With that he turned and climbed down the stairs and walked out into the sunlight.

CHAPTER 16

I had to work my way to the corner, pushing away cardboard boxes full of old electrical supplies, cartons of cracked, dusty pottery, a wooden keg of half-rusted nails. I brushed away cobwebs and was forced to bend farther over as the roof sloped. It was hot and I was stirring up motes of dust—I could feel the particles in the back of my throat when I tried to breathe through my mouth.

Finally the weak light caught the raw pine of a crate lying flat in the deepest part of the corner. I pulled up one edge and was able to stand the piece on one side. It was about as long as the distance from my shoulder to my fingertips and as wide and deep as a piano bench. It was more awkward than heavy. I wrestled it out of its hiding place and backed out, carrying it to a cleared spot on the floorboards.

The wood was dry and clean but almost brittle with age. I used the bar and pried off the entire top panel. The contents were packed in a dried moss of some kind, not much different from the paper confetti used today. I pulled it away and uncovered a long scabbard made of dark leather that was cracked and split. I untied the top flap but before reaching inside, I looked around and found a ripped but dry section of old towel and covered my hand. Then I carefully withdrew the stock half of a Winchester .405 Takedown. The rifle had to be nearly a hundred years old and was stunning. The plating on the fixed box magazine was tarnished, but the scrollwork along the lever action was gorgeous and as intricate as any I'd ever seen. I reached back into the scabbard and from a separate compartment slid out the barrel half. The base was threaded, and even with some spots of rust showing, I was able to twist it smoothly into the receiver. It was the same kind of gun that Teddy Roosevelt had used in his African hunting exploits.

I didn't touch the surfaces of the gun but laid it down on the opened scabbard while I checked the rest of the crate. Buried in the moss at one corner was a small wooden box of ammunition. The cartridges were at least three inches tall and the tips big and heavy. Roosevelt had called the .405 cartridge "Big Medicine" for its power to drop a water buffalo, gator or man. At the other end of the crate I found a leather-bound book. The initials JWJ were stamped in gold relief into its nearly black cover. The pages inside were yellowed and felt like dried leaves between my fingers, but the faded markings and tooled letters were still legible. It appeared to be some kind of ledger. Rows of calculations were on some pages, along with entries for quantities bought or sold and the amounts. On other pages were diagrams and drawings of machines and plans for buildings. The light was poor, so I stood and cradled the book in one hand while carefully turning the pages. When I finally determined the dates, I skipped forward to 1924.

Among those pages I found a crude map. Its dominant feature was a straight hatched line, apparently depicting a rail line. I could make out the west terminus as Everglades City, while the opposite end was scratched "Miami." Along the hatch marks, childlike drawings of tree palms were spaced at odd intervals, and at each of these was a cluster of faded X's. Two at one spot, three at another, six farther to the right toward Miami. The spots also bore numbers above the tree drawings, which I recognized as longitude and latitude indices. And beneath the X's were dollar amounts much like the prices marked in earlier pages. The left, and I assumed western group, where there were two X's, was marked "II—$600.00." The three X's were marked "III—$900.00." The eastern grouping was marked "IIII I—$1,800.00." I began to feel nauseated as I stared at the figures and went down on one knee, with the book still balanced on the other. Sweat was now running in rivulets down my back, and I pulled at the front of my shirt to tighten the fabric and soak up the moisture between my shoulder blades. I wiped at my eyes and carefully turned the page to the subsequent rows of the ledger. There, listed under the name "Noren," were the same figures, dated and grouped "ea./$300 + .15 ammunition." Gator hides, I knew, were going for $1.50 a foot in those days. John William was not killing alligators for three hundred dollars apiece. Even the most luscious and illegal flamingo plumes did not bring those kinds of prices.

I placed the book back in the crate, rewrapped the Winchester and tamped the panel back into place on the crate. I used the pry bar to reset the nails, and with the crate held tight against my chest, climbed back down the staircase and snapped the light off. The reverend Jefferson did not show himself again. He may have been in the house, having lunch with his wife. He may have been out in the back rows of his garden. He may have been somewhere quiet and cool where he went to pray alone.

I carried the crate to my truck and slid it into the space behind the seats on top of my bag. I climbed in, started the engine and kicked on the AC. The reverend's sedan and family van were still parked side by side, and I watched the front of the house as I backed away but saw no movement at the curtains or the door. As I drove away I kept my eyes on the rearview mirror until the dust billowed up and the house and the oaks disappeard.

When I got to Billy's it was late and the overnight desk manager looked long and hard at the crate under my arm as he passed me through.

"Good evening, Mr. Freeman," he said with his stiff British accent. "Mr. Manchester is still out for the evening."

I nodded and continued to the elevator.

"Do you require the freight elevator, sir?" he said, still looking with disdain at the wooden box, judging perhaps its rough corners and the damage they might do to the paneled walls.

"No. I'm fine," I said as the regular elevator doors slid open.

The apartment was lit, although the lamps and recessed spots were dimmed. Billy remembered well his days in a chopped-up tenement building in North Philly, where the lights would be shut down sometimes for days because of blown fuses or blown deadlines for making the payments. He never wanted to come home to a dark house again.

I laid the crate on the carpeted floor and went to the guest room and found a large bath towel in the bathroom linen closet. My own image in the mirror stopped me. The light blue oxford shirt I'd worn to church that morning was creased and rumpled, and so was the face above it. The skin was deeply tanned, left even darker by the unshaven stubble. The crow's-feet were pronounced and pouches of skin hung beneath my eyes, the exhaustion of hours on the road. I leaned in closer. I didn't have a mirror at the river shack and sometimes didn't look at myself for weeks at a time, and even then, not closely or seriously. The reverend's last words had followed me for the entire drive back, and I looked into the black irises of my eyes. Was my father in there? And if so, which one? The relentless cop who wouldn't let a child-killer go unpunished? Or an alcoholic racist who beat his wife? Or both? Or neither? "We leave more than DNA behind," the living William Jefferson had said. But how much more? The answers weren't in the mirror.

I took the towel with me out to the living room and spread it out on Billy's polished wood dining table, then carefully laid the crate on it. I used a screwdriver from the utility drawer to pry the top off and took out the ledger. Under better light I sat at the kitchen bar counter and studied the pages while sipping cold bottles of beer from the refrigerator. The man had been meticulous. If my interpretations were right, John William had recorded every dime he had paid out or taken in from the time he landed in Everglades City until 1962, when he'd blown his brains out in his barn one late summer night. The entries were filled with figures, dates, mileage, the running costs of supplies and their changes from year to year. But there was not a single sentence of opinion or emotion or aesthetic description in all the dry, yellowed pages.

It was past midnight when I gently closed the book and took a fresh beer out onto the patio. There was an uncharacteristic chill coming in on the northeast ocean wind. I could hear the surf chopping at the sand, and interrupted moonlight caught on the swells at sea far from the shore. Weather was kicking up. I took another long drink from the bottle and found it difficult to focus on the lights of a ship at sea. Then from behind me I heard my name being called.

"M-Max."

Billy was looking down into the crate when I came in through the sliding doors. Diane was at his side, barely a step behind. Billy was in a tuxedo and black tie, and looked every bit like a version of the most recent Academy Award winner. Diane was in a long gown, an expensive-looking lace shawl still around her shoulders. Billy looked up at me.

"M-Max. What the h-hell is this doing in my home?"

I hesitated only a second. My mind might have been muddled at the moment, but it was made up.

"That, my friend, may be the murder weapon used to kill our Mr. Cyrus Mayes and his family."

I drank coffee after that, standing next to the pot in the kitchen. Diane tasted a glass of chardonnay and Billy drank bottled water as they sat on stools on the other side of the counter going carefully over John William's ledger. Billy had pulled on a pair of thin latex gloves before handling the book and Diane only looked over his shoulder, letting him touch the pages.

I narrated the story of John William Jefferson as it was told to me. They listened, interrupting only for clarification, which lawyers do, and even that happened less and less as the coffee sobered me. When he got to the pages showing the diagram of the trail, Billy spent several minutes staring at the markers.

"Jesus, M-Max," he said.

Billy had come to the same assumption that I had: the possibility of grave markers. X's where bodies where buried or simply left some eighty years ago.

"Yeah. But not enough to get a warrant for all of PalmCo's records pertaining to their part in building the road, is it?"

The two attorneys did not look at each other but both were subtly shaking their heads.

"N-No names. No use of the word 'bodies.' No description of killing or the three hundred dollars b-being the rate for the d-disposal of a human being."

"Any attorney is going to argue that those entries could represent anything from rattlesnakes to bobcats," McIntyre said.

"We could use it as m-more ammunition to get PalmCo to consider a settlement, but that's n-not what Mayes wants. Or anyone else," Billy said, looking at me.

"We still need the bodies," I said.

"Eighty years old?" McIntyre said, not bothering to hide her skepticism.

"Yeah. The bones, teeth, skeletal remains. Hell, even the bullets themselves could still be there. And now we may have the treasure map."

I'd already written down the coordinates from the ledger. Billy could lay them out on a relief map of the Glades in the morning while I made a call to the Loop Road hotel and got a message to Nate Brown. If John William had borrowed the technology of the road surveyors and was meticulous with his markings, we had a chance.

"I also h-have to get this to our d-documents expert for a t-time analysis," Billy said. "Is that going to b-be a problem with your reverend Jefferson?"

"I don't think he even knows it exists," I said. "I doubt he ever even opened the crate. Maybe his father had, but it was like a Pandora's heirloom that they didn't want to destroy but didn't want to acknowledge, either. It was like they were waiting for someone to take it out of their hands."

The statement left us all quiet. Billy had long ago shed his jacket and tie but somehow still looked as sharp as a razor crease. McIntyre was barefooted again and in her concentration had dragged her fingers through her thick dark hair enough times that it left her looking rumpled.

"Tomorrow," Billy finally said, as his hand subtly went to McIntyre's neck and they rose together. He started to turn but stopped. The Winchester Takedown was still on his dining table. No one had even looked at it after we'd started concentrating on the book. Billy's aversion was not political or liberal; it was personal. His past was not without its own flashes of violence and what always comes with it.

"I'll take it down and lock it in my truck," I said quickly.

"OK, M-Max. T-Tomorrow we can put it in p-proper storage. And I'd l-like to get our f-friend Mr. Lott to take a l-look."

They retired to Billy's room. I closed up the crate and went and closed the patio doors. I then snagged two bottles of beer, picked up the crate and carried it down to my truck. I draped a rain jacket over it in the back behind the seats and took out my emergency sleeping bag, then locked up and walked out to the beach.

The wind had died some but the surf was still kicked up. The lights from the shorefront buildings caught the white foam of the breakers and illuminated them as they rolled and tumbled and eventually died on the sand. I walked up into the breeze. I could feel the moisture of the salt air on my arms and hands. When I found a swatch of dark beach where the building light was blocked by a partial dune, I sat in the sand and wrapped the sleeping bag around my legs and opened the first beer. I took a sip and stared out at the eastern horizon, thought of what John William may have left behind, and waited for the glow of sunrise.

The next day I showered and shaved upstairs while Billy made one of his gourmet breakfasts. The weak nor'easter had blown itself out overnight. The ocean had begun to flatten out and the partial cloud cover had been replaced by a hot clear sky that was difficult to look up into for too long without hurting one's eyes.

When I came back up well after seven, Billy and McIntyre were on the patio drinking coffee and absorbing sections of *The Wall Street Journal*. By the time I'd cleaned up, Diane had gone off to court.

"The girl's a workaholic," I said to Billy as I sat down with coffee in the patio chair she had abandoned. He was still in the kitchen, on the other side of the threshold.

"She's seriously considering a run for a judgeship in next year's elections. I think she's testing her stamina," he said, the physical barrier removing his stutter.

"She's tough enough, and sure as hell smart enough," I said.

"Yes," he said, coming out to place plates of hard scrambled eggs with scallions and diced red peppers and sides of homemade salsa on the table.

"So, is there a concern?" I said, reading the tone of his voice.

"It's an elected p-position. Which m-means it's political by nature."

"Yeah?"

"I'm n-not sure the South left in South Florida will accept a woman c-candidate who is carrying on a long-term, interracial relationship."

It was not an area that Billy brought into conversation often. He had been able to overwhelm any overt racism in his own life by the strength of his intelligence and ability to command a great respect for his services. His business sense and knowledge of the markets had also made him wealthy, and the economic world of dollars and cents was truly color-blind. He did not give a damn about racism directed toward him. If confronted, he turned his back on it; the loss wouldn't be his. But when it showed against others less powerful, he seethed because he knew it was not just about him.

"Don't tell me she's deciding between you and the judgeship," I said.

"N-No. She says fuck them," he answered, and the curse word sounded alien coming from his mouth.

"So what's the problem?"

He waited, squinting out into the sun and taking a long sip of hot coffee without wincing.

"I m-may ask her to m-marry me, Max."

CHAPTER 17

I followed Billy to his downtown office, where we locked John William's rifle away in a vault where he kept a variety of items for his client's cases. Billy alone knew the combination, and it kept his anxieties in check. The next day I would take it down to Lott's forensics lab and let the expert take a look.

We then went to work on printing out a topographical map of the Everglades corridor along the Tamiami Trail and a two-mile border on either side. The satellite imagery that was used to create the map was detailed enough to show the curve of Loop Road. It showed the Everglades National Park visitors' center at Big Bend and the Gulf Coast visitors' center just outside Everglades City. Without too much map-reading expertise, you could make out the larger groups of hardwood hammocks and cypress stands. When Billy used the longitude and latitude notations from John William's crudely sketched book, the corresponding points were stunning. The groups of X's he had recorded under a pen squib of trees came up in three groupings of existing trees found by the satellite. All were less than a mile as the crow flies south of the existing roadway. By simple choice of elimination, I focused on the spot with the three X's. If a father and two sons were buried there, the chance of finding some sign of them had been enhanced dramatically. But we were still talking about hundreds of square feet, and then only if the figures were exact.

While Billy checked more calculations, I used one of his office lines to call the Frontier Hotel.

"Bar, can I get cha?" said the woman's voice after eight rings.

"Josie. This is Max Freeman, the tall guy who was in the other day meeting with Nate Brown?"

"Yeah. I know who you are—always pullin' trouble behind you."

"Yeah, well, I need to get a message to Mr. Brown, and he said you'd be able to contact him."

There was silence on the other end.

"If he comes in, I'll contact him," she finally said.

Right, I thought. Maybe next month. But what was I going to do?

"OK, fair enough. If you contact him, can you give him this cell phone number and tell him to call me as soon as possible?" I read the number off to her, going slowly, pronouncing clearly, not knowing if she was even bothering to write it down.

"OK?" I said.

"OK. I got it. But I don't think Mr. Brown ever used a phone in his life. He usually finds folks when he wants to find them."

"Yeah, I know. But these were his instructions, to call you, Josie, OK?"

"He said me? By name?"

"That's right."

"OK, then. I'll get it to him," she said, and might have let some point of pride slip into her voice.

"Thanks very much, Josie. I owe you," I said, but hung up before she could ask me how much.

I went back to the map. Billy had marked off mileage

amounts along the roadway, and distances from recreation turnouts to the X's.

"It's g-going to b-be very inaccurate," he said, maybe not knowing, since he had never been in the Glades himself, how obvious the statement was.

"You plan to say anything to the Mayes kid about all this?"

Billy shook his head.

"N-Not him. N-Not PalmCo's people," he said. "We keep it to ourselves and see wh-what we come up with. This way we keep it out of the p-press. No one knows what we're after or where we're l-looking."

I thought of getting my truck swept again by Ramón and his crew. I thought about the look of satisfaction on Nate Brown's face when he'd ditched us into the mangroves and lost the helicopter tail.

"You're optimistic," I said.

"I'm a lawyer," he responded. "It's w-what I do."

I used his phone to page Richards and then rolled up a copy of our treasure map.

"I'll let you know when Brown gets in touch with me," I said.

"Good h-hunting."

I was in the truck trying to think of a good place to take a nap when Richards answered the page.

"Hey. What's up?"

"Dinner tonight?"

"You beat me to it, Freeman. Can we just have something at my place? I've got someone staying with me and it might help to have you there, you know, to give your perspective on things?"

"Sounds like your friend in denial," I said. "She too scared to go home now?"

"You're quite the detective, Freeman. Can't talk now though, I'm in the shop. How about six-thirty or seven?"

"I'm there."

"Good."

My brain was feeling clunky from lack of sleep, too much alcohol and too much grinding. I drove south on A1A until I got to the entrance of a beachside county park, paid the seven dollars to get in and then found a quiet parking spot in the shade of a line of Australian pines. I rolled both windows down for a cross-breeze and then put my seat back. Within five minutes I was asleep.

The squawk of a bird woke me, or maybe the yelp of a child, or the clatter of beach chairs being loaded into a car. It took me a moment to realize where I was, but then I banged my knee on the steering wheel and the quick shot of pain cleared my head. I checked my watch. It had been two hours. I climbed out of the truck and took a few minutes to stretch out the kinks in my back and the tightness in my hamstrings. Behind me the western sky was smeared in soft washes of burnt orange and purple. To the east, through the trees, the surf was slushing up onto the beach. I walked to the park rest room and stood at the sink splashing cold water into my face and finger-combing my hair. You'll be quite the date tonight, Freeman.

I took A1A down to Lauderdale, stopped at a doughnut shop, just for the coffee. I passed the spot where the Galt Ocean Hotel once stood, where Joe Namath made his outlandish promise at poolside that he would beat the Colts in Super Bowl III and then went out and did it. I made a special pass by the Elbo Room, the corner bar where spring break was immortalized in the 1960s. It was a cool and lazy evening, and I was in an unusually buoyant mood until I parked in front of Richards's place and heard a harsh, guttural yell coming from the garden entrance at the side of the house. There were two unfamiliar cars in the driveway, a two-door Toyota and a black Trans Am with a spoiler on the back and an air-scooped hood. I was running the possibilities through my head when the man's barking sounded again.

"Goddamnit, Kathleen. I need to talk with you now! I know you're in there!"

I started up the driveway, shifting into cop mode, feeling the trace of adrenaline trickling into my bloodstream. Signal 38. Domestic disturbance. Worst and most unpredictable call a patrolman gets.

I came around the corner and his back was to me. He was dressed in civilian clothes, jeans and a tank-top T-shirt. He had one arm over the top of the wooden fence gate to Richards's backyard, searching, I assumed, for the lift latch that would unlock it.

"Come on, Richards," he said, taking his voice down a notch in volume but not in anger. "I know what the fuck you're doing. Stay out of it and let her come out and talk, just talk." He lowered his voice further and whispered, "you fucking bitch."

I took a few more quiet steps, set my feet and said, "Nice talk about a superior officer, McCrary."

His head twisted around like he'd been bitten in the ass and when he recognized me he slowly came off the fence and squared up.

"This ain't your business, P.I.," he said, and I could see the muscles in his jaws flex. Here was something male to put his anger on, something he could understand.

"I believe you're trespassing, officer. Not a pretty charge to show up on a report to your sergeant," I said, measuring the distance between us and moving just slightly to my right away from his dominant hand. I had spent too many years at Frankie O'Hara's father's gym in South Philly, first as just a kid in the neighborhood fascinated by what went on inside, and later as a sparring partner for the professionals who worked there. You never forget the fundamentals or the moves after they'd been punched into you by professionals.

"And you're just the kind of prick who'd write one up on another cop, aren't you, P.I.?" I watched his hands flex at his sides and then curl into fists.

"It might be a good time for you to relax a bit, McCrary, and take a walk. I think—"

He swung with the right hand I was expecting, throwing his weight behind it and throwing himself off balance. The distance I'd kept made him reach and I slid behind the punch and chucked him with two hands in the shoulder to keep his momentum going. In the ring I would have fired an overhand hook into the back of his ear as he passed. But I just stepped back as his elbow went down on the hood of Richards's car and he regained his balance.

"You want to stick 'assault on a civilian' into the report, too, McCrary? You're a real bright guy."

This time his hands came up in a real fighter's pose and there was a calculated rage in his eyes. But like most amateurs, he carried his right fist too low, and a combination of calculated punches was already clicking in my muscles when I heard a metallic snap and the groan of hinges behind me. I saw McCrary's eyes change.

"You're a solid asshole, McCrary. Back off! Now!"

I took a step back out of his range and cut my eyes over to the sight of Richards, her 9 mm extended in both hands, the bead on McCrary's chest.

He opened his hands first, and then his mouth as he stepped back.

"OK. OK. Shit. OK," he stammered, and I watched the emotion flush out of his face.

"You're out of fucking control, Officer," Richards barked, and McCrary nodded his head and showed her his palms. He was breathing hard. We were all breathing hard.

"OK. OK. Look, I'm sorry," he said, visibly gathering himself. But Richards did not lower her gun.

"None of that sorry shit, McCrary," she snapped back at him. "That doesn't wash with me. You've assaulted two of my guests on my private property. I have already cut you way too much of a break by not calling this in and having you cuffed in the street. You will back off and leave the premises right now, and you'd better have a long, hard talk with your sergeant tonight, McCrary. Understand?"

"OK. OK. Fine. Look. Just put the weapon down, OK? Look. . . ."

"Now!" snapped Richards, cutting him off.

McCrary may not have had a full appreciation for Richards's limits, but I had witnessed her pull a trigger, and I had seen the result.

"OK. OK," he said, and this time he began to step back. I watched him nodding his head in acquiescence, but I also picked up a flicker of sharp light in his eyes. Richards lowered her gun but did not move as we watched him get into the Trans Am, back out and, maybe to his credit, or maybe not, pull away slowly and disappear down the street.

Richards was now looking down at the ground, the gun

hanging from her fingers.

"How you doin'?" I said, and she looked up at me.

"Just swell. You?"

"A little wired," I said. "You know, a little *macho interruptus.*"

"Can't let you boys have all the fun," she said, but the joke was forced.

"You think it was a good idea not to just have patrol come pick him up?" I said.

"What? And have his boys come over and slap him on the back and tell him to chill and take him out for a few beers and make sure nothing gets written up?"

There wasn't much I could say. I'd seen it work that way myself.

"No. I called his sergeant and then the captain. You start working up the chain of command and those guys aren't going to swallow a black mark on their own jacket for the sake of some dipshit patrol officer."

"Yeah, well, you hope not," I said, and that's when she finally looked into my eyes and seemed to click over to who she was talking to and the background my father's story brought with it.

"You hungry after all that, Freeman?" she said, changing her voice. I followed her through the gate and relocked it behind us. When we walked through the back French doors, she quietly put her gun into a kitchen drawer and slid it shut. There were a couple of lamps lit deep in the living room and sitting on the couch with her legs curled up under her, clutching a pillow to her chest, was a woman with long, strawberry-blond hair. I balked at the sight and the memory that jumped into my head. Richards crossed the room and sat down beside the woman, and they talked softly to each other. I stood at the kitchen counter letting the remnants of the driveway adrenaline leach away and eyeing the automatic coffeepot in the corner. There were several boxes of Chinese food lined up and untouched on the counter.

"Max."

I put on a pleasant face and walked out for introductions.

"Max, this is Kathleen Harris."

"A pleasure," I said, taking the woman's hand.

She stood and looked a bit taller than Richards, and bigger-boned, solid, like a basketball or lacrosse player. Her grip was surprisingly strong.

"Nice to meet you," she said, looking me directly in the face. Her eyes were red-rimmed, but she did not look away until she added, "I'm sorry about all that," nodding her head to indicate the driveway. She wasn't wearing any makeup, and there was a spray of freckles across her nose and cheekbones. Country girl, I thought.

"Nothing for you to be sorry about," I said, and left it alone.

Richards warmed up the Chinese and I squeezed past her and made the coffee. The three of us then sat at the low coffee table in the living room, and I told Harris the impersonal side of my life as a Philly cop. We all ended up swapping stories about academy training, rookie assignments, embarrassments on the job and the various criminal sideshows we'd run into over the years.

Richards told the story about the bank heist where the mastermind wrote the stickup note on the back of his own overdue electric bill and the cops were waiting at his house when he showed up with the loot. We were all shaking our heads over Harris's "ass-man" story, about the Middle Eastern guy who was using a home remedy for hemorrhoids during the anthrax scare. When he showed up at the E.R. with a bottle of white powder lodged up his rectum, the yet-unknown concoction of powdered laxative, talcum and baking soda had a dozen cops, hazardous material firemen and federal agents scrambling for hours. Harris was a smart cop, an intelligent, driven, strong woman. She was attractive enough to have dealt with men in social situations. She was experienced enough to have run into plenty of jerks. She forced you to kick out the false stereotype of abused women as so weak, mousy and dependent that they'd put up with it just to hold on to a man, even if he was a shit. The "just leave him" solution does not factor in the unknowable ways of the heart and each person's understanding of love.

When we were done eating, they gathered up the leftovers and I went outside to get my bag out of the truck. I shut off the overhead light in the cab as I went through the bag, unwrapped my Glock and snapped a loaded clip into place. I checked the safety and slipped the gun back in under a fold of clean clothes. I closed and locked the truck and then stood in the darkness, listening, checking both ends of the street. Everyone in this house had seen people at their worst under stress. No one knew what McCrary might do if he felt his back was up against it, if his career and his future were threatened. A lot less can kick a guy over the edge. I was thinking worst-case scenario again. It was a bad habit I wished I could kick.

Back inside, Richards slid a videotape in and the three of us watched a movie called *Meet Joe Black*. Harris fell asleep on the couch at about the point where Anthony

Hopkins's millionaire was explaining life to Brad Pitt, who was playing the role of Death, and Richards punched the TV off. We went outside onto the patio and sat in the hammock. There was no breeze, and the smell of night-blooming flowers hung in the thick humidity. I could hear traffic moving along the streets in the general stillness, but chose to ignore it. Richards's warm skin was against my own, and she was staring up into the night sky.

"You think I should have had him arrested, don't you?" she said.

"I suspect it wasn't just your decision."

"But you know what the brass will do."

"They'll make him go to counseling, if they're smart. Let the shrinks at him awhile, see if he can admit his control problem or whether he denies it."

"That's it?" she said, and I was surprised by the snap of anger in her voice.

"I said that's if they're smart. They could just fire his ass and put an angry guy with weapons training out on the street."

There was a sigh of concession from her.

"What if he threatens her, or comes back at her again?"

"Have him arrested, just like anyone else. He got his chance."

This time her long silence worried me. I lay back into the ropes and closed my eyes. Soon I felt her move and do the same. She curled against me, her hair smelling of shampoo.

"Have you ever hit a woman in anger? I mean your ex-wife or a girlfriend?"

I could tell the recent revelations about my father were still tumbling in her head.

"The children of abusers becoming abusers themselves is not a blanket sociological axiom," I said. "Sometimes it works the other way. The act is so repugnant that the witnesses to abuse grow up to loathe the very idea."

I felt her wiggle herself back tighter into me, and even without seeing her face I could tell she was grinning.

"OK, Professor Freeman," she said. "But you still haven't answered the question."

I put my arm over her waist and rested my wrist on her chest, the backs of my fingers against the soft skin of her neck.

"No," I said. "The answer is no, I never have."

We did not fall asleep for at least another hour.

CHAPTER 18

It would be two days before I heard from Nate Brown. The bartender from the Frontier Hotel called at noon.

"Mr. Brown says meet him at Dawkins's dock at eight tomorrow mornin'. You know that's over on Chokoloskee? Right?"

"Yeah, I know. And thanks."

"How much do y'all owe me now, Mr. Freeman?" she said with humor in her voice.

"I'll talk to you soon," I said, disappointed that she now had my cell number. I wasn't sure which I was concerned about more, the guys from PalmCo tracking my calls or the Loop Road barmaid getting friendly.

There was no trace yet of dawn in my rearview the next morning as I drove west. This time I used Alligator Alley, a straight concrete shot from the suburbs of far west Fort Lauderdale to their identical twins in Naples on the other side of the state. The Alley was the second gouge across the gut of the Everglades. It was constructed in the 1960s with better machinery, better technology, and supposedly better working conditions. It was the thirty-year span of inter-mittent carnage that gave the alley its reputation. Originally two lanes with nothing to break the hypnotic mo-notony of endless acres of sawgrass, head-on collisions were frequent and almost always fatal out here, where the sound of wrenching metal and screaming passengers was quickly lost in the silence. In the 1990s the state expanded the road. They doubled and separated the lanes, and acquiesced to the environmentalists by tunneling under the roadway to allow water and animals to pass through. Imagine the bonanza for the predators that would quickly figure out the migration flow of untold numbers of species forced to funnel through a ten-foot-wide passageway.

I kept myself on a constant flow of caffeine from my oversized thermos, and went over the search possibilities or impossibilities that I was asking Brown to undertake. I'd gone to an army/navy supply store two days ago. In the back of the truck I had a high-end metal detector similar to the kind used by anthropological investigators and emergency rescue teams; a new-generation handheld GPS; an expandable trenching tool with a knife-sharp spade and a chisel-head pickax. I also brought a variety of evidence bags—optimistic—as well as Billy's digital camera and a new satellite cell phone with a different number and carrier from any of the others.

By the time I hit Route 29 I had to flip my mirror up to keep the rising sun from blinding me. The top few feet of the sawgrass had gone a fiery orange in the early rays, and for a mile I watched a trio of swallow-tailed kites swooping down into the grass. The sharp forks of their black tails and pointed wings showed hard against the clear sky, and one came up with a wriggling snake in its beak, the ribbon of flesh outlined against the bird's pure-white belly. I made the exit and turned south and rode along a canal that drained the water and gave high ground to the tiny communities of Jerome and Copeland. I passed the old road prison where convicts were held after long days of clearing the roadsides of overgrowth with their bush-axes and machetes while guards stood by with their rifles at port arms. Would even a desperate man try to run out here?

Farther south the road hit a blinking-light intersection at the Tamiami Trail and then continued all the way into Chokoloskee. When I pulled into the shell-lot of Dawkins's dock, both of his boats were gone. Nate Brown was sitting out on the end of the wood-plank dock. I knew he was dangling a hand-line into the water, just as I knew he had heard me and marked my arrival. I parked out of the way of the forklift's worn path and walked out to meet him.

"Anything biting?"

"They's always somethin' bitin', Mr. Freeman."

He looked up at me and then back into the water, waiting. The early sun was dancing off the surface, the southeast wind rippling up the surface. I sat down next to the old Gladesman and unfolded one of Billy's computer-generated maps.

"This is what we figure, or what we think is possible so far," I started. Brown first looked down at the map and then up at me.

"Anythin' is possible, son."

I nodded and began.

"Let's assume that Mayes and his sons go to work for Noren somewhere about here," I said, putting my finger on the map. "The letter indicates they're some distance out of Everglades City. It's early summer and you know the heat and mosquitoes are just starting to get unbearable, making the crew more miserable by the day.

"We know through some reports and writings in local newspapers that the dredge is making about two miles of road a month when things are going well. We figure these X's here coincide with Mayes's letter of June third, when the two workers slipped out at night to make their way back and his son heard the gunshots."

Brown touched the spot with the rough tips of his fingers. It was a delicate gesture that made me pause and look up at the side of his face, wondering what he was thinking.

"These trees here an' the elevation mark means they's high ground, right?" he said.

"Yeah."

"Curlew Hammock," he said. "An' then this one here's got to be Marquez Ridge."

His fingers slid over to the spot where the three X's were marked.

"Where'd y'all get this here map?"

Now he was looking directly into my face but his own was blank.

"William Jefferson," I said. "John William's grandson."

He did not let any recognition or surprise show, but he did not take his eyes off mine, waiting, expecting more. I told him about using his information on the grandson's cleric possibilities to run down a list and then about the discovery and evasiveness of the reverend up in Placid City. I told him William Jefferson's recounting of his grandfather, his strange silence and the perception at least by the reverend, and obviously his own mother, that John William had an evil aura about him.

"They ain't nothin' you're tellin' that don't fit," Brown finally said. "I recall the boy being awful close to his religion. The girl brought him to that and a lot of folks thought of it as savin' him from what his grandfather done."

Nate waited again, not saying more, just looking out on the water, maybe remembering a small boy running a bit too scared into the trees of the island, talking a little less than any other kid, and turning away when adults and then other children began whispering his grandfather's name.

"So that's where you got these here coordinates and such?" he said.

I told him about the crate and its contents. His face only changed when I mentioned the rifle, the infamous gun that outshot his own father and gave the community a solid thing to tie all the rumors to.

"You think John William Jefferson was capable of killing these men for three hundred dollars?" I finally asked him.

"Men out here in them days done a lot of things for that kind of money," Brown said, and I knew that included him. In my encounter with the old Gladesman three years ago, Billy had run what background there was on him and found that he had done time in prison on a manslaughter charge. In the late sixties an Everglades National Park ranger had been chasing Brown through the islands, trying to arrest him for poaching gators. Snaking his boat through the dizzying waterways just as he had done with the helicopter, Brown had led the pursuing ranger into a submerged sandbar. The government boat slammed into the unforgiving sand. The ranger pitched forward out of the cockpit and broke his neck. Brown turned himself in three days later when word spread that he was being sought for killing the man.

"I s'pose I know why ya'll asked me to help you, Mr. Freeman. If you're askin' if these here X's are the graves of them boys and their father, they is only one way to know," he said, standing up and rewinding the fishing line around his palm. "So let's go.'"

Brown's boat was cleated at the dock and this time he had

his homemade Glades skiff tied off on the back. I loaded my supplies and then locked up my truck. Within minutes we were moving north, the skiff slapping behind us on the end of a line. We headed into the sun, its early brightness burning white-hot. Brown pulled his billed cap low, shading his eyes so they were difficult to read, and I thought of the similar description of John William. They were men who worked and lived in water-reflected sunlight all their lives. They chose to exist in a desolate place where sociability was not a part of their everyday existence. The reasons they came may have been different, but why they stayed was not: they didn't like anyone else's rules or some other leader's vision or expectation. Eighty years of that independent blood had not yet been washed out by the generations.

"Yonder is where my daddy run a still in the twenties," Brown said, interrupting the drone of the motor and the slap of water against the hull. "Him and a half-dozen others had their fixin's on the smaller shell mounds. First they was in by Loop Road. Then the law started crackin' 'em an' they had to come further out. Daddy and them weren't too acceptin' of others comin' into their territory."

I'd learned to let Brown talk on the few occasions that he cared to. He was making his own point, under his own logic.

"Same thing happened to the gator hunters. You could take a dozen gators in a three-night trip. Sell the hides for a dollar fifty apiece for the six- to eight-footers.

"Then in '47, Harry Truman hisself come down and they drew up the boundaries for the Park and one day the best gator-huntin' spots was now illegal, and to hell with you if you and your daddy before you been livin' off that for forty years."

While he talked I unfolded Billy's map and tried to gauge our progress. But even with the detailed, satellite-aided photos, the myriad water trails and green islands were an impossible puzzle. I was lost when we suddenly came around a bend onto open water that was Chevalier Bay.

"They call it progress, Nate," I said, my tone flat and nonjudgmental.

"I know what they call it, son," he said. "That don't mean I got to like it."

The morning heat was building. A high sheet of cirrus cloud was not going to offer any respite from the blurred sun. The air was beginning to thicken with that warm, moist layer that rises up from the Glades like an invisible steam. It was as if the earth herself was sweating, and it carried the not unpleasant odor of both wet and drying plants and soil and living things. As we approached the northern boundary of the bay, I checked the map again and saw no obvious place to go. But Brown kept a steady course to a spot in the mangrove wall that only he could see. It wasn't until we were thirty feet from the green barrier that he pulled back on the throttle and I picked up the eight-foot-wide opening that he'd been heading for all along. We slid through the tunnel of mangroves for thirty minutes, the motor tilted up, the propellers burbling through the dark water. When we got to a broad opening to the outside again, Brown stopped the boat before moving out into the sun. I was checking the coordinates with the handheld GPS. If I was matching them up correctly, we were not too far, maybe two miles, south of the point where John William had marked the three X's on his crude map. Brown cut the engine and stood upright and silent, listening. He seemed to be holding his breath. I could hear nothing.

"Airboat," he said, not looking back me. "This ain't no place airboats usually come."

I waited for an explanation, which also didn't come.

"Check that skiff line if you would, Mr. Freeman. We gon' try to put some speed to 'er."

I went back and tightened down the cleated line; then Brown restarted the motor, moved out onto the wide channel and inched up the throttles. Each second he seemed to get a better feel for the depth and the rhythm of the curves and put more gas to it. I stood up and tried to check above the grass line, looking for the distinctive rounded cage of an airboat engine and the usually high-riding driver. The contraptions are designed to let the operator sit above the sawgrass so he can watch the landscape and curves of the canals instead of just guessing and navigating by pure instinct as Brown was doing. It also makes them more visible. I could see nothing behind and only another dark hammock of trees ahead in the distance. We were carving through the water trail now like a slalom skier, and Brown backed off the throttles only on the tightest turns—the skiff behind us was swinging on the rope and actually fishtailed into the grass several times. A small gator, maybe a four-footer, raised its head in the middle of the canal as we came roaring up. Brown never flinched or slowed and the gator flicked its tail and dived deep just before the bow clipped him. Our destination was clearly the hammock, so I concentrated on the horizon behind us. After a few minutes I turned and was surprised at how fast we'd moved up on it.

"Git your stuff, Freeman, 'cause we gon' grab up the

skiff and hightail it north as soon as she stops. Hear?"
Brown steered one long curve around a jutting piece of
semi-land and then plowed headlong into the greenness,
pulling the same slide and crash he'd done when the helicopter had followed us.

This time I was prepared and rode the lurch. I was out
into the knee-deep water as soon as he cut the motor. I
snatched up the skiff line and then he was beside me, both
of us dragging the flat-bottom boat across the shallows. We
were deep in the cover of tree shadow when I finally picked
up the sound of a burring airplane engine, the noise growing from the direction we'd come. We stayed shoulder to
shoulder. It was easier moving through the dense undergrowth this time. We were following a low path, almost like
a riverbed with only inches of water in it. Maybe when the
rains fell, the path actually ran like a river, because it
seemed to cut directly south to north across the elongated
hammock.

"Them boys cain't bring that airboat through here an'
it's gon' take 'em plenty of time to go all the way round to
git to the other side," Brown said, his breathing under control despite the exertion of pulling the skiff and stomping
through the roots and muck of the path.

"How do you know they're following us?" I said, dodg-
ing a dripping curtain of air-plant roots that hung gray and
mossy like the wet hair of an old woman.

" 'Cause they ain't no reason they should be. I heard 'em
forty-some minutes back there, keepin' enough distance to
stay back, not fast enough to catch us. They're just trackin'."

We were both watching the route ahead. The canopy
above was much less dense than on my river and light
sliced through in sheets and created oddly spaced planes of

209

shadow. It was difficult to see where the end of the path might be. Brown kept pulling, and each time I thought of slacking I reminded myself that the guy was at least twice my age, and the embarrassment of it pushed me on. At times the skiff would hang up on a slab of drier ground or get hooked on a stump and the load would yank at our arms and Brown would look back, judge the angle, and lean his meager weight into it. I would copy him until we freed it. After a half hour without slowing, I picked up the glow of open sunlight walling up a hundred yards to the north. Brown stopped and I thought he'd heard something, because he was staring to one side of the trail. But his eyes were focused into the trees. I tried to match his angle but could see only an odd stand of ancient gnarled pine, with one limb that seemed to have been broken crossing through the crotch of another. The knot where they met looked like it had grown together over the years.

"What?" I said, but the sound of my voice seemed only to snap him out of his trance. He shook me off and kept moving. Soon the creek bed began to fill with deeper water, and after several more minutes we were at the edge of open water again. The old man looked east and west. Nothing. Farther to the north another hammock sprouted up a quarter-mile away.

"You want to find out how bad they want you?" Brown said to me, his head cocked slightly to the side. I could tell he was listening both for the airboat engine and for my answer.

After a few seconds I said, "I want to know who they are."

He tightened up the slack on the line and moved out into the sunlight.

"Let's push on over to Curlew Hammock yonder then, and take 'er easy gettin' there," he said, nodding to the patch of green to the north.

When we got into enough water to float the skiff, both of us stepped up and in. Brown took up the long pole and pushed off, working the wooden staff hand over hand, shoving off the muck bottom and then efficiently recovering the length of the pole. Even on the grass-covered shallows he seemed to slide the boat gracefully over thirty yards of water with a single stroke. I kept cutting my eyes east to west, waiting to spot the airboat coming around either side of the hammock we were leaving behind. Brown kept his attention forward.

When we came within fifty yards of the smaller lump of trees that he'd called Curlew Hammock, Brown stopped poling and for the first time checked behind us. We were still out in the open.

"Need 'em to see us so's they'll follow us in," he said.

"You want them to know where we are?"

"They know where we are, son. They always knowed."

CHAPTER 19

Brown was looking west when he narrowed his eyes. I caught the bobbing figure in the distance an instant later. Above the grass the dark shape seemed to rise and fall erratically, like a black bird at first. As we watched, it grew in size and the jerking turned into a more fluid movement. A man's torso soon took shape against the backdrop of the sky and then the gridwork of the circle-shaped engine cage became visible. I could barely hear the low, harmonic burring of the machine, but it too was growing. Brown waited a full five minutes and then started poling again toward the small hammock. He pushed us at a slower speed than before. When we were finally up against the edge of the hammock, Brown shipped the pole and jumped out.

"Got to hope they'll follow us in," Brown said. "Bring in your supplies so's they'll figure we're workin' it."

I shouldered one pack and Brown took the satchel with the metal detector and we worked our way through the low grass and muck to the tree line of the hammock and stood in the shade of a clump of cabbage palms and looked back. Now I could see the body of the driver, sitting up on the raised driver's seat. Below him I could make out the heads of two other men who must have been crouched on the deck, down a bit out of the wind, their billed caps pulled hard on their brows.

"They seen us," Brown said. "Let's go."

The old man seemed to have a destination in mind. He

moved efficiently in under the trees and about forty yards later stopped and surveyed the layout.

"Hold up there, son," he said, and I watched him walk off to the north, stepping into a pile of brush and shuffling his feet around, then moving off to a downed poisonwood trunk and stopping to deliberately scrape his boot sole against the mottled bark. He moved on another twenty feet and took off the satchel I'd given him and laid it carefully at the base of a tall pine in full view. Then he returned.

"If they is half-dumb, they'll move that way an' you can take a look at 'em from back here," Brown said to me. I turned in a circle, not seeing a way to hide.

"Down there in the gator hole," Brown said, pointing to a low, half-exposed depression filled with mud and standing pools of water. He stepped down into the pit and showed me how the gators had burrowed down below the roots of the trees and swept out a shallow cave. It was dark in the shadows and I could not see the back wall.

"They ain't in there now, son. Water's high enough for 'em out on the plain. They use this here one when it's the only wet place left for 'em. I hunted it plenty of times. Took three or four six-footers outta here in '63."

I was still looking down at him, trying to work out the logistics. If we tucked ourselves down in the gator hole and the airboaters moved past us to the spot where Brown had baited them with the satchel, I might get a look at them. One more piece to work with. A visible threat is always better than one you've never seen.

The sound of the airboat engine put off my grinding. The rough mechanical noise echoed into the hammock even after the motor was suddenly shut down, until the shadows and greenness swallowed it and the place fell silent.

I slipped down into the gator hole with Brown and we both crouched below the cover of leaves and ferns and listened. My knees and the toes of my boots pushed six inches down into the mud, and the water began to soak the back of my jeans. Brown was also getting soaked but he didn't move a single muscle, save for his almost imperceptible breathing. His eyes were focused. I shifted my hips uncomfortably, but he didn't react. After several silent minutes, at some unseen or heard signal, Brown turned and motioned me deeper into the gator hole. He went to his hands and knees and slid himself down under the rough lip of the root line and into the darkness. I followed. The muck squeezed up between my fingers and the dripping root tendrils dragged across the back of my neck. The hole smelled of wet, rotted wood and decayed leaves and an odor I could not identify. My imagination placed it as the cold, fetid breath of some reptile, lying in the back, his mouth starting to salivate with this sudden home-delivery of a fleshy meal.

I had to go lower as the cave narrowed. It was pitch-black now and I was on my elbows and knees when I felt my hip bump against something that bumped back. "Got to listen for their voices," Brown whispered. I could feel his breath on my cheek when he spoke and then the touch of air disappeared. Outside I heard the rustle of vegetation. A branch snapped under the pressure of something heavy. I closed my eyes and envisioned the three men moving along the same path we had, looking down at our tracks and then several yards ahead. One of them spoke, the words indistinguishable. The slap of hands against palm fronds and the soft sucking sound of a boot being pulled out of the muck were audible. They had to be just above the gator hole opening. More movement and then silence. They had gathered at one spot, and I could tell it was the same plot of land where I had stood watching Brown plant the satchel. I could hear more mumbling, too low to make out, but then one of them raised his voice: "They didn't just leave it behind for no goddamn reason!" The man got shushed by another. "Oh, fuck you, Jim. That's probably the damn spot right there and they went off to scout a way out. Shit, I'm gettin' tired of this fucking boar hunt."

"Let's go get a reading on it and then get the hell out of here," said another voice.

"Hell, let's get a reading and then cap these two fucks and put a real lid on it," said the first voice.

The water was up to my hips now and had gone cold. Loose dirt from the root system above crumbled and fell across my face. Still we did not move, but we heard them begin to. Footfalls vibrated through the ground, and the voice of yet another response was muted and farther off in the distance. I heard the sound of a dull, solid thump on wood and in my head saw the downed poisonwood trunk. Brown moved and started to slurry out toward the light and we both got back to our positions just below the leaves and ferns and looked out at the backs of the three men.

Two of them were next to the satchel. One, the smaller, was twenty feet away, next to the poisonwood trunk, inspecting Brown's scuff marks and then looking up to sweep the area left to right but not behind. He was in blue jeans and high rubber boots and an off-white, long-sleeved shirt. The driver, I thought. The others were bigger, in black cargo jeans and vests with pockets like they were on safari or on some photo shoot for an outdoor clothing magazine. They were older men, both thick in the shoulders and waist. One was taller and I could see the silver in his hair. I'd heard one name used, "Jim," and put it on the taller one.

I didn't like the look and could feel the adrenaline moving hot into my ears. I slipped my hand down into my mud-covered pack. I was feeling for the Glock and my fingers found an unfamiliar shape, a metallic box the size of a cigarette pack. I flashed back to Ramón the bug man and the cheap tracking device he'd removed from my truck. They'd gotten it into my bag without my knowing. I'd brought them right to us. It pissed me off even more. I found the handle of my gun and pulled it out. Brown looked at the weapon, looked into my face, and like the old infantryman he once was, mouthed the words "I'll flank 'em" and started to move silently off to the left.

I gave him time to get into position, watching the closer man who was now rubbing the chafed bark of the downed tree and again swinging his head from side to side, tilting his head up like a bird dog trying to catch a whiff of game in the air. The others appeared to come to some agreement and walked back to the driver, and when all three began moving in my direction, I came up out of the gator hole, the gun in both hands in a combat position and yelled, "Police! Don't fucking move, boys! Just freeze it and don't . . . fucking . . . move!"

I probably didn't have to swear, or tell them to freeze. The sight of me, a tall, lanky man covered head to foot in slimy black muck coming up out of the ground with a 9 mm pointed and ready to fire was enough to shock their nervous systems into a temporary lockup. They didn't move until I did. When I took a few steps forward I saw the bigger man's arm start to move behind his partner to use its cover for whatever he was thinking, and I fired. The barrel of the 9 mm jumped and the round struck the poisonwood trunk with a whack, spitting up splinters of wood and jerking all three of their heads to the left. The sound of the gun echoed through the trees and was quickly swallowed up.

"One step away from each other, *now!*" I said, locking on to the big man's eyes. "No fucking way you win, fella. You're the first one to die." I could hear the anger in my own voice, and wondered briefly why I was letting it build.

Both of them were city men. Their clothes were too new. The boots were the type a hiker or a weekend woodsman would wear. The big man's complexion was newly burned from the sun, and his eyes had a hardness that said former cop, or former felon. I put the sight bead on his chest. When he stepped away from the other man, his hand was still empty.

"You ain't no police," said the other one, the driver. In just four words I could tag the country in his voice, and it was familiar. He cocked his head to the side, again like a retriever that didn't understand. "I know all the law round here an' you I ain't never seen," he said. His naïveté might have made me chuckle under different circumstances, but I could sense the muscles in the other two tensing. Whatever they might have been thinking was again scrambled by a voice from the side.

"Shut the hell up, Billy Nash," said Brown, and now the heads of all three spun to the right. "You already in this deep, boy. Don't y'all keep diggin', jest listen to what the man tells you."

The young one's eyes went big, just like the kid on Dawkins's dock when he recognized Brown.

"Lord o' Goshen," he whispered. "Nate Brown? Got-damn, that's Nate Brown," he said in an awe that had little effect on the two men beside him when he looked back to spread his recognition.

Nash looked back at the old Gladesman, bowed his head a bit and slowly turned it back and forth. I could see a grin come to the corners of his mouth.

"Damn, Nate Brown. I shoulda figured. I knew we was trackin' somebody special," Nash said, looking up again at Brown in admiration. "Ain't a man alive could move a out-board through the channels like that. It was too fast and too damn smooth. It was like we was going after a Glades otter or somethin'.

"Didn't I tell you boys," he said, again looking back. But the others were not listening. They had turned their silent attention back to me and the Glock and did not care to know about some old mud-covered fisherman. "When you two jumped to the skiff an' I seen you all the way over to here, I knew somebody was handlin' that thing like the olden days."

Then Nash seemed to realize that no one, not even Brown, was paying any attention to him. He also seemed to realize that he was suddenly on the wrong side of his world.

"An' they didn't tell me it was you, Mr. Brown. Honest. They never said a word that I was supposed to be trackin' a Gladesman. I didn't know, sir. I didn't."

"Shut up, Billy Nash," Brown answered.

Brown had not moved. There was a thick swatch of palm fronds obscuring him from the waist down and he carefully did not show his hands, keeping the other two men from determining whether he was armed or not. I also had not lowered the 9 mm.

"Tell me exactly what they did ask you to do for them,"

I said to Nash, who stepped away from his old partners and turned to face them. He looked once over at Brown before he spoke.

"They come out to the Rod and Gun askin' for a guide who knew the area. First said they was followin' some migratory bird, but I could tell they weren't no birders. Then when we got out of Chokoloskee this mornin', they kept secret, like checkin' some electronic thing in their bag. Tol' me it was a GPS but hell, I use one them my own self and I knew it was some kinda tracker. Then they got nervous when we found you'd ditched your boat, Mr. Brown, and after that they didn't want to lose sight of y'all.

"And I didn't. Y'all almost slipped me through the Marquez, but I caught ya," he said with a kid's overblown pride in his voice as he looked over shyly at Brown.

"How much they pay you, Billy?" I asked.

"Five hundred."

"And whose name is on the expense account, Jim?" I said turning back to the other two without focusing on either one, so my use of the overheard name would put them off guard.

"Fuck you, Freeman," said the big one. "You're just a hired P.I.—you know we don't give up the name of a client. Besides, nothing illegal has occurred out here unless you consider you pointing that piece at us is worth an aggravated assault charge that we could file against you."

"All right then, boys. What's the name of your licensed agency and I'll be glad to get a hold of you at a later date after I get my equipment scanned and figure out where you planted your directional tracker. You two were the ones watching me have dinner the other night in Fort Lauderdale, yes?"

The other one moved to his left, as if he was starting to sit down on the poisonwood trunk, and I snapped, "Hey!" and bobbled the tip of the gun to keep him on his feet. He was well out of his element. Beads of sweat had formed across his pate and the heat was flushing his face a dull red. But his eyes were as black and hard as marbles when he stared back at me from under the bill of his cap. He reached back and put his right hand on the tree trunk and then turned back to me.

"Hey, fuck you, Freeman. And that hot little cop you're hosing on the side." He was all New Jersey, the accent, the tough guy thing. But like a bad magician, the mouth was supposed to distract me. He made it look like he was sitting down, a motion that shielded his right hand, but I saw the crook in his elbow go high.

I'd like to say it was the disparagement of Richards that got me. I'd like to say I was thinking of Cyrus Mayes and his boys. I'd like to say I could control the bloom of violence that was spreading in my chest at the sound of another street asshole somehow tied to the death of good men. But I couldn't. It was just a guess.

I shot him in the right thigh. The 9 mm jumped slightly. I had been aiming for the knee. Both of the guy's hands went to his leg, like he could cover the new hole there and make it go away. The other one's hand went to his vest and I had the warm muzzle of the Glock in his face before he could get through the unfamiliar zipper.

"No, no, no, Jim," I said. "Bad move, considering that you now know I don't give a shit about your rules, or your standing with the Better Business Bureau, or your lives at this point." I'd used the name right, guessed which one it belonged to. I could see it in his eyes.

"Now, hands on your heads, boys, fingers laced together."

I heard Brown move in the brush beside me. The Nash kid had been frozen again by the second gunshot of the afternoon. The big man put his hands on his head and I went in close and took a .38 from a shoulder holster under his vest. Then I stepped behind him and patted him down, found a cell phone and put it in my pocket. Satisfied, I moved the other one. He'd laced his bloodied fingers together on top of his hat. He was breathing short, whistling breaths through his mouth and his jaw was clenched up with the pain. He'd stumbled back against the tree trunk when I shot him and was now leaning with his good haunch against it. I found the 9 mm Beretta I'd guessed he was reaching for still clipped to his belt in the small of his back.

"All right, let's start with names," I said, moving back in front them. Neither said anything.

"Jim?" I said, pointed the gun at his face again.

"Cummings," he said in a tone void of resignation.

"Jesus Jim, don't . . . ," said the other one through his teeth.

"It's only money, Rick. It isn't worth it," Cummings said.

"Yeah? Since when isn't money worth it to you?"

I switched my aim to Rick's face.

"He's a smart man, Rick. I could shoot the two of you just like you would me and leave you to rot out here in the middle of nowhere and nobody would know—forever and ever," I said, not once considering the irony of what I was saying.

"Rick Derrer," Cummings said, and his partner scowled at him.

"Who hired you?"

Again silence, but this time it felt tighter.

"OK, then," I said to Brown. "Let's go."

The old man was looking from me to them but did not hesitate to move back toward the way we'd come.

"Y'all are with us, Nash," Brown ordered the young man, who'd been unsure of what ground he'd landed on, but knew to answer to a legend.

"Yes, sir, Mr. Brown," he said, and moved with the Gladesman.

I held my Glock in my left hand and with my right heaved Cumming's .38 and then Derrer's Beretta out into separate parts of the wet hammock. Without a metal detector, neither was ever going to be found.

"Now, I figure big Jim there might make it the fifteen miles through the swamp to the trail. He looks fit enough. Probably did some hunting in his time. But your boy Rick here, he's in for a long trek with that leg. He makes it a mile and it'll be something," I said.

"But fuck you, Freeman. That's what you both said, right? Ought to cap both of us, right?"

I turned and walked away and Brown and Nash walked with me. We were ten steps away when Cummings spoke up. "All right, Freeman. It was the PalmCo attorneys."

I took a couple of steps back and waited.

"They hire us on occasion, when their regular loss-prevention guys can't handle the job. They're lawyers so they don't tell us it's for PalmCo, but we've done enough shit for them over the years, we know who pays the bills."

Derrer had taken off his belt and vest and was strapping the Eddie Bauer ripstop cloth over his wound.

"What was the job?" I said.

"To tail you. Find out where you went, who you talked to. Typical stuff. The only twist was trying to follow you out here. Not exactly our neighborhood," Cummings said, raising his hands. The movement caused me to raise the Glock to his chest. He turned his palms out and continued.

"We figured you knew about something that PalmCo wanted. That's the usual story. When you picked up the old guy and started moving around in the Glades, we figured you had the location of some damn oil deposit or something.

"We were supposed to map everywhere you went and record any spot where you spent much time. They said if you started digging anywhere, we were to contact them right away and record the location."

He wasn't cowering. He wasn't spilling his guts. This was business for him, and he was playing out his hand with the goal of not being left in the swamp with little chance of getting himself and his partner out alive.

"What about the guns, the chopper, the cell intercepts and bugs on my truck?"

"Standard corporate security procedures," Cummings said. "I saw your jacket, Freeman. You were a street cop for a long time. The corporates, they've got stuff we never dreamed of back then."

My guess that he was former P.D. had been right.

"You the guys who went to the Loop Road bar and took the picture off the wall?"

He was silent for a few seconds, thinking, I knew, trail of evidence. Everything he had said so far could be denied by the company lawyers. Something physical couldn't be. I turned again to walk away.

"They told us to pick up anything we ran across that

had to do with construction of the road, especially the old stuff," he said to turn me around. "We turned it over to them."

Now it was my turn to be silent. It was a cruel game because I knew I had the better cards this time. And he didn't know it was more than just business to me. I called the young airboat driver back to me and frisked him to be safe.

"Help your clients get to your boat, Nash," I said. The kid looked at Brown once and when the old Gladesman gave him a nod, he moved.

Brown and I watched as they shouldered Derrer and walked him like an injured player between them off the field. I shouldered our satchel with the metal detector. When they were far enough ahead I searched the ground where I had been standing and found the spent cartridge that had ejected from my gun when I shot Derrer. When I stood ready to go, I caught Brown staring at the side of my face, an unusual act for him. I caught his eyes.

"You're a hard man, Freeman. I knowed men like you," he said. "All of 'em in the past."

I could find no way to respond. If it was a compliment, I didn't take it as such.

CHAPTER 20

Nash had run the airboat up onto the grass only yards from our skiff. I climbed aboard first and searched through their supplies. I left them their fresh water and food and the first aid kit. I took another 9 mm from one pack and an old but beautifully preserved 16-gauge shotgun from a scabbard strapped up behind the driver's seat. Nash whined about the gun, begging that it had been passed down from his father, but Brown again informed him to shut up.

They propped Derrer up against the gang box at the base of the elevated driver's chair and Nash climbed up and started the big airplane engine. The one called Cummings did not look back at me. His business was done. The mist of spray kicked up as the airboat pulled away felt cool against my face, and Brown and I waited until the sound faded. Then the old man stood up on the skiff to get a higher angle to watch them. I sat on the deck, my legs crossed, and took out the map and my GPS and Derrer's tracking unit.

"You ain't worried about that feller goin' back and tellin' the police you shot him?" Brown said, continuing to look out after the airboat. I scrolled through the unit's stored coordinates and could not find anything that coincided with the longitude and latitude of John William's records.

"There would be a lot of explaining to do. Some jurisdictional matters. Permission from the men who hired those two. My guess is he'll be compensated and quiet. PalmCo isn't going to want to bring any more scrutiny out here, especially law enforcement scrutiny."

Brown just nodded and watched me working the map and the GPS. The encounter with Cummings and Derrer had thrown me off and I realized the spot we'd been looking for was back toward Marquez Ridge. We had passed it while leading the airboat to the hammock.

"We've got to backtrack," I said to Brown as he stepped down into the muck to spin the skiff.

"Yep," he said, and did not offer another word, or ask a question about where we needed to go. Instead he poled us through the open grass between the two mounds of trees, and I actually lay back in the skiff and stared into the sky. My head was throbbing. I was trying not to replay the last hour through my head. I'd shot a man, maybe out of necessity, maybe out of anger or frustration. When you're a cop, you're trained that whenever you fire your gun, it's a use of deadly force, meant to kill. You aren't on TV. You don't try to wound. When the citizens start whining after every fatal police shooting about why the cop couldn't have just winged the asshole with the knife, they're out of our loop. Danger is a pissed off guy with a knife and only a wound. The killer in the subway and now some P.I. who just happened to piss me off. Somewhere inside me I had that capacity, and I wasn't sure what that fact told me.

I registered the change in light on my closed eyelids before I felt the skiff slide up into thicker grass and come to a halt. Brown had poled us into the shadows. We would once again have to pull the boat by a line to follow the riverbed path. I checked the GPS and looked ahead. Brown wasn't waiting for instructions. I put the unit away and we pulled together.

After twenty minutes, he stopped. I knew it wasn't because he was tired. I found my water bottle and took a long drink and sat on the edge of the skiff. Brown was still standing, staring at the stand of ancient pine, the single limb that had been broken but remained alive as it fell perpendicular through the crotch of another. The knot where they met had grown together, and now that I looked at it as a whole, it was the perfect representation of a cross.

"This is it, Freeman," Brown said. "Git out yer map or your metal finder. This is it."

I checked the GPS and plotted it on the map. The alignment was close but not perfect, but I wasn't arguing. I assembled the metal detector and adjusted the settings while Brown gave me his rationale, a lot of it based on his gut instinct, which I had long learned to trust out here where everything, even the earth herself, had a way of shifting and moving.

"If them last letters were written in the summer, then it'd be the rainy season," Brown said, scanning the area around the trees, but looking up anxiously at the form of the cross.

"The rains'll raise this water another four, five inches and this here bed'll fill up. We ain't but two mile from the Tamiami Trail," he said.

I'd known how close we were because I had been working the map as we came up from the south. I thought of how disappointed Cummings was going to be when and if he found out how close they'd actually been to civilization when I threatened to leave them.

"If Jefferson had loaded them dead men into his skiff, he'd of been able to pole his way down here on the high water and come right on in here on that current."

I climbed up to the tree formation and then started working the metal detector from the base of the cross in a circular motion. I was slow and careful and exact in my movements.

"If he knew these Glades as well as my daddy, he could of made it easy in the dark, even without a moon," Brown said. "It's the way I woulda done 'er."

I expanded the concentric circles with the tree base as my epicenter. Nothing showed on the attached screen. It was all vegetable, no hard mineral. The detector was designed to pick up anything impenetrable—a belt buckle, a necklace, coins, a pocketknife.

"You think John William snapped that pine limb and marked the grave?" I finally asked Brown, knowing it was on both our minds. The old man let his eyes rest on the image.

"I ain't a religious man, Freeman. That there coulda formed up on its own like that. Maybe it's got God's hand on it. Maybe not. They's things I seen in war and nature and men that made me swing both ways over the years. Best I can say is, it don't hurt not to discount the Almighty altogether."

I was eight feet out from the tree base, due south, when the detector beeped under my hand. I stopped and swung the pad back to a cover of maidenhair fern and it beeped again. The readout showed a depth of two and a half feet. Brown brought the trenching tool over while I cleared a big square of vegetation and studied the cover of slick muck and plant roots. I got down on my knees and scraped away the top layer with my hands, watching for anything foreign, anything out of place, anything. After a few minutes I started in with the shovel, carefully coming up with one spade of thick, wet earth at a time and flopping it onto a rain poncho that Brown had brought from the skiff. The old man scanned the pile with the detector like I'd shown him and then went through it with his fingers. He knew what bone looked like. Every couple of spadefuls we would sweep the hole I was creating, and the beep still registered.

My digging was a good two feet down when Brown said, "Bone." He held up a dull gray chunk between his dirt-stained fingers. It was the size of a poker chip and about the same thickness. We both stared at it—the possibilities, the reassurance that we were not wrong, and the dread that came with it.

"Could it be an animal?" I asked.

"Could be," he said. "I ain't no expert."

We swept the hole again. Still beeping.

We found four more pieces of bone, which Brown carefully put aside in one of the plastic evidence bags I'd brought. I made sure we marked the depth of each one taken from the hole. Then the shovel blade hit something tough, but not hard. I reached down and felt with my fingers and found fabric. In one of Billy's books I'd come across a study of the Glades that remarked on the preservation power of the thick muck. Because the layers were set down by rotting, microbial vegetation, the muck was so dense that little air penetrated the lower levels. If it was airless, the breakdown of any nonorganic material would be greatly slowed. I set aside the shovel and went down with both hands, using my fingernails to scratch away the dirt, exposing more and more of what I soon realized was leather.

It took another thirty minutes or so for me to free the

remnant of a work boot from the muck. The thick sole was nearly intact, but the leather upper was the fragile consistency of wet cardboard. I brought it up with a layer of muck from beneath its resting place and placed it on the poncho. Brown waved the detector over it. It beeped.

Brown crouched nearby while I carefully separated dirt from leather. I went inside the boot with my fingers. It had filled with muck, and I brought out a handful at a time. Brown went through each small pile, studied it, and then swept it away. But as I got farther in toward the sole, he began to find bone; small phalanges that he recognized as foot bone. I was deep into the front of the boot, where the hard toe cover was remarkably intact, when my fingers touched metal. I curled them around the object and came out with a rounded, ancient, pocketwatch.

I stared at the piece lying in the palm of my hand. Brown exhaled deeply and then went to the skiff. I hadn't moved when he came back with his jar of water and poured it over my hand, washing away the dirt while I turned and rubbed the timepiece with my fingers. The metal was a dull yellow gold. I pushed the locket release but had to work my fingernails in under the lid to finally pry it open. Brown poured more water in to wash out the dirt that had penetrated inside, and I rubbed my fingertips over the inside of the lid to expose an inscription:

The Lord is thy Shepherd my son, let him lead you, and the Kingdom of God will by thine forever.
Your loving father, Horace Mayes

I sat with the disk of gold in my hand for some time, trying to connect the little I knew of Cyrus Mayes with this,

his final resting place. A good and righteous man and his innocent sons had lost their lives to another being who was their polar opposite. If John William Jefferson had marked this death bed with a cross for some deeply warped recognition of a God, he had gained no mercy. If that deeply buried sense of religion had passed into his future gene pool and led his progeny to swing to his moral opposite, perhaps there was some hope in evolution. But his own son had ended his own life, and I could not help but think that the stain of John William's acts had stopped spreading.

Brown and I packed up the boat. I recorded the GPS coordinates of the gravesite in the unit as well as on paper tucked away where it wouldn't be lost or electronically wiped out. We were obviously overmatched by the crime scene. Billy would convince law enforcement to bring their own forensic paleontologists out to grid the sight and recover the remains of the Mayes family, and to try and determine the details of their murders. We made a feeble attempt to stake the poncho over the three-foot-square excavation we'd completed, but all we could hope for was a day or so without rain. I dropped the watch into another evidence bag, wrapped it up with the boot and the bone fragments, and tucked the whole thing into my pack. We pulled the skiff south to the spot where Brown had tied up his boat, and I was mildly surprised to see that it had not been scuttled by the PalmCo P.I.s.

We made the boat switch, tied off the skiff, and then Brown cranked up the engine and turned her back toward Chevalier Bay. I sat on the transom and calmly dropped the tracking device that had been planted in my satchel into the water behind us. The vibration of the engine hummed through my bones and told me how every tendon and muscle ached. When we finally hit open water the sun was slipping down and the blueness of the sky was already darkening. I focused on the old man for the first time in hours and noticed the crusted mud and grime and stink that covered his clothing. He appeared to be some caricature on a kid's slime show. Then I looked down at myself and saw that we were twins, and I began to laugh. Brown hadn't said a word since I'd pulled Cyrus Mayes's pocket watch from the rotting boot. He now turned to look at me with as close a look of merriment on his face as I had ever seen him carry. He then turned back into the sun, pulled down the brim of his hat and began to whistle. "It's a Long Way to Tipperary." And he stayed with the melody for a good part of the trip back to the docks in Chokoloskee.

CHAPTER 21

When we got to the docks the sun was down and the last clouds on the horizon were bloodred. Dawkins's boats were still out on the water. I pulled out some clean clothes and a towel from the cab of my truck and showered off with a hose that the boat captain used to spray the salt off his decks. I tossed my ruined jeans and shirt and boots into the truck bed. When I was dressed and half human again, I sat in the cab and called Billy.

"I don't quite know what to say, Max," Billy said when I told him of our discovery of the grave, as well as the PalmCo investigators and their admission that they were working for the attorneys who had offered him the bribe. "I suppose I had little optimism that it would go this far when we started. I'm pleased, but saddened."

I told him I was convinced the investigators didn't know about the grave and were just following instructions to follow and mark me. I also told him that we let the P.I.s leave before finding the grave and that I doubted they'd be able to find it on their own. I didn't mention the shooting.

"I have some prosecutor friends in Collier County," he told me. "With the evidence, I should think we can get a recovery team and a group of forensics people out there tomorrow."

"All right. I'll stop over in Lauderdale and see if Sherry has any pull with the homicide guys over in Collier—she can get them excited about an eighty-year-old cold case."

"Speaking of Richards, she left a message earlier today, something about one of her fellow deputies getting a call about you from the sheriff up in Highlands County. That's the Reverend Jefferson's region, right?"

"Yeah. I ran into the sheriff while I was up there. Curious guy. Paranoid about some string of shootings in his jurisdiction."

"Well, he's apparently curious about you and was checking out your credentials," Billy said. "Richards said it might be nothing, but she was anxious to tell you about it. I tried calling her back, but I haven't been able to get through."

"All right, I'm heading that way. Let me know about the forensics response. I don't think we're gonna have to worry about intercepts anymore."

"Be careful driving back, Max," Billy said, and clicked off.

I went back down to the dock to say good-bye to Nate Brown. The old man had removed his shirt and used the hose to soak his head and chest. I tossed him my half-wet towel and he thanked me. While his face was in the towel I noted the scars on his back and under his rib cage. His chest hair was thick and snow white, and a stark tan line ran around his neck where his collar protected him from the sun. The wrinkles in his loose skin were pronounced and his stomach looked sunken and unhealthy.

"I'm heading back, Nate. I want to thank you for helping me, and I want to tell you not to worry about what happened out there with those company men. You're clear."

He did not answer.

"There will probably be some cops and scientific people out there tomorrow, and they'd probably pay to have you guide them back to the site," I said, even though I could anticipate his answer.

"Don't bother bringin' my name into it if you don't mind," he said. "Them boys'll take that GPS and find 'er just fine. Take 'em a while, but they'll get it."

He gathered up his shirt and tossed it into his boat, then handed my towel back to me.

"I'm a go check on that Nash kid. Like to get his daddy's shotgun back to 'im if I can."

I watched him lower himself down the ladder into his boat as smoothly as a surefooted cat. But I had the definite feeling that Nate Brown was not long for this world. He'd seen too much of what I had flippantly called progress. He didn't like it, and I had a feeling he was ready to leave it.

He started his engine and tossed off a line and the boat drifted back into open water. He pulled the bill of his cap, pushed up the throttles, and was gone.

During the drive back across the state I tried Richards's phone three times. I let it ring eight or nine times before hanging up. Her answering machine didn't come on. I set the cruise control on the truck when I got into the eastbound lanes of Alligator Alley, but the cut of my headlights through the middle of the vast darkness on either side ended up hypnotizing me instead of keeping me alert. Twice I caught myself drifting out of my lane, my head snapping up with the realization that even though my eyes were open, I was seeing nothing. I rolled down both windows and turned off the cruise so I would have to concentrate on the speed, then searched for a Stevie Ray Vaughan CD that I had buried in the glove compartment. I popped it in, loud.

By the time I hit the traffic of west Broward County, it was after nine, but the city lights and the bustle recharged me. I drove straight into Fort Lauderdale, and when I pulled around the corner to Richards's street and saw the kaleidoscope of spinning red and blue emergency lights, my heart felt like it had suddenly doubled in mass and dropped down into my rib cage.

I didn't remember parking. I tried to control myself, like a cop, a professional. I walked around the news trucks and patrol cars and gawking clumps of neighbors. I caught a glance of a yellow tarp draped over a body on Richards's front lawn. I passed two uniformed officers who must have mistaken my demeanor and stride as belonging to their brotherhood, but before I got to the house someone grabbed my elbow.

"Excuse me, sir," said the man's voice. "Do you have an I.D., sir?"

I could not take my eyes from the yellow sheet, and I instinctively pulled my elbow out of the questioner's grip.

"Who is it?" I said, still not looking at the cop behind me.

"I'm gonna need some I.D., sir. This is a secure crime scene, and . . ."

I spun on him and the kid took a step back, a touch of alarm in his face. Then I heard her voice behind me, from up on the front porch.

"It's OK, Jimmy. He's with me."

She was still in her work clothes, a light gray suit and black heels. But she was disheveled in an uncharacteristic way. She said something to a man in a shirt and tie with a clipboard, then came down the steps to meet me. We walked together around the corner of the house by the driveway gate entrance. I wanted to step in to her and hold her, but held back.

"McCrary," she said, looking down at first, avoiding my eyes. "Kathy called me and asked if she could come over while I was still on duty. She was crying and said she needed a place to stay, so I told her where the key was and that I got off at six."

I bent my head down so that our foreheads were almost touching. We were having a discussion, quietly informational, not intimate.

"Didn't take McCrary long to figure out where she'd gone, and he shows up in uniform and starts banging on the front door. The neighbors see a cop and figure, hell, he's got something going on."

She looked up and I could see the tears welling up, even though she was fighting them.

"He put his shoulder into the door, splintered the lock and came at her."

"She shot him?"

"Yeah," she said, quickly wiping at her eyes with the sleeve of her jacket, hoping no one would catch the movement. "With her service weapon. The neighbors heard the shot, saw an officer lying in the yard and called in a 911 officer down."

"Cavalry time," I said.

Richards nodded, took a deep breath, and gathered herself.

"She's still inside, talking with homicide. Can you wait until they're gone?"

"Of course. Sure."

We went through the gate around back and Richards went inside through the French doors. I saw a knot of men huddled around the end of the couch where Harris had sat watching a movie with us just a few nights ago. Richards closed the doors behind her and I sat down heavily on the steps. The pool lights were on, but the aqua glow seemed to have gone cold.

I listened to the murmur of low, male voices and tried to blank it out because I knew what they would be saying. Did he threaten you? Did you fear for your life? Had he crossed the threshold of the doorway? Was he backing away or coming forward when you fired? I had been through it all before. So had Richards. After another hour I heard the door close, and cars out front were started. It was several more minutes before Richards stepped out with a steaming mug of coffee in her hands. I thanked her without saying so.

"She wanted to stay with me but IAD thought it was a bad idea, like we would stay up all night and concoct a story," she said, sitting in a chair next to me and pulling her feet up beneath her.

"She have a place to go?"

"Her grandmother is up in Pompano Beach."

"You get here with everyone else?" I said.

"Right along with the rescue squad and about thirty other cops coming in from every damn patrol sector in the city."

"He dead when you got here?"

"Yeah. Right there on my front lawn. Bastard."

I let the quiet sit uninterrupted for a while. Richards had already been through the mill, and no doubt would have another session with IAD in the morning, when they would want her to take them through Harris's relationship with the deceased. After a time I tried to offer some solace.

"He deserved it," I said.

I had expected a quick agreement, but Richards was thinking, thinking in that way good detectives think, without letting emotion get in the way of seeing the scene.

"She said he stumbled back out of the door and fell after she shot him." Her tone was unconvincing. I let her think about it. If she wanted to share, she would.

"One shot. In the mouth," she said after a few seconds. "She would know enough to take a head shot. She'd know he was wearing a vest."

"He still deserved it," I said, and then shut up. If Richards wanted to work through her question of premeditation versus an act of fear and self-defense, she was entitled, but I wasn't going to join her there. I set my cup down and reached out and put my warmed fingers on her wrist and listened to the night. She sighed and I thought I finally heard her give it up.

"Billy tell you that the Highlands County sheriff was asking after you?" she finally said.

"Yeah. What was that all about?"

"A sergeant friend of his with the office called me, knowing that I knew you. He said the sheriff had met you and wanted to verify some background. I gave him the basics. Hope you don't mind."

"I met the guy outside a café up in Placid City when I went up looking for the Reverend Jefferson. Seemed a bit inquisitive for a small-town sheriff."

"My friend says the guy is as thorough as any cop he knows but a little obsessed. He says Wilson's on the hook for four homicides in the last fifteen years. All similar. All unsolved."

We were talking shop again, but I let her go on, hoping

it would keep her mind off the possibility that her friend Harris had committed a justified but illegal assassination in her own home.

"He says they were all killed by the same big round. A heavy caliber. Possibly all from the same gun."

I stopped drinking the coffee and the look in my face must have confused her.

"What?" she said. "Max? What?"

"He tell you the exact caliber?" I said while digging the cell phone out of my pocket.

"No. I'm not sure the sheriff told him, exactly."

I speed-dialed Billy's home number and got the machine. I tried his office. He picked up on the first ring.

"Hi, Max. Any luck getting Richards?"

"Yeah, I'm at her place now."

"Good. I've been able to contact the prosecutor in Collier I told you about. He's willing to get a forensics team together, but he'd like to get some interagency cooperation. Maybe Sherry can help us with that."

"That's great, Billy, but we might have a more urgent problem," I said, trying to hold back my speculation. "Did Lott get back to you with anything on that old rifle?"

"No. My guess is he just stored it away. We didn't put any priority on it. What's up?"

"We need him to check it, Billy. We need to find out how recently it's been fired. Now."

The attorney went quiet for a second while he did his logic thing.

"Max, what's up?"

I told him about my encounter with Sheriff O. J. Wilson up in Placid City. The way the little bulldog had charmed me into letting him look for a weapon in my truck. Then I filled him in on how Wilson had tried to check me out, through Richards's friend and the string of homicides that had made him so paranoid.

"All large caliber. That could be anything, Max," Billy said. But he was too good a lawyer to dismiss it as coincidence that easily. "Did you call this Wilson and let him know about the gun in Jefferson's barn and its history?"

"It's my next call, Billy. If I can get the guy this late at night."

"Try hard, Max," he said. "Earlier this evening I had a conversation with Mark Mayes. I filled him in on what we found and told him you'd discovered his great-grandfather's watch. He seemed quite dumbstruck by the whole thing."

"You told him about Jefferson?"

"I told him about the grandfather and the son. He was quite intrigued about the grandson having become a minister."

"He thinks it's his destiny," I said, thinking out loud. "The letters with his grandfather's deep beliefs, the whole search for what happened and that thing about forgiveness."

Billy was reading me from the other end of the line.

"You think Mayes will try to contact Jefferson? To somehow bring the thing full circle?"

"Yeah, I do. But I'm not so sure that William Jefferson is so forgiving. You know where Mayes is now?"

"I'll try his number."

"Let me know," I said.

The next call I made was to information, looking for the number to the Highlands County Sheriff's Office. When I dialed it I got a computerized answering service giving me the office hours and instructions to call 911 if this was an emergency, or to press 1 for the county dispatcher.

"Highlands County dispatch," answered a woman with a tired and bored voice. When I asked for a way to speak to Sheriff Wilson, she repeated the office hours and asked me to call back in the morning. That's when I identified myself as Detective Richards of the Broward Sheriff's Office and told her it was a matter of importance. She was much more agreeable, asked for a callback number, and said she would page the sheriff. I did not like to lie often, but I was very good at it when I did. Richards was staring at me when I put the phone down. Her night had been bizarre enough. I started to explain when O. J. Wilson called me back.

"Detective Richards, please," he said when I answered.

"Sheriff Wilson, this is Max Freeman," I said. I gave him a couple of empty seconds, figuring if he didn't hang up right away, I might have a chance to hold him.

"I'm sorry to have deceived you, sir, but I really need to speak with you on a matter that I think may be of concern to you."

"Must be important, Mr. Freeman, for you to have misrepresented yourself as a working law enforcement officer."

"Yes, sir. I am told by sources, sir, that you have been trying to solve a number of homicides that you think are related. And my understanding is that the link you have is the use of a large-caliber rifle."

Again the line was silent, and I could picture the man's small eyes working beneath that furrowed brow.

"Four of them to be exact, Mr. Freeman," he said.

"Have you determined the caliber of the weapon used, sir?"

"We think so. The sheriff at the time of the first shoot-

244

ing found a shell casing in the area. It's pretty distinctive. But we haven't been so lucky in the other three, and in two cases we weren't even able to find bullets. The wounds were through and through and the rounds were never discovered."

"Was the shell casing an old .405?" I said.

This time I had turned the sheriff in a direction I had not meant him to go.

"Mr. Freeman, if there is something you would like to tell me, or talk to me about, I would much rather do this in person. I could come down and meet you first thing in the morning. Maybe you would like to arrange something at the Broward Sheriff's Office down there?"

"Well, sir, I'm headed in your direction momentarily. In fact, I can be there in a little more than two hours."

Before letting him jump to any more conclusions, I gave him a truncated version of the Mayes case, how the great-grandson had come to us, how I had tracked down the name of John William Jefferson and then Placid City's own Reverend Jefferson. I then told him the secret that the reverend had been keeping in his barn, and that the rifle he turned over to me was indeed a .405-caliber weapon meant to take down large animals, including people.

"You said the first shooting was fifteen years ago?" I said, working the long conversation I had with the reverend around in my head.

"Yes. Before I got here," Wilson answered.

"You might check with the morgue and get the date of the reverend's father's suicide. He told me it was fifteen years ago. I'd be interested in seeing how close the days match."

There was silence on the line.

"I think the great-grandson, Mark Mayes, is coming to visit the reverend. I'm not sure I'd trust the pastor's reaction," I said.

It was this bare accusation that pushed the old sheriff over the edge.

"Freeman, you got some set of brass ones on you, fella," he said, his tone, even over the cell phone, turning icy. "The reverend Jefferson has been a blessed and solid citizen in these parts for more than a decade. Why, that man even presided over my own daughter's wedding.

"Son, I have checked out your record, and according to my own damn sources, you might have gone off the deep end yourself up north in Philadelphia when you shot a young boy in the back. Then I understand that you came down here to Florida and got yourself twisted up with a child abductor and ended up killing him, and that some innocent park ranger went down at the same time. Then not too long ago you were apparently found beating a suspect nearly to death, and another cop was forced to shoot and kill another suspect before that one was over.

"You've got a bloodlust or something, Freeman, and I'm not sure I even want you in my jurisdiction unless I've got you up here as a suspect."

I had not had my recent past raked into a pile with such an efficient stroke before. And Wilson didn't even know about my most recent wounding of PalmCo's hired man, nor could he have been aware of my subway encounter with an evil that I obviously held in my memory. The list made me wonder if I truly knew the man reflected in Richards's kitchen window as I looked out on the light of the pool.

"Do you have a fingerprint on the shell casing found in the first shooting?" I asked him.

He waited to answer.

"Damn right I do."

"Do you have a sample of the reverend's prints?"

Again he waited a couple of beats.

"No. He has no criminal record that I know of."

"No, he wouldn't," I said, then added, "I'll be in town as soon as I can get there, Sheriff."

When I punched off the cell, Richards had her head down, staring at the large stone tile on her kitchen floor.

"I've got to go," I said.

CHAPTER 22

I drove the first half of the trip at seventy-five miles-an-hour. After Billy called me on the cell phone, I did the rest at eighty-five. He had been unable to find Mayes. He was not answering the cell number Billy had for him. His room at the small mom-and-pop motel he had been staying in was empty. The manager said he'd last seen Mayes's small, two-door sedan sometime this morning. He had said something about going to church.

"I called Professor Martin up in Atlanta, and he talked to Mayes yesterday," Billy said. "He said he told him about your discovery of the burial site and the watch. He said Mayes seemed resigned to the truth and glad that it was finally over, that he had some answers."

"Did he tell Martin about Jefferson—the reverend, the religious connection?"

"Martin said he told him he thought he'd made up his mind about the seminary and would pray on it at church today, and that was it."

"What church?"

I could tell Billy was putting it together faster than I was. There was an anxiety in his voice, and the sound of it was racheting up my own nerves.

"I did get in touch with Lott," Billy said with an even tighter tone. "I got him out of a late-night place where he was moderately intoxicated, but with the right promise of a bonus remuneration, I convinced him to open the lab.

"He took a look at the rifle and said that there were several patterns of rusting going on in the barrel. One layer was very old from the samplings he took, but it had been disturbed at least a couple of times since forming. New rust had apparently started, and it too was marred. His quick conclusion was that it had been fired and then stored away for a long period of time and then fired again. He'll have to do more extensive analysis to give any kind of timeline, though."

The reverend could have used his grandfather's gun four times or even more. He would not have had to clean and oil it. Without any particular fondness for its past or maybe because of that past, it could have been a simple tool to him.

Billy had also done some computer searching.

"I found archived newspaper accounts of four homicides in and around Highlands County that were the result of gunshot wounds that fit your sheriff's timeline. The victims in each case were not exactly upstanding members of the community," Billy said.

All four were convicted felons. A rapist. A child abuser. A domestic batterer. And a man with more convictions than the paper had space to go into. His last crime was beating and choking a woman because he wanted her red sports car.

"He was awaiting trial when he was shot in Sebring, only a few miles up the road from Placid City," Billy said.

"So the reverend is a man on a mission to rid the world of evil?" I said.

"Maybe. But Mayes isn't evil. He wouldn't be a target."

"That's your opinion, Billy—the opinion of a rational man," I said.

I swung north from the bottom of Lake Okeechobee and my headlights found the sign that read OUR SOIL IS OUR FUTURE. I pressed harder on the accelerator.

When I got to Placid City the eastern sky was showing the soft gray glow of dawn, but it was still early, even for the rural farm folk. I passed Mel's and could see that there was a light on deep in the building somewhere. Maybe it was for security. Maybe an early cook was dicing up breakfast ingredients. If Sheriff Wilson was somewhere awaiting my arrival, I saw no sign of him, and I doubted that it would be his style to hide himself. I continued through town and out to the Church of God.

When I turned down the entry road, the sun's first rays sheared over the horizon and the huge oaks caught the light in their upper branches. There was dew in the grass and it was disturbed by three sets of footprints, one going and coming back, the other leading from a van to the front steps. I remembered the van as Mrs. Jefferson's. I got out and could tell from the moisture on the van's hood that it had been here awhile. The windows were layered with a wet sheen, but I could see through the windshield. No one was inside. I took the precaution of rubbing a clear spot on the back window and checking the floorboards in the backseat. Nothing.

I turned to the church. The high steeple was slightly afire with the early sun and all was silent, save for the ticking of my truck engine cooling after its hours of abuse. I followed the tracks in the grass and got to the porch before realizing that the front door of the church had been left open, not enough to peer inside, but enough to show that the bud of metal on the catch mechanism was not engaged.

My right hand felt empty. I had left my Glock behind.

I moved to the side of the building, looking for any other vehicles that might be parked in back. I checked the height of the windows and quickly gave up the idea of peeking inside. I went back to the front, stepped quietly across the porch boards, held my breath and eased the door open. The inside was dim but my eyes adjusted and I could see the shape of someone sitting in the first seat off the aisle in the front pew. The head was bowed as if praying and did not move. I swept the room as I moved down the center but noticed nothing out of place. I was halfway up the aisle when I said, "Mark?"

When she lifted and spun her head to look at me the movement scared the hell out of me. My knees flexed and my heart jumped in my chest.

"Why, Mr. Freeman. What are you doing here?"

I don't think I exhaled until I sat down next to her. Margery Jefferson was wearing a dark shawl over her shoulders. Her eyes were red-rimmed and her face was pale. She maintained her quizzical look, as if she'd been expecting someone else.

"I'm sorry, Mrs. Jefferson. You OK?" I finally asked, looking away.

"Yes, of course, sir."

"Uh, is the reverend here, ma'am?"

"My husband is at home, Mr. Freeman," she said. "Are you looking for him or for your Mr. Mayes, sir?"

It was my turn to be anxious.

"Has Mark Mayes been here?"

"He was waiting outside when I arrived," she said, turning her face back to the altar. "We spoke for some time. He was very comforting, Mr. Freeman. He told me of the things you had found out for him, the past about his family. He reminds me very much of Mr. Jefferson when he was that age. Full of questions and wonderings."

I stayed silent and scanned the polished wood floor, the open door to the back of the church, the pure white cloth covering the altar.

"I don't know whether to thank you or to despise you for bringing out these truths, Mr. Freeman. I am asking the Lord to guide me."

"Yes, ma'am," I said, standing up, not knowing how else to answer.

"I suspect you will find Mr. Mayes at our home," she said. "I gave him directions."

"Thank you, ma'am," I said.

My tires spun in the wet grass when I pulled away from the church. I drove back through town and then west on the blacktop road, thinking that my speed might alert the local law. The sun was up full by the time I pulled in between the oaks in Jefferson's front yard. When I got out I quietly closed the door. The air was still and the dust I'd raised caught up and settled around me. The reverend's car and Mayes's small sedan were parked side by side next to the house. The veranda was empty and the front door closed. I took a survey of the windows before moving to the side of the house. I hesitated before rounding the corner, then stepped out onto the two-track that led to the barn. In the distance the angle of the sun threw a shadow across the half-opened barn door. It was forty feet of open ground, and I felt naked without a weapon.

"Reverend?" I called out with no expectation of an answer. "Mark Mayes? It's Max Freeman."

The call returned nothing, and I had little choice. I

walked upright and slowly toward the barn, concentrating on the shadow and any possible movement. The air held the smell of sun on grass and the odor of turned dirt. When I got to the door, I hesitated again, then scanned the back of the house, unnerved by the flash of sunlight on the panes of glass.

"Mayes?"

When I stepped into the space of the open doorway, the smell of cold dust touched my face. The windowless room was dark and I pulled on the metal handle to let in more sun. The low, waist-high swatch of light caught the shined black leather of the reverend's shoes.

He was in his dark suit. The coat unbuttoned. The black shirt wrinkled up with the twisted position of his body. The white cleric's collar stained on one side by dirt from the rope. He had fastened one end high at the top of the center beam that ran from ceiling to floor. The joists that formed the floor of the second story had provided the crosspiece, and it appeared as though the reverend had measured carefully so that his chest was positioned at the intersection. I had seen enough dead men to know that to cut him down would be fruitless.

"He didn't wait for my forgiveness, Mr. Freeman."

The words snapped my head around, and for the second time that morning my heart jumped.

Mark Mayes was sitting cross-legged on the floor behind me, exactly where the shock of the sight of a hanged clergyman had probably dropped him to his knees.

"Why would he do such a thing, Mr. Freeman? The Lord would have long ago forgiven what his grandfather had done."

I helped Mayes to his feet and backed him out of the barn and into the sunlight.

When we got back to the front of the house, I sat him down on the steps of the porch, opened my cell phone and called O. J. Wilson. Mayes didn't flinch when he heard me ask the dispatcher to send the sheriff to the Jefferson home.

"You know, after Mr. Manchester told me about my great-grandfather's watch being found, it was like everything in my head just fell together," Mayes started.

"He hadn't run out on his family. He had been true to his beliefs. Ever since I was a kid I had this ache to believe in God, and I wondered where it had come from, how it had gotten inside me. I guess I wanted to know it was him, Cyrus Mayes.

"Then, when Mr. Manchester told me about the Jefferson in the letters and what you'd found, Mr. Freeman, I couldn't get it out of my head. The grandson of Cyrus Mayes's killer chose this, the ministry? How? I looked up the address of the church and drove over. I talked with his wife and asked her if I could talk with him, to maybe, I don't know, maybe offer some kind of forgiveness."

The silver crucifix he wore around his neck was out of his shirt. He had been handling it while he sat quietly in the barn and prayed. The glow of his innocence bothered me. Maybe I was jealous.

"Yeah, maybe you did," I said.

CHAPTER 23

Wilson showed up with a squad car following him into the driveway. He greeted me coldly.

We stood in the shadow of the big oaks. Mayes deliberately avoided looking back at the open barn door, and the uniformed cops, one with sergeant stripes on his arm, seemed at a loss as to what to do with the bristle they carried into the place. The sheriff's face held a look of tight-lipped resolve.

"Hank, keep these two separated, please, until I can get their independent statements," he said, and then spun on his heel and headed for the barn. I went to sit in my truck while one of the deputies took Mayes to the squad car. The sergeant started over to me but when I looked up and met his eyes, he saw something in them that made him stop short, and he took up a position about fifteen feet away. I didn't say a word. After a time I watched Wilson step out of the barn door and head back our way. He bypassed us and went to the trunk of his Crown Victoria and popped the trunk. He came up with what I recognized as a fingerprint kit and I watched him return to the barn. He was gone several minutes more and then came out with the kit and again disappeared into the trunk of his car, concentrating on something there. When he was finished, he called me over and my guard came with me.

"I am not a man who likes to be wrong, Mr. Freeman, but my daddy taught me to at least admit it when you are."

There was no question in the statement, so I did not feel compelled to say anything in return.

"I have taken enough latent print courses at the FBI to make a good guess that the fingerprints of the now-deceased Mr. Jefferson appear to match those on the .405 casing that we found at the first murder scene," he said. "We'll have to get them over to the expert in Orlando, but I'm guessing we've got some shaking out to do with all this, Mr. Freeman. So why don't you and I sit down and talk a bit."

Wilson used his cell phone to call the county medical examiner's office. When he was through he gave his deputies instructions on how he wanted the scene sealed off, and then turned to me.

"Come take a knee with me, sir."

He led me over into the shade of the oak, and when the sergeant started to follow, he waved him off.

"It's OK, Hank," the sheriff said.

"If you don't mind, Mr. Freeman, I'd like to leave your friend there in the car."

I looked over at Mayes, and when I turned back, the sheriff read the confusion in my face.

"Gotta do this one by the book, sir."

We settled under the tree and I told him how I had arrived at the church at 6:10 and found Mrs. Jefferson there. I described where and how I had found Mayes and how I had left the scene out back just as he found it, except for my adjustment of the barn door.

He nodded, and then it was his turn.

"You must have left the church just before we got there, son. Mrs. Jefferson called Judy down to dispatch and told her she'd found her husband hanging dead in the barn when she got up. She said she didn't know what to do but to go to the church and pray."

She had known he was dead before I had arrived. I tried to rerun her words and wondered why I hadn't caught it.

Wilson then gave me a short version of his own ten-year investigation into the Highlands County murders. The facts weren't much different from those that Billy had come up with in his research, but from the lawman who had lived the cases and had obviously let them burn in his head for so many years, it was painful to see him try to accept the truth. The reverend had carried out the killings as some kind of warped retribution against evil. The twitch of violence in his bloodline had surfaced in a way he could somehow justify.

While we spoke a van from the medical examiner's office arrived with another county squad car. Wilson's sergeant spoke to the driver and he backed down the driveway to the front of the barn. The van emitted a piercing beep for as long as the transmission was in reverse. I cringed with each beat, and saw Mark Mayes squeeze his eyes closed.

"I have seen Reverend Jefferson two or three times a week for a decade. Attended many a prayer meeting at his church," Wilson said, looking off in the direction of the van. "I'm having a hard time with all this, Mr. Freeman. What possesses a man?"

I wasn't qualified to answer such a question, and when I remained silent, he stood and put his hand on my shoulder.

"I need to speak to Mr. Mayes, and then you two can go. I will eventually need that rifle that the reverend gave you."

"I'm sure the ballistics reports on the weapon will be extremely thorough, Sheriff."

While Mayes was being interviewed I called Billy's office and home before finally reaching him on his cell. The connection was bad.

"I'm down in Miami-Dade," he said. "The lawyers for PalmCo are trying to get an injunction to block any excavation of the site that we put in the probable cause filing. They're trying to use some angle about sacred Indian burial grounds through the name of some Miccosuki tribesman they dug up, excuse the expression."

"Christ," I said. "Lawyers."

"It's a stalling tactic," Billy replied. We've already got a Collier County sheriff's detail out there securing the site, and I've warned the PalmCo boys that if they play us on this, we'll be glad to get the media involved."

"We built Florida on the bones of our workers."

"Exactly," Billy said.

I told Billy about Reverend Jefferson's suicide and the sheriff's preliminary fingerprint analysis.

"Is Mayes all right?"

I looked over to the patrol car where Wilson was still talking with the kid. Mayes was nodding his head, being deferential and polite.

"The kid's got some faith," I said. "And finally some answers."

"And more to use it on than he bargained for," Billy said.

When the sheriff was done talking to Mayes he escorted him over to where I was standing and shook my hand.

"I'll have to have both of you come in later to make official statements. I hope that won't put you out much. I know you'll have some pressing engagements down south," he said.

Mayes climbed into his car just as another squad car was pulling in. I could see Mrs. Jefferson's profile through the backseat window.

"May we go back to the church for a few minutes, Mr. Freeman?" Mayes said, watching the car through his window. I nodded and he pulled out ahead of me without waiting.

When we pulled down onto the dirt drive to the church, a worn and rusted truck was parked in the grass. I stopped next to Mayes's sedan and got out.

"Can I suggest that you get a hold of Billy as soon as you can?" I said. "He's going to have some things to tell you. There's a forensics team working the spot in the Glades where we found your great-grandfather. Billy can probably arrange to have you taken out there if you want."

He waited a few seconds and then said, "I don't think I'm going to have to, Mr. Freeman." We were still standing next to my truck when a couple came out of the church. He was big and round-shouldered with thick, workingman's hands. The woman was small and angular and sagging at the shoulders with some invisible weight. The man opened the passenger-side door of the truck for her and then got in and drove away.

"I'm going to go inside for a minute if you'd like to join me," Mayes said, and turned away.

I watched him disappear through the church door and then sat back looking at the sun filter down through the leaves and onto my hood. I had been up for nearly forty-eight hours, and my head felt filled with cotton though I couldn't call it sleepiness. I was bone-tired, but my grinding had not stopped. I reached back behind the seats and found the bag I had stuffed there after hosing myself off at

Dawkins's dock and took out an evidence bag.

Mayes was in the front pew when I joined him inside. His hands were folded in front of him, but instead of bowing his head he simply stared up at the cross behind the altar. I sat down beside him and tried to match his gaze but couldn't hold it for long. I took the gold watch out of the plastic and held it out in my palm beside his knee and he finally shifted his eyes down and reached out to take it. He held it with the tips of his fingers as though he was afraid of a brittleness that was not there.

"It still opens," I said.

He found the catch and flipped it open, then turned it so he might read the inscription. A single tear rolled down his face, leaving a shining streak. He looked back up at the cross.

"He was a good and pious man, wasn't he, Mr. Freeman?"

"I believe so."

"Then I should forgive him," he said. It was not a question, and I did not feel the need to answer.

CHAPTER 24

When I got back to Billy's penthouse I slept for fourteen hours, the first six or seven in my clothes. I woke late in the evening and took a shower with the full intent of staying up, but when I lay back on the bed I turned my head into the pillow and was gone again for another six or seven. It was still dark when my eyes snapped open, my heart thumping in fear that I didn't know where I was, nor did I have any concept of the correct day or even the year. My fingers went involuntarily to the soft disk of scar at my neck. I reached over and turned on a bedside lamp, and it took me several minutes to calm myself.

I pulled on a pair of shorts and padded out into Billy's kitchen. The only light came from the dimmed recessed spots that glowed above the counter space and at the front entryway. I had a magnificent headache, and my immediate guess was caffeine withdrawal. I had gone without coffee for longer than I had in many years. I set a ten-cup pot to brewing in Billy's machine and stepped out onto the patio to wait. The ocean was black, and against all odds I couldn't see a single light on the ocean. There were no fishermen, no freighters and no way to judge the horizon—or even the era. There was only the sound of the surf on the sand, the way it has moved up onto land for millions of years. For the rest of the night I sat with coffee, waiting out the darkness and watching light come into the world.

Shortly after dawn I heard Billy moving about inside,

and he joined me with an obscene concoction of blended fruit and vitamins and a copy of *The Wall Street Journal.*

"Welcome b-back, Mr. Van Winkle." We clinked mug to crystal and caught up.

The judge in Collier County to whom the PalmCo attorneys had presented their injunction had apparently not been the recipient of enough PalmCo political money, and they squelched their argument. The excavation had already begun. Billy had sent Bill Lott to be his representative. The old CIA man was grumpy as hell over having to spend days in the Glades fighting mosquitoes and the heat, but he was fascinated by the project.

"He c-called last night to tell us they had already f-found an intact skull. They weren't sharing too m-much with him until he convinced them of his experience with l-law enforcement. Then they l-let him have a look," Billy said.

"They can't tell in the field if it w-was one of the b-boys or Cyrus, but there was an obvious shattering hole in the back of the skull. They've already ruled it a h-homicide.

"Lott thinks a lot of the b-bones and fragments will be spread out from the animals that would have g-gotten to the bodies. B-But in that insect-rich environment, he says it t-takes only a few days for a body to be st-stripped to the bone. So they th-think they'll find the others."

"That ought to get PalmCo spinning," I said.

"It already h-has. There are three agencies in on th-this, including someone from the park service. One of them is already l-leaking info to PalmCo. And an acquaintance of m-mine at the *South Florida Sun-Sentinel* called on a t-tip he got, so the press is onto it, too."

"So there goes our media threat."

"Doesn't m-matter," Billy said, looking a bit pleased with himself. "Their attorneys left a m-message with my office today. They w-want to meet."

I let him enjoy his lawyerly reveling for a couple of minutes before asking him his opinion on what they might do.

"They will p-probably offer some c-compensation to the families. Not b-because they had any direct h-hand in the deaths, but b-because it w-was their project years b-back and they want to show r-respect for the working m-men who sacrificed their lives to b-build the trail."

"Christ, that's repulsive," I said.

"It's called spin, Max. And due to the fact that w-we don't have anything sp-specific to tie their old company Noren to John William Jefferson, it m-might be the b-best we can do."

"And that's going to be enough for you?" I said, wondering if my friend had gone soft. But I should have known.

"No. We'll d-demand that they continue to f-fund any extra c-costs for the forensics investigation into the other b-burial spots on John William's m-map. And if there is anyw-way to identify them, their f-families will also have t-to be compensated.

"We will also ask that a m-memorial to the men who lost their l-lives d-during the building of the Trail be purchased by them and s-set in a prominent p-place on land that they will provide."

"And that's going to be enough for you?"

I had succeeded in dampening some of his gloating.

"We will m-most likely n-never see their internal documentation from that time. If it even ever existed, they would have sh-shredded it by now.

"They may even h-have the n-names of the other m-men Mayes's letters sp-spoke of. But I doubt that even a h-homicide investigation is g-going to find them."

When Billy mentioned Mayes's letters I thought of the young man. At the church I'd asked him if he would be driving back to the coast. He said he didn't know. When I stood to go, he handed his great-great-grandfather's watch back to me.

"You'll need this for evidence, yes?"

I told him he'd get it back as soon as possible.

"Yes, I know."

When I left he was still sitting in the front pew, his head bent forward in prayer, but I didn't know for whom—his family or the Jefferson's.

"How much is he going to get in compensation?" I asked Billy.

"I'll ask for a m-million, and they'll give it," he said. "But it won't m-matter to him, you know? He c-called to say he'd enrolled in the seminary.

"Yeah, I figured," I said. "The truth shall set you free."

I spent the next two days at the beach, swimming in the surf, reading travel books I stole from Billy's shelves, and then falling asleep with warm salt air in my lungs and uneasy thoughts in my head. I talked with Richards on the phone and gave her a recitation of the details of my wounding of the P.I., the revelation of the reverend's own possible killing spree, and the discovery of his suicide.

She told me about the removal of McCrary's body from her front lawn. That she had spent two hours with internal affairs, documenting what she knew of his relationship with her friend, Deputy Harris. It was shop talk, and even over the phone I could sense an uncomfortable hesitation in her voice. I asked if I could drive down and see her. I asked if she could come up, get away for a day in the sun. She said Harris was now staying with her and she didn't want to be far away. They were talking late into the night, and the woman was in a fragile place.

"You OK?" I asked the last time we spoke.

The phone felt awkward in my hand and I could hear her breath in the receiver.

"I've been doing a lot of thinking about lives caught in circles, Max," she said, without offering more. I tried to out-wait her again and kept swallowing back words.

"We could talk about it together," I finally said. The phone was quiet on the other end, and I winced with a physical ache in my chest that I was losing something.

"Yeah, maybe," she said. "Gotta go." And the line went softly silent.

I wiped the sweat from my left eye with the shoulder of my shirt on the upstroke. When I switched to the other side of the canoe, I did the same on the right. I was pounding down the midline of the river in the open water, reaching and pulling with a ferocity I thought I'd left behind long ago. The sun was high and hot and even my raptor friend in the dead stalk of the tall palm was hiding somewhere in the cool shadows. I'd packed the boat with extra supplies. My intention was to make it a lengthy stay this time. I had had enough of bodies and bones, concrete and air-conditioning, recollections and remembrances. I needed to get back onto my river.

I didn't stop my angry paddling until I reached the cavelike mouth of the upper river, and by then I was gasping to fill my overwrought lungs and the blood was pounding in my ears, and when I finally gave it up I bent forward and was nearly sick in the bow. The canoe coasted along with my final kick-stroke and drifted into the shadows. I laid the paddle handle on one gunwale, the blade on the opposite side, and crossed my arms over it. I rested my head on my slick forearms and closed my eyes. I could smell the leaves and roots rotting on the banks, taste the tannin in the tea-colored water, and feel the shady greenness cooling my back. I wanted to stay in that position forever. Then I heard the distinctive sound of a hammer on hard wood coming from the distance.

I took up the stroke again, and along with it, my head began its speculation. I couldn't work up the same speed as before; the winding trail of the water through the cypress knees and clustered oak tree trunks slowed me. My exhausted shoulder muscles would not loosen again.

The hammering became louder, overwhelming any other sound in the forest. It had no rhythm—six or eight hard strikes, then quiet, then four more. I knew where it was coming from, but not why. When I got to the columned oaks that marked the water trail to my shack, the hammer reports stopped. I turned the canoe in and strained my eyes through the cover of tree limbs and ferns to see if I could catch any movement and surprise whoever was chopping at my home. I crept in slowly, taking care not to let water drip from the paddle blade. Thirty feet from the dock I could make out a rowboat through my cover. It was tied and anchored at one of the rear support pillars. Oddly, an aluminum extension ladder was set in its stern, and I could see that it was leaning up onto the northeast wall and was lashed to the column. Straddling the top of the ladder was Ranger Griggs. He had a plank of newly cut wood in his hand, and I watched him place it carefully against the corner wall of the shack and then take out his hammer from a ring on his tool belt. Before he could set another nail I called out to him.

"How much you charge for this kinda work?" I said.

My voice startled him. The ladder shifted and swayed and started the wide rowboat to rock.

"Jesus!" he yelped.

I paddled over while he settled his own heartbeat and waited for him to climb down. I lashed the canoe on his stern cleat. He was obviously embarrassed, and I made him more so by not saying anything.

"I, uh, came across some Dade County pine and, well, I figured I could use it," he said, stumbling on his words.

"Yeah?"

"Well, I saw the state order warning that the building may not be inhabitable after the fire, and being somewhat familiar with the code, I figured it wouldn't take that much to fix."

"Yeah?"

He sat down on the port gunwale and reached down to open a small cooler. He hooked his fingers around the necks of two iced Rolling Rocks and offered me one. I took it.

"I had the day off with not much else to do so . . . I hope it's OK."

I twisted the top off the beer and tipped my head back as I drank.

"It looks like you know what you're doing," I said, keeping my eyes up on the corner where he had already set three planks after tearing out the blackened remains of the originals.

"Well, my father was a carpenter, and his father before him," Griggs said. "So I come by it honestly."

We sat in an uneasy silence for a few seconds, both looking up and avoiding what truth might be in either of our eyes. The boats were gently rocking below us both. The quiet was a shared salve.

"Well, then," I finally said. "Let's carry on."

ACKNOWLEDGMENTS

I would like to thank the following people for their fine work and support. Many thanks to Mitch Hoffman, a young editor with an old editor's work habit of making stories better, and to his colleagues at Dutton, particularly Erin Sinesky, the finest publicist in the business. Also to my agent, Philip Spitzer, for including me in his legendary stable.

My wife and children for their sacrifices to my mental and physical absence. My friend Michael Connelly, for his inspiration and immeasurable help. My longtime newspaper editor, Earl Maucker, for giving me the freedom to make this happen. And Richard Hall, my grassroots marketing machine.

I would also like to thank the many booksellers I've met in these first few years who have introduced my stories to their readers, especially my local friends Joanne Sinchuk and Rob Hittel.

All Orion/Phoenix titles are available at your local bookshop or from the following address:

Mail Order Department
Littlehampton Book Services
FREEPOST BR535
Worthing, West Sussex, BN13 3BR
telephone 01903 828503, *facsimile* 01903 828802
e-mail MailOrders@lbsltd.co.uk
(Please ensure that you include full postal address details)

Payment can be made either by credit/debit card (Visa, Mastercard, Access and Switch accepted) or by sending a £ Sterling cheque or postal order made payable to *Littlehampton Book Services*.
DO NOT SEND CASH OR CURRENCY.

Please add the following to cover postage and packing

UK and BFPO:
£1.50 for the first book, and 50p for each additional book to a maximum of £3.50

Overseas and Eire:
£2.50 for the first book plus £1.00 for the second book and 50p for each additional book ordered

---

BLOCK CAPITALS PLEASE

name of cardholder _____

address of cardholder _____

delivery address
(if different from cardholder)
_____
_____
_____

postcode _____   *postcode* _____

☐ I enclose my remittance for £ _____

☐ please debit my Mastercard/Visa/Access/Switch (delete as appropriate)

card number ☐☐☐☐☐☐☐☐☐☐☐☐☐☐☐☐

expiry date ☐☐☐   Switch issue no. ☐☐

signature _____

prices and availability are subject to change without notice